LATE FOR HIS OWN FUNERAL

LATE FOR HIS OWN FUNERAL

Elaine Viets

**SEVERN
HOUSE**

First world edition published in Great Britain and the USA in 2022
by Severn House, an imprint of Canongate Books Ltd,
14 High Street, Edinburgh EH1 1TE.

Trade paperback edition first published in Great Britain and the USA in 2022
by Severn House, an imprint of Canongate Books Ltd.

severnhouse.com

British Library Cataloguing-in-Publication Data
A CIP catalogue record for this title is available from the British Library.

ISBN-13: 978-0-7278-5029-4 (cased)
ISBN-13: 978-1-4483-0931-3 (trade paper)
ISBN-13: 978-1-4483-0925-2 (e-book)

All Severn House titles are printed on acid-free paper.

Typeset by Palimpsest Book Production Ltd.,
Falkirk, Stirlingshire, Scotland.
Printed and bound in Great Britain by
TJ Books, Padstow, Cornwall.

For my friend Carol Berman – with thanks.

ACKNOWLEDGMENTS

In this age of DNA and dental records, can someone really be misidentified, like the man who was *Late for His Own Funeral*?

It happens, and more often than you think. As this book goes to press, a man in Orange County, California, was misidentified. Eleven days after his funeral, his family discovered he was alive. No one knows quite how the mix-up happened, but officials may have used an old driver's license photo.

There are other cases across the globe, from Australia to Brazil. And now, in fictional Chouteau County, Missouri, home of the one percent.

Writing a novel seems like solitary work, but it took a team to produce this book, and I want to thank them.

Detective R.C. White, Fort Lauderdale Police Department (retired) and licensed private eye, and Synae White gave me many hours of advice and help. Thank you to death investigator Krysten Addison and Harold R. Messler, retired manager-criminalistics, St. Louis Police Laboratory. Gregg E. Brickman, author of *Imperfect Friends*, helped me kill off my characters. These experts did their best to make this novel accurate, but all mistakes are mine.

Many other people helped with *Late for His Own Funeral*. My husband, Don Crinklaw, first reader and critiquer, was the most important.

Thanks also to my agent, Joshua Bilmes, president of JABberwocky Literary Agency, and the entire JABberwocky team. Joshua reads my novels and gives detailed suggestions to improve them.

Thanks to the Severn House staff, especially commissioning editor Carl Smith for his skillful editing, as well publishing assistant Natasha Bell and copyeditor Katherine Laidler. Cover artist Jem Butcher perfectly captured my book.

Some of the names here belong to real people. Sarah E.C. Byrne made a generous donation to charity to have her name in this novel. She's a lawyer from Canberra, Australia, and a crime fiction aficionada. Valerie Cannata is a friend and race-horse lover.

I'm grateful to Alan Portman, Jinny Gender, and Joanna Campbell Slan, author of *The Friday Night Mystery Club*. Alison McMahan, and Marcia Talley, author of *Disco Dead*, were especially helpful.

Special thanks to the many librarians, including those at the Broward County, St. Louis, and St. Louis County libraries, who answered my questions, no matter how strange they seemed. I could not survive without the help and encouragement of librarians.

I hope I haven't missed anyone. I also hope you'll enjoy Angela Richman's latest adventure. Email me at eviets@aol. com

ONE

I sat six feet away from Sterling Chaney's closed coffin, wondering how much of the dearly departed was actually in that golden casket. Not enough to fill a briefcase, I thought. Not after Sterling's Porsche missed the curve and slammed into the rock face at a hundred and ten miles an hour.

I didn't actually see Sterling's mangled remains. He wasn't my case. I'm Angela Richman, a death investigator for Chouteau County, Missouri – home of the one percent. I work for the county medical examiner's office, and I'm in charge of the body at the scene of murders, suicides, and unexplained deaths.

I'd heard the deceased driver was seriously spiflicated, and hoped he didn't feel a thing when he met his awful end.

Camilla, his widow, was giving her husband what's called the 'Golden Send-Off' – she was burying him like a rock star in a stunning Promethean casket. Sterling's remains rested on plush velvet. The casket's exterior was actually solid bronze, hand-polished to a mirror finish. It shone like gold.

Michael Jackson, James Brown, and Aretha Franklin all went to their reward in a Promethean casket. And now, Sterling Chaney. His casket, covered in roses like a Derby winner, looked incredibly gaudy in the austere Episcopalian church in Chouteau Forest, the largest town in Chouteau County.

I could hear the shocked murmurs and appalled whispers as the funeral home attendants rolled the garish casket up the aisle. The churchgoers would be even more shocked if they knew it cost thirty thousand dollars. In the pew behind us, a sturdy black-clad matron gasped, 'Good heavens!'

I wondered why Sterling's socialite widow had chosen such an ostentatious six box. It wasn't her style. Camilla was tastefully dressed in a black dress and long-sleeved jacket, her blonde hair pulled into a sedate chignon. A small black hat with a discreet veil hid her pale face.

Camilla and Sterling's closest relatives were long dead, and she'd asked me to ride with her to the funeral in the limo and sit next to her at the church. Sterling must have had plenty of friends – or drinking buddies. Every seat was taken, and the crowd spilled outside.

The new rector, Father William Winthrop, didn't know the dead man, which was probably just as well. Father Win looked exactly the way an Episcopalian priest should: tall, blond, and beak-nosed.

Father Win intoned a comforting verse from Revelations: 'Never again will they hunger; never again will they thirst.'

That was good, I thought. Sterling had been born one drink behind and never caught up.

Silent tears rolled down Camilla's face, and she blotted them with a black-bordered handkerchief.

Father Win said, 'The sun will not beat down on them, nor any scorching heat.'

For Sterling's sake, I hoped that was true. Between the boozing and the womanizing, the general opinion was that Sterling was headed somewhere hot.

'And God will wipe away every tear from their eyes,' the priest said.

Camilla burst into noisy sobs and tried to stifle them. Fortunately, the soloist launched into a powerful rendition of 'Amazing Grace.' Camilla wept harder, but most people couldn't hear her.

I knew she was estranged from her husband. Maybe Sterling's death reminded her of all the reasons why she'd married him – or all that could have been. Sterling had been handsome and charming. Camilla's tears seemed genuine. I patted her hand, and she gave me a watery smile.

I went to high school with Camilla, which was unusual in Chouteau County. Most upper-crust children went to private schools, but her family was more egalitarian and sent their only daughter to public high school, where she mixed with the likes of me, the daughter of servants.

Camilla and I bonded over our hatred of gym class and

became good friends. I was a bridesmaid in her wedding ten years ago, and we marched down the same aisle now blocked by Sterling's golden casket.

When they first met, Sterling had seemed awed by Camilla's cool elegance, and she fell in love with his humor and energy. I'd had my doubts about the match, especially after Sterling hit on me during the rehearsal. I often wondered: if I'd said something to Camilla back then, would she have gone through with the wedding? But I'd kept quiet, and she'd married Sterling, for better or worse.

Mostly worse, as it turned out. Much worse.

Sterling started the marriage with a tidy fortune, which he quickly turned into a large one, thanks to the telephone service he started. While Camilla's family fortune declined, Sterling's money grew. He poured money into worthy causes and soon had an honorary doctorate from City University and membership in the prestigious Chouteau Founders Club. He was at every charity event, loud and boisterous. The only time he was quiet was when he was seducing some woman.

As the years passed, Camilla seemed to grow thinner and sadder, though she was still a glamorous beauty at forty-one. I wondered if her life would improve now that her philandering spouse was dead. Although I'd never ratted out Sterling, Camilla knew her husband was unfaithful. In the limo on the way to Sterling's funeral, she'd told me, 'I'm just relieved there wasn't a woman in the car with him.'

Across the church aisle, I could see the black-clad dowagers studying the crowd with beady eyes. I'd bet my next paycheck they were trying to figure out which of the younger women had slept with Sterling.

Camilla had opted not to do any of the funeral service readings herself, or to have any of Sterling's friends deliver a tribute – a wise decision considering the unpredictable boozers he befriended.

Instead, Father Win launched into an earnest eulogy. He was doing a good job of it, too. He'd managed to capture the deceased's personality.

'Sterling was a vital man,' he said. 'He was larger than life and cast a long shadow. We can feel his presence here today . . .'

'You betcha, Reverend,' said a loud voice from the back. Framed in the church doorway was a man who looked a lot like Sterling Chaney.

At first, my brain denied what I was seeing. Yes, the man was six feet tall, and his skin had a drinker's flush, just like Sterling's. His hair was blond and slightly too long. He wore a perfectly cut dark-blue Tom Ford suit and he had Sterling's wicked grin.

In fact, it *was* Sterling.

The blood had drained from Camilla's face. 'No,' she whispered. 'You're dead.'

But he wasn't. Sterling strode up the aisle and examined the gaudy gold casket.

'Why, Camilla darling' – he flashed white teeth at his wife – 'you did follow my last wishes and got me the swanky coffin I wanted, even though I know you think it's painfully tacky.'

Camilla whimpered. She was way too white, even for a Forest Episcopalian. I patted her shoulder.

Sterling sized up his stunned wife and said, 'Black really isn't your best color, Camilla. It washes you out.'

Sterling was enjoying himself. He turned to address the congregation.

'I was in the Bahamas for a business trip,' he said. 'I left at the last minute and didn't check in with my lovely wife.' He didn't mention that they hadn't been living together at the time. 'In fact, I was totally out of touch. No phones, no news media. No nothing.'

Hm. I wondered if he was in the Bahamas chasing women.

'At the airport, I'd left my Porsche in long-term parking,' Sterling said, 'and when I returned from my trip, I couldn't find it anywhere. Looked high and low. That's when I called the police. We concluded that my Porsche had been boosted. Then I learned I was supposed to be dead.' His laugh was a drunken hee-haw. No one laughed with him. They stared at him with frozen faces.

Sterling patted the gold casket. 'I guess the poor bastard who stole my car is in here.'

He was warming up and putting on quite a show. 'I had to take a cab to my own funeral. I had the driver stop for some sustenance.' He held up a bottle of Johnnie Walker Black Label. 'This was the best we could scare up. Blended scotch.' He took a long swig.

I could feel Camilla trembling. I thought she might be going into shock.

'Well, my momma always said I'd be late for my own funeral, and damned if she wasn't right.'

Sterling turned to his former widow and held out his arms. 'Camilla, honey, I'm home.'

Camilla screamed and fainted. I managed to catch her before she hit the floor.

TWO

All hell broke loose at the church after Sterling Chaney came back from the dead. I didn't know whether to call the cops or an exorcist. The air was filled with shouts, murmurs, and gasps of 'Oh my.' Most of the black-clad women looked appalled. They hastily gathered their belongings and raced for the door.

Camilla Chaney had fainted. As she fell, she hit her forehead on the hard wooden pew. The *thunk!* was loud and worrisome. I stretched her out in the pew, thankful that the needlepoint cushions were heavily padded. I called 911, then piled hymn books under her feet to elevate them. The poor woman was as still as death. She was out cold. There was a smear of blood above her eyebrow. This was not good. I loosened her tight dress jacket to give her some air. The church was heavily air-conditioned, and I took off my own suit jacket and wrapped her in it so she wouldn't be chilled.

Meanwhile, Sterling was being backslapped by his barfly buddies. A scrum of tubby, balding white men in somber suits were laughing, hugging, and high-fiving one another.

Sterling set the bottle of Johnnie Walker Black on the gold coffin like it was a bar top, then stepped back to admire what was supposed to be his final resting place.

'I must say, that's a beauty, isn't it?' he said, slapping the casket's golden side as if it was a new car. 'Can I open it up and see the squatter camping in my casket?'

'No!' I shouted. 'That casket is now a crime scene.'

'Says who?' Sterling was just drunk enough to be belligerent. I walked over to him and looked right into his red eyes. We were the same height. I could smell the liquor on his breath. I wondered if he was too drunk to remember me.

'I do. I'm the Chouteau County Death Investigator, Sterling. We need to determine who the dead person is.' He backed down, but he still seemed to be looking for a fight.

'And who is the idiot who misidentified me?' Sterling asked.

I looked at the church's stained-glass St Michael for inspiration. Could the angel with the fiery sword protect me from this temptation? Should I reveal the force's criminally careless detective in a church full of Forest fat cats? I remembered all Greiman's sly insults and ugly comments. I turned my back on the angel and said, 'It's Detective Ray Greiman.'

Sterling grinned. 'Oh, hell, I know Ray. Nice guy. He helps me home when I've had a little too much.'

Of course Ray did. Forest big shots got special treatment from Ray. The detective would give the loaded lushes a gentle warning and escort them safely home.

'I bet I've got Ray's number somewhere in my cell phone,' Sterling said, scrolling through its menu. 'Let me find it and I'll give him a call. I'll give him a good razzing, too.'

Meanwhile, I had to make some quick decisions: Who was I going to call?

If I called Chief Buttkiss, I'd be going over Greiman's head, and the detective would be ticked at me. If I called Greiman, he'd be happy that I didn't call the chief, but the heck with him. I didn't owe Greiman any favors. I decided to call the comm center. I braced myself to repeat the message several times and made the call.

After the nasal-voiced operator answered, I said, 'Hi, this is Angela Richman. That's right, I'm the death investigator. I'm at the funeral of Sterling Chaney at the Episcopalian church. We've got a weird problem here. Sterling just walked into the church. Alive and well. Yes. You'd better send somebody because I don't know who's in the casket, but the guy they think is dead is very much alive. Yes, that's right, Sterling Chaney is alive.'

I had to repeat the message three times before the operator finally understood. 'Well, this is a first,' she said. 'Please secure the casket until we can send someone to bring it in.'

I tried calling Evarts Evans, Chouteau County's chief medical examiner, but he wasn't at the office. It was a sunny weekday afternoon in June, and I figured he was golfing. I left a message for him to call me but didn't say why. There was no way I could explain this situation in a short message.

Next, I called my friend, Dr Katie Kelly Stern, the assistant medical examiner, and told her what was going on. This time, I only had to repeat myself twice. Katie said, 'You have got to be kidding me. Thank gawd this wasn't my screw-up. Greiman and his useless sister, Regina, worked that case.'

Regina was another death investigator, hired because of the Forest's strict nepotism policy: if you were related to someone in the government, you were hired. No matter what your qualifications – or lack of them.

'Evarts completed the fuckup trifecta by doing the autopsy and not checking for DNA,' Katie said. 'This is gonna be a major shitstorm.'

'Lawsuit city,' I said.

Meanwhile, Sterling was yelling into his phone, 'Hey there, Ray. How's it hanging, you old bastard?' I winced at this language in a church.

'Yeah, this is Sterling Chaney. I understand you think I'm dead. My friends and family are here at my funeral. Well, let me tell you . . . There might be a body in that casket, but it sure as hell isn't mine. What the heck is going on? Oh, and by the way, I'm hurt you didn't come to my funeral. I thought we were friends. Especially after that nice Christmas present I gave you.'

I added accepting bribes to Greiman's misdeeds.

By this time, Father Win had recovered enough to hurry over. Sterling was taking selfies with his friends in front of his casket. They were passing around the bottle of Johnnie Walker Black. The red-nosed George had just posed for a selfie with Sterling and the casket.

'Hey, Father, take a selfie with me by my coffin,' Sterling shouted.

'Mr Chaney,' Father Win said, his voice soothing. 'Naturally, we rejoice that you are alive—'

'Damn right we do,' Sterling said. 'Nobody more than me. Hey, George? Any more of that booze left? Quit guzzling and hand me that bottle.'

'Mr Chaney' – Father Win's voice was more commanding – 'while we are happy that you have survived, you might want to attend to your wife. She's suffered a terrible shock. Then we can offer a prayer of thanksgiving.'

'My wife?' Sterling looked confused. 'Oh, right. Camilla.' He put away his cell phone and came over to the pew where his pale spouse was lying on the cushions.

He turned to me. 'Is she OK, Angela?'

'Of course she's not OK,' I said. 'Camilla's had a horrible shock. You're alive.' I realized how that sounded as soon as I said it. 'She hit her head on the pew and her forehead is bleeding.'

Sterling squeezed into the pew and began slapping Camilla's cheek. 'Hey, Cammy, wake up. It's OK. I'm alive.'

Camilla remained unresponsive. Finally, I had to evict the lout from the pew.

'Is it serious, Angela?' he asked.

'I'm no doctor, but it's a head wound and she hasn't come around yet.'

'Aw, she'll be OK,' Sterling said. 'Her head is as hard as her father's.'

Sterling glanced outside the open church doors and shouted, 'Hey, somebody called the TV stations! I've gotta talk to them.'

And he was out the door, all thoughts of thanking God forgotten.

'Here I am, ladies and gentlemen,' he said. 'The man who was late for his own funeral.'

I could hear the reporters shouting frantic questions. Sterling's booze buddies must have called the media. Their questions were drowned out by the sirens. The police and ambulance were almost here. Finally. Camilla would be cared for.

'Wait till you see my casket,' Sterling said. 'It's gold! Come inside and have a look.' Actually, it was polished bronze, but Sterling wasn't going to clear up that technicality.

Father Win barred the door and announced, 'While we all share the joy of Mr Chaney's return, I must remind you that another person is dead inside that casket, and we must respect that. The authorities are on their way. Ladies and gentlemen, you'll be able to photograph the casket when it is carried out.'

Sterling looked disappointed. Then he was cornered by

Kelly Morton, a curvy TV reporter with national connections. Sterling swiftly promised her an exclusive interview, knowing he would be on network TV by nightfall.

Father Win gave them permission to talk in the closet-sized anteroom off the vestibule. I couldn't hear Kelly's questions, but Sterling's drunken voice boomed through the church.

'See, Kelly, I was in the Bahamas on business . . .'

Monkey business, I thought.

'And I didn't get home until about noon today. I tried to find my Porsche in the airport parking lot, but it was missing. How the hell do you lose a red Porsche? I called the police and we concluded it had been boosted.'

A slight pause, and then Sterling said, 'What? Who took my car? Beats me.'

Another pause before Sterling said, 'My wife? What about my wife? Oh, she did exactly what I wanted for my funeral. Followed my last wishes to a T. She got me this fancy gold-looking casket. Cost thirty thousand buckaroos. I know she didn't want to buy me one. Camilla has good taste – she married me, didn't she? Haw, haw! – but I knew she wouldn't like that flashy exterior. Anyway, Camilla got me the same kind of casket that all the big stars are buried in – the Promethean. It's supposed to be special order – takes two weeks. It's all hand-polished, you know. I have no idea how she did it, but that's my Camilla.'

Another pause, and Sterling said, 'Oh, you meant, how did my wife feel about me coming back from the dead? She fainted. Passed out. From sheer happiness. Yes, sir! When she wakes up, she's gonna be one happy woman!'

THREE

Paramedics carried the unconscious Camilla out on a clanking stretcher, right past the room where her fatuous husband was being interviewed by Kelly Morton.

I heard the TV reporter say, 'As soon as you found out about your funeral' – she stopped to giggle – 'did you call your wife, Sterling?'

'I tried to, but her phone was off,' he said. 'She was in church – at my funeral.' Kelly and Sterling both guffawed as the senseless Camilla was rolled by. I longed to open the door and slap the man silly, but Camilla needed me. I was worried that she hadn't awakened yet. If she'd simply fainted from shock, she should have been conscious by now. Did she have a brain bleed from her fall? Or worse, a stroke?

I told the paramedics that I was Camilla's sister, so she wouldn't be alone at the hospital. I held her cold, clammy hand all the way to the Sisters of Sorrow emergency room, and prayed that the bluish tinge would leave Camilla's lips and her eyes would open.

Sterling's funeral had started at ten o'clock. It was now noon, but it seemed so much later.

At the ER, I gave the admissions clerk all the facts I could muster about my friend, including why she'd fainted – the clerk gasped when I told her – and that Camilla had hit her head on a church pew. Again, I said I was her sister, so I could stay with her as her next of kin.

When I finished with the paperwork, I learned that my friend had been whisked deep into the hospital for tests. I paced the ER while I waited for news, all the while wondering where Camilla's worthless husband was. It was two o'clock. He should have turned up by now.

By four o'clock, I caught up with Camilla in an ER cubicle. She was still unconscious and laid out like a corpse in a hospital gown, an IV line in her hand. Her face was deathly pale. The cut on her forehead had been stitched. She'd have a heck of a bruise there.

A helpful ER nurse told me, 'We gave your sister the works. She had a CT scan, an MRI, an X-ray, blood tests, and more. Your sister didn't have any sign of a brain bleed or a stroke. That's good news. She's being given intravenous fluids in case she's dehydrated. Do you know if she's had any food today?'

'I doubt it,' I said. 'She was too upset to eat.'

'That could be part of the problem,' the ER nurse said. 'Decreased fluids mean decreased blood supply, and that means less oxygen to the brain.' She patted my hand. 'Don't you worry. Your sister will come around when she's ready. That woman has had a horrible shock.'

Finally, a bed was free and Camilla was admitted to a room upstairs in the hospital. The doctors wanted to keep her until she woke up and then for observation. I sat by her bed, reading a *People* magazine so old that Brad Pitt and Angelina Jolie were still married.

About five o'clock, I heard a slight groan, and then Camilla's brown eyes opened.

'Angela?' Her voice sounded weak.

'I'm right here, Camilla.'

'Is it true? Is Sterling really alive?'

'Yes.'

'Damn!' She closed her eyes as if she was in pain. Then she quickly added, 'I didn't mean that, Angela. I don't want my husband dead. I just want him out of my life.'

Camilla stayed so still I thought she'd fallen asleep again. Finally, in a voice that was more a sigh than a whisper, she said, 'He isn't here, is he? He's not at the hospital.'

'Sterling? No. Last I saw, he was being interviewed by a TV reporter.'

'Of course he was,' Camilla said. 'He loves the limelight. A lot more than he loves me.' A single tear trickled down her face.

'Do you want to divorce him?' I asked.

'I still love him,' she said. 'At least, I love the man I married. You know that. You were in our wedding. He was so charming, funny, and likable.'

And she'd looked so happy. A memory of their wedding flashed in my mind. Camilla was a radiant bride, almost floating up the aisle in her white silk and lace gown. Sterling held his arms out for her. He was slender and golden-haired. His bespoke morning coat was perfection.

The couple exchanged their vows, and when the rector said, 'You may now kiss,' the older women in the church smiled at their torrid kiss. We bridesmaids were close enough to feel the electricity crackling between the couple. As was the fashion then, the bridesmaids wore black. Perhaps it was an omen.

'When did things go wrong?' I asked.

'About six months after our wedding,' she said. 'I learned that Sterling had hit on most of my friends.' She looked at me. 'Did he hit on you, Angela?'

'Uh . . .' I stalled.

'He did, didn't he? At the rehearsal or the reception?'

'Rehearsal. But I didn't take it seriously. He was tipsy.'

'You mean drunk,' she said. 'He uses that excuse a lot. Most of my friends weren't as kind or forgiving as you were, Angela. They made sure to tell me "for my own good." I didn't want to know. I liked my dream world. When we'd been married six months, I wanted to surprise him at his office. Sterling said he had to work late. I showed up with his favorite dinner, wearing nothing under my raincoat. I walked in on Sterling having sex on the desk with a so-called friend of mine. I was humiliated. I dropped the food on the floor and ran home, crying myself sick.'

Camilla was still teary-eyed over the painful memory. I patted her hand.

'Sterling came home an hour later with a diamond necklace from Tiffany. He sweet-talked me into forgiving him, and, well, I'm ashamed to admit it, but the make-up sex was spectacular. I'm such a fool.'

She was crying now, harsh sobs. I feared for her fragile health and was about to call the nurse when Camilla's tears dried up, like the sun coming out after a hard rain. She sniffed a few times. I handed her the box of tissues on her bedside table, and she dabbed at her eyes.

She gave me a weak smile and said, 'So that's been my life

for the last ten years, Angela. We'll go along happily for several months, and then I'll find out he's been unfaithful. He'll ask forgiveness and give me another expensive bauble from Tiffany, or Van Cleef and Arpels – and once, a spectacular canary diamond necklace from Harry Winston. On my tenth anniversary, I realized I had an overflowing jewelry safe, a permanently hurting heart, and an empty head for going back to that man.'

I opened my mouth to make a suggestion, but my friend shut me up with, 'Please don't tell me to get counseling, Angela. I've tried that. More than once. He's addicted to adultery and I'm addicted to make-up sex.'

She paused for a moment and looked at her long, slender fingers, then said, 'Sick, huh?'

'But you are separated, aren't you?' I asked. 'You had the strength for that.'

'I did. He had a threesome in our marriage bed. That was too much for me. I called a lawyer and made Sterling leave the house. He found himself a bachelor pad – and another woman in the Bahamas. That's where he was when I thought he'd been killed in that car crash. I can't manage to make a final break.'

I shrugged. 'I know you loved him – right from your first date.'

She smiled, a sad, rueful smile. 'Yes, I did. We had dinner in the rose garden of a little French restaurant – and a whirl-wind courtship. We were engaged six months later and married a year after we met.

'I was so relieved when I thought Sterling was killed in that car crash. I was ready to start my life over. This time, my decisions would be sensible. I'd regain my self-respect. And then he walked into the church and it was like a nightmare. A living nightmare.' Camilla cried again, loudly and freely. She was out of tissues, but I found more in my purse.

'Camilla, if you'd like some time to think, you can move in with me. I have a guest room. You can decide your next steps and figure out how you want to make a living.'

'Make a living?' This time she squeezed my hand and gave me a lopsided smile. 'Oh, Angela, I don't have to worry about money. Sterling took the money his father left him and invested it in that telephone service. He's making tons of money – so much that it worries me.'

'Why?' *How could anyone have too much money?* I wondered.

'I'm afraid he's doing something that's not quite legal,' she said. My friend had a little color in her face. Her blonde hair had come loose from its chignon and she looked like a delicate figure on a cameo.

'May I get you some food?' I asked.

'Not hungry,' she said. 'I wanted to talk to you before the nurses show up. You're a good friend, Angela. I needed someone to listen to me.'

'Always, my friend.'

With that, there was a commotion in the hall, and I heard a loud, boozy voice demand, 'Where's my darling wife?' There was no doubt it was Sterling.

'Oh, no,' Camilla whispered, and closed her eyes.

Sterling – big, blond, and boisterous – burst into the dim hospital room, his arms loaded with red roses. 'Camilla, sweetheart, I've been so worried about you.' Sterling covered Camilla's bed with the rich red blooms. There was something odd about them, but I couldn't figure out what it was. He gathered his wife into his arms and covered her face with kisses, while I studied the roses and edged toward the door.

Finally, he looked up and saw me. 'Angela, I'm so glad you were here to take care of Camilla. Would you mind leaving us now?'

I looked at Camilla, and she gave me a tiny nod.

As I left, I took one more look at those roses. I saw traces of green florist's foam on the stems.

Sterling had brought Camilla the roses from his coffin.

FOUR

For the next two days, I couldn't escape Sterling. Every time I turned on the TV or the radio, there was another story about 'the man who was late for his own funeral.' Sterling was interviewed by the local and national media, from the *Forest Gazette* to NPR and *The New York Times*.

Reporters loved Sterling. His interviews evolved into comedy routines. Most started the same way, with Sterling saying, 'Let me tell you, it's a real shock to find out you're dead. But at least I got to attend my funeral and see that my darling wife, Camilla, had given me the funeral I'd wanted. She bought me that gaudy gold coffin. Camilla is a woman of refinement. I know she didn't like my flashy bone box. But I know she loves me.'

Soon he added a costume for his routine. Here's part of his interview with Merilee Thompson, a pretty blonde St. Louis TV host known for her fine mind and bounteous assets, which she fearlessly displayed. Merilee and Sterling were on the living-room set of her popular show, *Merilee's Afternoon Delight*, sitting on a red couch against a dark-blue background.

For the interview, Sterling wore a sober black suit with a vest, white shirt, and a black tie. The suit was the only sober thing about him. Sterling had obviously been hitting the bottle, and from the way Merilee was giggling, I suspected she'd also had a drink or two.

'What do you think of my suit, Merilee?' he asked.

'It's very nice,' she said, and giggled girlishly.

'Nice! Nice?' He leaned toward her. 'Nice doesn't begin to describe this suit. It's a freaking Tom Ford, the same suit Daniel Craig wears in *Spectre*.'

'My,' she said.

'Look at this suit,' he said, petting the fabric. 'It's a three-piece black herringbone. And here's something for you. This black has a blue cast.'

'It does, doesn't it?' Merilee widened her eyes and leaned forward, nearly falling out of her turquoise top. 'Most black suits have a brown or a green cast.'

'Damn right,' Sterling said. 'But this one is black as a bill collector's heart. Note the lapels.' He fingered them in a way that made me feel uneasy.

'Classic – wide and peaked,' Sterling said. 'The suit jacket has a single vent and five-button cuffs with the last button left open. The trousers have narrow tapered legs and no cuffs.'

'Oh.' Merilee seemed rather overwhelmed by the minutiae of male finery. 'I like your pointed collar shirt with the silver collar pin. I haven't seen one of those in years.' She leaned forward, and the camera dove into her plunging neckline.

'Ford brought collar points back, too.' Sterling didn't seem to realize no one was looking at his points.

'Your tie is black,' Merilee said, 'like a funeral tie.'

'You got it!' he said, as if she'd won a grand prize. 'The tie is black-on-black. This will be my funeral suit when I finally cash in my chips.'

'Which we hope won't be for a long time,' Merilee said, thrusting her chest out and giving all mankind a reason to live.

'I plan to go in style,' he said. 'I've instructed my lovely wife to bury me in this suit.'

'Speaking of your wife,' Merilee said, 'how is she? I hear she met with an accident when you walked into the church.'

'She did. She was overcome with joy and fainted dead away. Hit her head on the church pew and had to go to the hospital. She got three stitches. My wife's downfall was church pews. Mine is church keys.' He grinned rakishly and winked.

Merilee got the last word. 'I'm Merilee Thompson, keeping you abreast of the news.' The camera slid down her cleavage for the last time.

Sterling and Merilee cackled together as the *Afternoon Delight* theme played.

I was sick of watching Sterling – and worried about my friend. I had offered to take her home from the hospital when she was released, but Sterling's persuasive powers must have worked again. He drove Camilla home in his new red Ferrari and moved back in with her.

I visited Camilla the day after she returned home. She lived in her great-grandparents' 1898 Queen Anne mansion, a stately pile with wraparound porches and a gaggle of gables. It was ridiculously large for two people – ten thousand square feet, with glorious views of the formal gardens. Mrs Ellis, the housekeeper, showed me upstairs to Camilla's sitting room. Every table and the mantelpiece were covered with vases of those blasted red roses.

Camilla made a pretty picture in the sun-drenched room, reclining on an ivory silk chaise longue, wearing a soft pink robe and reading a book. Today, she had a little more color, but she still looked sad. She smiled when she saw me.

'Hey, Camilla, I brought you chocolate-frosted doughnuts from the Chouteau Forest Bakery.' I leaned over, kissed her cheek, and opened the box with a flourish.

Camilla burst into tears. 'You remembered,' she said. 'You remembered my favorite treat in high school.'

'How could I forget? The Forest Bakery got most of my allowance back then.'

This time, she laughed.

'I'll bring tea,' Mrs Ellis said, and hurried out of the room.

'Have a seat at the table by the window and let's demolish them,' Camilla said. For a moment, I saw a flash of the mischievous schoolgirl she used to be.

'I haven't had these in ages,' she said. 'They're so fattening.'

'That's what makes them good.'

Camilla looked like a wraith, walking toward the table. I started to get up to help her, and she said, 'I'm fine, Angela.'

She didn't look fine. She seemed frail, and there were dark bruises under her brown eyes. She'd fixed her blonde hair so it hid the stitches in her forehead. Up close, I saw that the color in her face was mostly skillful make-up.

As soon as Camilla sat down, she reached for a doughnut and took a big bite. 'Yum. As good as I remembered.'

'How are you feeling, Camilla?'

'Better, thanks.'

'Seriously?' I studied her face. 'You have a prize-winning bruise on your forehead. In festive shades of purple, yellow, and green.'

She shrugged, then winced.

'You're still hurting,' I said.

'I still have headaches, but they're getting better. The doctor wanted to give me Percocet, but I refused. Aspirin seems to be working fine.'

At that moment, Mrs Ellis returned with the tea tray. She was a plump woman with short gray hair, kind brown eyes, and a wide smile. She carefully placed the flowered china teapot on the table, then set out cream, sugar and lemon, cups, napkins and silverware, and two dessert plates.

She poured us hot, fragrant tea. 'I brought a serving plate so you don't have to eat those doughnuts out of the box.'

'Thank you, Mrs Ellis, but they taste better out of the box,' Camilla said, and smiled.

'We get to lick the chocolate frosting off the cardboard,' I said.

Mrs Ellis looked mildly scandalized. She set the plate on the table, then left.

Camilla reached for another chocolate doughnut and licked the frosting off her fingers. 'I've regressed to fifteen.'

We ate our doughnuts and sipped tea in comfortable silence. When Camilla finished her third doughnut, she said, 'I guess you think I'm an idiot for letting Sterling move back in.'

'No,' I lied.

Camilla clasped her long, thin fingers and twisted them into a knot. 'I can't help it, Angela. I still love him.'

I knew she did. I remembered her love-struck face on her wedding day. 'You don't have to explain anything to me,' I said.

'I'm trying to explain it to *me*,' she said. 'He drinks too much, he's unfaithful, and when he snaps his fingers, I come running back.'

Her voice had a bitter edge. 'He wasn't on a business trip to the Bahamas. He was seeing a woman who lives there – Nicole. Some kind soul texted me a photo of the two of them half-naked on the beach. But when Sterling came into my hospital room, his arms loaded with red roses, I forgave him. I love his romantic gestures.'

Would she love them quite as much if she knew he'd given

her the flowers off his coffin? The symbolism in that gesture made my eyes cross. I still wasn't brave enough to tell my friend the truth. I knew it wouldn't make any difference. Camilla refused to open her eyes and see the man she'd married.

'Do the police know who was in my husband's coffin?' Camilla stopped, then said, 'I can't believe I've just said that sentence.' She reached for another doughnut.

'I'll find out later this afternoon. I'm going to see the assistant medical examiner. Where's Sterling? Is he at work?'

Camilla chewed her doughnut thoughtfully and sighed. 'You didn't hear the hubbub when you showed up here? He's in his study, being interviewed by a big-deal network TV star, Valerie Cannata. Her truck's parked around back.'

'The star of the WNE News Network?' I was impressed. 'That woman is a knockout.' Valerie was, too. Five feet seven, most of it legs. Long dark hair. Razor-sharp mind.

'That's her. I don't know why she's interviewing Sterling,' Camilla said. 'She usually does hard-hitting investigative reporting.'

'Maybe she found out why Sterling was really in the Bahamas,' I said.

'A cheating husband? That's hardly network news.' She shrugged.

'How many interviews has Sterling had so far?'

'Thirty-one and counting, including *Good Morning America* and *USA Today*. He's quite the celebrity.'

'And how many news outlets have interviewed you?'

'None,' she said. 'He tells them I still haven't recovered from fainting at the church. That's fine with me.' She took another sip of tea, lowered her voice, and said, 'I'm worried, Angela. Really worried.'

I set down my tea and leaned in. 'What's troubling you?' I studied her pale face, crisscrossed with tension lines and the frown marks between her eyebrows.

'Sterling's business,' she said. 'He's making bales of money with his answering service. He paid for the renovation of my family home – including a zillion storm windows – and he still has money to burn.'

'What's wrong with that?'

'There are tons of answering services, Angela, and many are cheap. They cost thirty or forty dollars a month. There's no way Sterling could haul in the money he's making with an answering service.'

'Have you been to his office?'

'No. He says he's going to take me, but he always cancels at the last minute. It's in an office park by the highway.'

'What's the name of his company?'

'Sterling Service of Chouteau Forest. I've never seen an ad for it.'

Neither had I.

'And why hasn't he mentioned the company's name once – just once – in all those interviews he's giving?' she said. 'He's always introduced as the owner of an answering service. He's turning down free publicity, Angela. What business owner does that? Something's not right. I know it.'

FIVE

I managed to master the keypad to the morgue while balancing two large go-cups of boiling hot coffee.

The Chouteau County Medical Examiner's office was in the back of Sisters of Sorrow Hospital, surrounded by ranks of dumpsters and black funeral vans. The June afternoon was so hot the blacktop lot had turned sticky.

I carried the steaming cups of coffee straight down the gloomy beige corridors to the office of Dr Katie Kelly Stern, my best friend and the assistant ME.

At first glance, Katie seemed practical as a plain brown tote, but her lively brown eyes and wicked sense of humor made her captivating. In fact, she'd captured the heart of Montgomery Bryant, the handsomest bachelor in Chouteau County.

Katie's door was partly open, and I could see her working at her desk. She had sensible brown hair, comfortable shoes, and a starched lab coat over a plain navy pantsuit. The windowless room was brightened by an autumn forest scene that covered the wall behind her. Hidden in the foliage was a grinning plastic skull. See what I mean about her?

Katie smiled when she saw me. 'Is that coffee? You are definitely welcome.'

I squeezed into her office – I had bigger closets at home – and she grabbed the hot coffee like a lifeline. 'Just what I needed.'

She examined me with shrewd brown eyes. 'I imagine this coffee comes at a price.'

'It does. I want information about the body in Sterling Chaney's overpriced box.'

Katie lowered her voice. 'Shut the door, will you? This news is radioactive.'

I checked the hall to make sure no one was lurking, then closed the door.

As soon as Katie heard the click, she said, 'As I predicted, this is a screw-up of epic proportions. The only thing saving the worthless asses of Detective Greiman and DI Regina Greiman is that our chief, Evarts Evans, did the autopsy. Evarts calls this mess "a little problem," which is like describing the *Titanic*'s sinking as "a little boating accident."'

Katie paused for another drink, then said, 'Angela, I heard you were at the funeral and helped preserve the scene. Good work.'

'Thanks. That drunken idiot wanted to open the casket in church.' I told her the whole gruesome story.

'If we're lucky, Camilla won't sue the ME,' Katie said.

'I can definitely say there was plenty of pain and suffering,' I said. 'Mostly because her husband is alive, not dead. Did you do the autopsy on the body in the casket?'

'Yep,' Katie said, 'and there wasn't enough left of the poor bastard to spread on a cracker.'

I gulped and felt slightly queasy at Katie's forthright description. Another sip of coffee helped settle my roiling stomach.

'The undertaker just wrapped what was left of him in a sheet,' she said. 'Didn't even bother picking out all the car bits.'

'Could you ID the man?'

'Oh, yeah. There was enough for DNA. He was in the system. His name is Dante Densellante. A pretty name for a very bad boy. His juvenile record was sealed, but he started his adult criminal career at eighteen by raping a thirteen-year-old girl. By the time Dante died at twenty-nine, he'd spent ten years in prison and had a rap sheet a mile long, including assault and battery, and assault with a deadly weapon. But mostly, he boosted cars. He went out in a blaze of glory when he ran Sterling's car into a rock face at a hundred and ten miles an hour.'

I winced.

'Lucky for him, Dante was drunk out of his mind,' Katie said. 'They found the remains of a bottle of eighteen-year-old Glenfiddich single malt at the scene. I suspect Sterling kept that bottle in his car. I don't think Dante drank expensive scotch.'

'Does Dante have any family?'

'Not that we can tell. His parents are dead, and no one has come forward to claim his body. Looks like Dante will be buried by the county in the potter's field. He'll have the fanciest burial there – the usual plain wooden box, but Sterling is letting the deceased keep the "Velutra velvet" interior from the Promethean.'

Katie lowered her voice. 'Angela, you should have seen the inside of that casket. It was whorehouse red.'

'Is that the name of the color?'

'No, actually that was "Rumba Red."'

'Now there's a dignified name,' I said. 'I hope Camilla sues for pain and suffering just for having to pick out that gaudy casket.'

'I've never seen a casket interior like this one,' Katie said. 'The velvet was amazingly soft. And it was ruched, draped, flounced, and pleated, like some Victorian lady's dress.'

'I've never seen you this excited by a casket before,' I said.

'I guess what I'm trying to say is that casket is really something. It had an adjustable bed and mattress.'

'So if Sterling gets tired of lying flat on his back, halfway through eternity he can sit up?'

Katie gave me the stink eye.

'What's going to happen to that morbid marvel?' I asked.

'When our investigation is finished, Sterling is sending it somewhere to have it refurbished and a new velvet interior put in.'

'Does it need to be deodorized?' I asked. 'It had a body in it.'

'Beats me.' Katie shrugged. 'You know my nose shorts out when I'm working. Sterling still wants to be buried in that casket, and he says he'll put it in storage until the great day.'

'Maybe he'll keep the lid up to air it out,' I said.

Katie snorted.

'He's been parading around on the TV shows in his black funeral suit,' I said. 'Should look nice against that red velvet.'

'I saw the suit,' Katie said. 'He's more interested in his burial than an Egyptian pharaoh.'

'He's loving the publicity,' I said. 'Camilla told me he's

had at least thirty-one interviews. He was talking to Valerie Cannata today.'

Katie shook her head. 'That fool gave Valerie an interview? She'll eat him alive.'

'Sterling must be feeling brave,' I said. 'Valerie doesn't do puff pieces.'

'Fatally overconfident is more like it,' Katie said. 'When she finishes with him, he may wish he *was* dead.'

We silently sipped coffee for a moment before I asked, 'How did this debacle happen – Sterling's misidentification? I've read about wrong IDs happening in the old days. But that was before DNA.'

'This was the triumvirate of screw-ups,' Katie said. 'All three elements combined to create the flawless clusterfuck.'

She set down her nearly empty coffee cup and counted on her fingers.

'First, and most important, our laziest detective, Ray Greiman, answered the call. The uniform at the scene saw the expensive car and the Chouteau Forest Country Club sticker on the back bumper, and correctly deduced that this was a dead bigwig. Never mind that detectives don't go out on traffic deaths, Greiman was there, lips puckered to kiss any important posteriors.

'Greiman knew the car – it belonged to Sterling Chaney. He also saw the broken bottle of expensive single malt that was thrown from the Porsche and knew it was Sterling's brand. He checked the license and confirmed the car was Sterling's. Based on no other evidence, and against all rules, he declared the dead man was Sterling Chaney.

'Meanwhile, firefighters with the Jaws of Life were trying to remove the body from the car. It wasn't easy – the car folded like an accordion. By the time they'd removed what was left of the driver, the detective's sapheaded sister, DI Regina Greiman, arrived.'

I'd met this death investigator a few times. Regina was a horse-faced version of her handsome brother. There was no love lost between us.

'So we have the worst detective and the worst DI on the case,' I said.

'That's what I was trying to tell you.' Katie sounded impatient. 'Big brother Ray told his little sis that the deceased was Sterling Chaney, and she believed him. The body was so mangled it was difficult to do a proper death investigation. So she didn't. The remains were shoveled into a body bag.

'Our boss Evarts wasn't playing golf that day, so he did the autopsy – and did nothing to confirm the dead man's identity. That's how a rapist and car thief wound up reposing in a thirty-thousand-dollar casket.'

She finished the last of her coffee and tossed the cup into the trash. Time for me to leave before she started asking about my love life. I finished my coffee and reached for my purse.

'Check the hall carefully before you go out my door, Angela,' Katie said. 'And whatever you do, don't go to the DI office.'

'There's no need,' I said. 'I have today off.'

I also have a unique work situation. Most death investigators go into an office at the medical examiner's and hang around when they're not in the field. Not me. My office space was taken when Evarts wanted a Swedish shower. He expanded his office into the corner formerly occupied by my desk. By unspoken agreement, I was allowed to stay out of the office as long as the detectives could reach me. Evarts and I were both happy with that arrangement.

'How are you and that hunky cop doing, Angela?'

Uh-oh. This was getting personal. When Katie started asking about my love life, it was time to finish up and leave. I was a widow, but I'd been dating a Chouteau Forest uniform, Christopher Ferretti, and Katie was an amateur matchmaker.

'Fine,' I said.

'Have you moved into his house?'

'Of course not,' I said.

'But you're there six nights a week.'

'Five,' I said.

'What are you keeping at his place?'

'Just a toothbrush.'

'And?'

I squirmed under her gaze like a pinned butterfly. 'And some underwear, a work suit, and some casual clothes. That's all.'

'Why are you still wearing your wedding ring?'

'Because I'm not ready to take it off,' I said.

'Donegan has been dead how many years?'

'He's not dead to me,' I said.

'So you're sleeping with one man while wearing the wedding ring of another,' Katie said. 'Are you wearing that wedding ring to ward off your new lover – or to tempt Chris into replacing that ring with one of his own?'

I didn't answer. I grabbed my purse and ran.

SIX

I fled Katie's office as if the devil were after me, and didn't stop until I unlocked my car and turned the air conditioner on high. I breathed in the cool air and waited for my heart to stop pounding.

Only then did I think about Katie's statement, the one that bedeviled me.

So you're sleeping with one man while wearing the wedding ring of another.

It was true. I still wore my late husband Donegan's ring. I couldn't take it off. Donegan had been a teacher at City University, and he'd died too young of a heart attack. After his sudden death, my own broken heart never quite healed.

It took Officer Chris Ferretti months to slowly coax me into dating him. I'd been a widow for two years when I'd met Chris. Someone had tried to run me down in a parking lot, and I'd narrowly escaped. Chris was the officer on call. He courted me sweetly and patiently, and I slowly came back to life. I even told Chris I loved him.

But could I take off my ring and tell Donegan goodbye forever? Was I ready to do that?

I rolled my Dodge Charger carefully up my driveway, avoiding the bushes at the entrance that would scrape its gleaming black sides. It was brand-new, and I didn't want any marks on it. My last car had been destroyed in a wild chase.

My home was gilded by the slanting late-afternoon sun and surrounded by summer flowers: purple phlox, red hibiscus, and a rainbow of zinnias. The two-story white stone house with the gingerbread porch was a former guest house on the Du Pres estate. My parents bought the house, and I inherited it. It was filled with happy memories of my parents and Donegan. Chris and I had never spent a night here. I didn't want to think about that, either.

Inside, I poured myself a glass of cold white wine and

opened a can of cashews. To stop the thoughts swirling in my head, I settled on the leather couch in the living room and switched on the TV.

A big red *SPECIAL REPORT* flashed across the screen. The bottom dropped out of my stomach when a sleek Valerie Cannata appeared on the screen. I didn't like the sly smile on her face. Not one bit. I took a sip of wine to drown my unease.

Valerie stood in front of the Forest Episcopal church and said, 'You've heard about Sterling Chaney, the man who was late for his own funeral. Unless you've been living in a hermit's cave, you can't have missed that story.'

Valerie's reddish-brown, shoulder-length hair was perfect. She wore a tight gold-brown dress and four-inch heels, and climbed the stone church steps backward, without holding on to the rail. I thought she deserved an Emmy for that feat alone.

When she was framed against the closed church doors, Valerie said, 'Sterling gives a great interview, and we've all laughed at his quips.'

She showed a brief clip of Sterling boasting about his gold casket. 'It's a little over the top to be six feet under.' He guffawed at his own joke, showing too many teeth. He looked like a rube.

Valerie continued her narrative. 'Sterling is a man of substance in Chouteau Forest, Missouri. He belongs to the prestigious – and all-white, all-male – Chouteau Founders Club.'

Uh-oh. I took another soothing sip, but my stomach was still fluttering. Maybe some salty cashews would calm it.

'He received an honorary doctorate from City University, and according to our records, in the last three years he has given more than ten million dollars to charity.'

That's good, I thought, and felt slightly calmer. But I knew Valerie's special report was just beginning.

'His wife of ten years is Camilla Chaney.'

Their wedding picture was on the screen, with Camilla as a radiant blonde bride.

'The glamorous Camilla is equally generous with her money and her time. She serves on all the important Forest committees.' Sarcasm dripped from Valerie's words.

I felt hot acid surge into my stomach. My friend didn't deserve this. Camilla did devote her life to good deeds – and she worked, she didn't just write checks. She volunteered at a soup kitchen to feed the homeless. She worked at a shelter for battered women, sorting clothes and other donations. She taught reading to grade-schoolers struggling with their books.

Valerie didn't mention these worthy activities. Instead, she asked, 'So where does all the money come from? Well, as Sterling told me . . .'

Another clip of Sterling flashed on the screen. He was sitting in a wingback chair in his study, and for once, he wasn't bragging. He looked into the camera with all the sincerity he could muster and said, 'My daddy left me some money and I started a little telephone service.'

Valerie was sitting across from him in a tailored black suit, a blood-red scarf slashed across her throat.

'A little telephone service' – Valerie gave a cruel smile – 'that brings in fifteen million a year.' She widened her eyes. 'My, my, that must be a special service indeed. What could it be?'

I didn't know what the service was, but I didn't like her tone. This time I took a huge gulp of wine.

Valerie paused dramatically, then leaned in, confiding to her audience, 'Well, as we all know, sex sells. And that's what our model citizen does. Sterling Chaney sells sex. Men – and, I suppose, some woman – call a special number, and for ten dollars a minute, women with sexy voices read risqué stories. Let's listen in – at least as long as the FCC permits – on a phone call between a female employee of Mr Chaney and our show's intern, Patrick Smitt.'

An old-school telephone appeared on the screen, and then we heard a sultry voice. 'So, Patrick, would you like to hear what I'm wearing?'

A pause, then a reedy voice said, 'Yeah, sure.'

I knocked back another gulp, then grabbed the wine bottle out of the fridge.

'I'm wearing a black lace bra and sheer black panties, Patrick, and my womanhood is wet and throbbing.' The sexy voice was panting passionately, filled with desperate need. 'I want you, Patrick. I'm young and firm and hot. Oh, so hot,

Patrick. I know that you are strong and hard, and you will rip
aside the thin black fabric and thrust—' The sultry voice was
cut off in mid-pant.

'That's all we're permitted to air, viewers, but young Patrick
quickly ran up a two-hundred-dollar bill. Ask yourself: Who
else is contributing to Mr Chaney's wealth – your husbands?
Your brothers?'

The camera showed the bar at Solange, a restaurant and
watering hole for the wealthy. The men's faces at the bar were
in shadow. I drank more wine, but it wasn't killing my fear.

'Or' – Valerie made another dramatic pause – 'your sons?
There's no age limit on who can listen to these so-called
"stories."'

That was shown over an artful shot of the Chouteau Forest
Jaguars, the local Little League team, playing baseball in the
park. The boys looked angelic, but I couldn't make out a single
face. I needed another drink after that.

Next was a photo of a credit card bill with an item for 250
dollars circled in red. Valerie positively cooed as she said,
'Oh, and the charges won't appear on your credit card state-
ment with the service's real name: Sterling Service of Chouteau
Forest. No way. They're billed as the Sterling Superior Steak
House.'

Good grief. Every woman in the Forest would be checking
her credit card statements, looking for that restaurant charge.
How many men just lost their appetites? I knocked back more
wine.

Valerie grinned and said, 'While Sterling Chaney is making
millions, his thirty female employees are making a measly
seven dollars an hour.'

Erin O. McBride was on the screen next, in a neat but
modest apartment. Erin's words were as fiery as her long red
hair, and her green eyes snapped with rage. 'Seven bucks an
hour. That's not even the federal minimum wage of seven
dollars and twenty-five cents. Hell, it's not even within hailing
distance of the Missouri minimum wage – eleven dollars and
fifteen cents an hour. We get so-called "bonuses" of twenty-
five dollars for every phone script we write. But Sterling is
raking in the dough while we're getting by on crumbs.'

Valerie was back, her voice soft and deadly. 'And some of Sterling's employees aren't getting by. Consider the case of Diana Dunn and her eight-year-old daughter, Abigail.'

Diana, in a prim white blouse and slim black skirt, looked like the last woman who would read lascivious stories for a living. She sat on a beige living-room couch with her arm around a thin, black-haired little girl so pale her blue veins were visible in her forehead. The child wore jeans and a pink polka-dot T-shirt, and had pink ribbons in her hair.

'This is my little girl, Abby,' Diana said. Abby smiled shyly.

'She has a leaky mitral valve,' her mother said. 'That means the mitral valve flaps in her heart don't close tightly and the valve leaks blood. Abby needs surgery to fix the valve and then she'll be just fine. In December, we asked Sterling for a raise. We wanted to make the Missouri minimum wage. Instead of a raise, Sterling promised us health insurance. I was thrilled. My girl needs that surgery.

'That was six months ago. Still no sign of any health insurance. Abby's not getting any better. She can't run and play with her friends. She's short of breath. Sometimes her heart beats so fast she gets scared. She misses school on bad days.'

Oh, man, this was a debacle. I wondered how my friend Camilla was, and drank another glass in her honor.

'Fortunately,' Diana said, 'my little girl likes to read.' Abby was holding a copy of *Charlotte's Web* and smiling adorably. The camera panned copies of Nancy Drew and the Clue Crew collection, including *Sleepover Sleuths*, *Scream for Ice Cream*, and the *Case of the Sneaky Snowman* on the coffee table, next to a bowl of pink silk roses.

Diana hugged her daughter and kissed her pale forehead. 'So my girl makes do with books, instead of playing soccer with her friends. Meanwhile, I found out Sterling spent thirty thousand dollars on a casket – a casket! – for his worthless carcass, when my Abby needs an operation to stay alive and healthy.'

Diana looked directly into the camera. 'This isn't my ideal job. Not by a long shot. But I'm a single mother and it allows me to stay home with Abby.

'I keep asking Larry where's our health insurance, and he

says it's coming soon. But I haven't seen hide nor hair of it yet, and it's been six months.'

Valerie was back, smiling into the camera, canary feathers on her red lips. 'And who is Larry, you might ask? Larry Perkins is Sterling's manager, the face of the business. I'll tell you more about him, after the break. Stay tuned.'

SEVEN

I drank through two commercials while I waited for Valerie to show us Larry, 'the face of the company.'

Some face. Larry was almost as pale as the ailing Abby, and nowhere near as pretty. He was completely bald, and his round head made him look like a fetus. A horizontally striped T-shirt did not add width to his narrow shoulders, but it beautifully emphasized his burgeoning belly.

Larry sat behind a beat-up gray metal desk in a dreary office, paneled with brown plywood. The single window was covered with dingy olive-green curtains. The snazzy space-age red-and-black leather chair and a giant TV screen on the credenza behind Larry's desk were the only bright spots.

Except for his smile. Larry was smiling proudly for the camera. 'Yep, Sterling started the phone service. And it took off right away. I'm what you'd call the main manager. Sterling put up the money, and I handle the day-to-day operations. I deal with the girls and sometimes they can be difficult.' He lowered his voice a notch. 'You know, at the wrong time of the month.'

Oh, jeez. The idiot didn't say that, did he? I downed the rest of the wine and opened another bottle.

'And just how do you know the *women*' – Valerie emphasized that word – 'are menstruating?'

'You don't have to be crude,' Larry said. Ugh. He was blushing. 'Their complaints are regular as clockwork, every twenty-eight or thirty days, so I figure they have to be on the rag.' I downed a full glass during that awful exchange.

'You don't think these women's complaints are legitimate?' Now Valerie was an avenging goddess, defending her sex.

Larry squirmed like the nasty little maggot he was. 'Well, uh, no, see, uh, Sterling tells me which complaints are OK. He's the one who said the girls could have health insurance.'

'So a man decides which of these women's needs are legitimate?'

Larry should have curled up and died in the acid bath Valerie dumped on him, but he gamely struggled on.

'Well, yes, he's the girls'—'

'*Women's!*' Valerie interrupted.

'Yes, ah, uh, the women's boss.'

Larry looked like he'd walked through Death Valley. I could see the sweat pouring off his massive forehead and the huge sweat stains under his armpits. Valerie looked cool and calm. I took another drink to stay calm myself.

'Anyway, the job isn't that bad,' he said. 'All they have to do is read for a couple of minutes.'

'Read what!' Valerie demanded.

'Just some stories,' he said.

'What kind of stories? Fairytales? Children's stories?' Valerie grilled him relentlessly.

'Uh, sexy stories,' the maggot finally admitted.

'And what kind of men listen to these stories?' she asked. 'Pillars of society?'

'Maybe,' Larry said, and gulped. 'Some are, yes.'

'What are these so-called pillars of society doing while the woman are reading?'

'Listening?' Larry sounded like a C-minus student trying to give the correct answer.

Valerie went in for the kill. 'And?'

'Uh, maybe pleasuring themselves?' Larry sounded tentative.

Valerie swooped right in. 'And you don't think that reading masturbatory material before a real person is difficult?'

Larry was trembling with fear. 'Yes. Yes.'

'And since those women bring in fifteen million dollars a year, don't you think their complaints need consideration?'

'Oh, definitely,' Larry said. His skin was wine-red and I wondered if he'd stroke out – not that it would be any great loss. I also realized I'd finished half the new bottle of white wine I'd been drinking. I poured myself another glass to calm down and chomped a handful of cashews.

'Now, about the health insurance,' Valerie said. 'Where is

it? It's been six months since Mr Chaney agreed to give them insurance.'

'We want to give the girls—' Valerie pinned him with a glare, and he said, 'I mean, the women, the best possible health insurance, but that takes time. There are so many choices. They'll get their insurance, though. I promise.'

Valerie swung him around in his space-age chair so he was facing the giant TV screen.

'This couldn't be the distraction, could it?' Valerie said. 'Ladies and gentlemen, Larry here has a sixty-five-inch TU7000 Smart 4K UHD TV and Nintendo Switch Limited Edition Bundle.'

She then began rattling off a slew of names, which made no sense to me, but must have been important.

'This bundle includes the TV, the Nintendo Switch *Animal Crossing: New Horizons* Edition, two joy-cons, joy-con straps, high-speed HDMI cable, Nintendo Switch dock, joy-con dock, joy-con grip, and Nintendo Switch adapter.

'Let me translate that for you, viewers. Larry is a video gamer. He's sitting in an expensive gamer's chair – the Secretlab TITAN Evo 2022 Superman – and this bundle costs sixteen hundred dollars. So instead of searching for life-saving health insurance for little Abby, he plays games.' Even the clueless Larry flinched at the contempt in her voice.

'I need to take a break from the pressures of dealing with customer complaints,' he said. Larry sounded so panicked that I knocked back more wine.

'What kind of complaints do you get?' Valerie asked.

Larry seemed to relax a little. 'Three main categories.' Larry held up three fingers, and I saw that his hand was trembling slightly.

'Sometimes we get complaints from parents that their young boy ran up a bill. We refund those charges immediately. We don't want any trouble with minors, so we always erase those bills.'

But there was no way to erase what those boys had heard, I thought – the passionate moans and salacious stories.

'And, second, some callers object to our fifty-dollar story fee that's added to their bill.'

'Do you tell them about the story fee?' Valerie asked.

'Oh, yes, it's mentioned right in the beginning, but most men don't pay attention to the notice. They're rarin' to go and not always thinking straight, if you know what I mean.' He smiled.

Valerie did not. 'So the women who write the stories only get twenty-five dollars, but you charge the callers fifty dollars,' she said.

'That's right,' he said. 'It's an agency fee. We're their agents.'

'And there's another complaint category?' Valerie's voice was smooth as silk.

'Oh, yeah. Our other big complaint is from gentlemen who get carried away when they talk to our girls and run up a big bill. They claim they didn't enjoy the experience and try to get us to refund their money. I say, "No way, sir. I know you enjoyed your phone call, and I have the audio file to prove it."'

Valerie looked shocked. 'So you record these calls?'

'Oh, yes, for quality control. And when I play the tape back and they hear themselves moaning and groaning, well, the problem is solved.' He smiled happily.

'Isn't that illegal?' Valerie asked.

'Oh, no.' It was Larry's turn to look shocked. 'Missouri has a "one-party consent" law. So if a company operates in Missouri, we can record a conversation or phone call if we're a party to the conversation. We don't need prior consent from the other party.'

'Unless you are recording to commit a criminal act,' Valerie said.

'Oh, we don't do anything criminal. Heavens, no.' Larry was wide-eyed with sincerity.

'Blackmail isn't criminal?' she asked.

'We're not blackmailing anyone,' Larry said. 'We're just reminding them of their fiduciary responsibility.'

'And do you also remind them that you keep the recordings?'

'Oh, yes,' Larry said. 'We're totally honest.'

Valerie's face was looking a little fuzzy. I reached for the clicker to adjust the picture and knocked the wine bottle off the coffee table. Fortunately, it was empty.

Chris called, but the answer button on my phone was blurry, so I let it go to voicemail.

I wanted to call Camilla, but the phone was slippery as a fish. She'd be OK. Things moved slowly in the Forest, and Camilla had a lot of friends. Her husband was a jerk, but they wouldn't hold that against her.

This would blow over soon, I thought, as I fell asleep.

EIGHT

I woke up on the living-room couch at nine thirty the next morning. My tongue felt like an old carpet. I sat up slowly and the room shifted and spun. Getting up was going to be difficult. I moved carefully so my pounding head wouldn't roll off my shoulders.

When the room righted again, I was sure I could stand up. Sometime during the night, I'd turned off the TV, but I'd never made it upstairs to bed. A flash of fear penetrated the hangover fog. I was on call today. I slowly reached for my phone on the coffee table and checked. No messages from work, but I had one from Chris. I'd call him when I was a little more coherent.

I carefully picked the two empty wine bottles off the floor, along with the empty cashew can, and carried them to the kitchen trash. A geyser of acid erupted in my gut. I hung on to the sink while I drank two glasses of cold water and felt slightly better.

My roiling stomach demanded real food, so I made coffee, toast, and scrambled eggs, and carried my breakfast into the living room. I switched on the TV to see if there were any repercussions from Valerie's interview last night. I prayed there was nothing. The Forest moved slowly, and I hoped this scandal would die quickly.

I was wrong. It was spreading like a bad rash.

My screen filled with video of shouting protestors circling in front of the locked wrought-iron gates of the Chaney mansion. They carried colorful homemade signs that screamed:

Keep Your Promise! We Demand Health Insurance!

A Little Girl Shouldn't Die for Your Golden Casket!

The group was led by the fiery-haired Erin, leader of the answering service workers. Her sign said, *You Live in a Mansion Paid for by Our Work!*

Erin was dressed in black with a green scarf in her long

red hair. She led the protestors in a chant: 'Hell no, we won't go! Not till you pay us what you owe!'

I counted twenty-one protestors, most of them youngish women.

A slim, earnest blonde reporter named Olive Nelson asked Erin for an interview. Olive approached Erin cautiously but respectfully, as if she expected the protestor to hurl a Molotov cocktail.

Erin's interview was an impassioned plea for her compatriots.

'We're going to stand out here until Sterling Chaney gives us our health insurance,' she said. 'We want everyone to see what a cheapskate he is. Look how he lives!' The camera obligingly shifted to the many-gabled mansion and the velvety green lawns.

'We paid for that lifestyle!' Erin shook her sign. 'And we're getting by on almost nothing. Nothing! Last night, Valerie Cannata gave viewers a glimpse of what's really going on in Chouteau Forest.

'Valerie exposed the corrupt heart of the Forest. Yes, it looks rich and pretty on the outside. But these fat cats got their wealth by exploiting people like us!'

Oh, boy. Erin was right, but certain powerful members of the Forest weren't going to appreciate that remark. When workers demanded more money, it was definitely bad for business. The Forest elite would quickly try to stamp out this small rebellion.

'We're sick and tired of it,' Erin said, while the other protestors cheered and waved their signs.

'We're not going back to work until we have our health insurance. Without us on the phones, Sterling can't make any money. He might actually have to work for a living.'

The protestors laughed and jeered as Erin went back to the angry circle.

Five of the protestors were black. One was a curvy young woman, Linda Connelly, carrying a sign that said, *Talk Isn't Cheap – Sterling Chaney Is*. Olive interviewed her first. 'My sign says it better than I can,' Linda said. 'It's the last word, as far as I'm concerned.'

Two older black women shyly shook their heads and declined interviews, but showed off their signs: *Pay Us What We're Due* and *Fair Wages for Women Workers.*

The fourth black protestor, Sheila Grafton, was so heavily pregnant it was painful to look at her. 'Are you OK, Ms Grafton?' the TV reporter said.

'Of course I am,' Sheila said. 'This protest is important to my future – and my child's.' She proudly patted her baby bump.

Olive interviewed Jenny Brown, a slender black woman with long braids and big brown eyes. 'I have an educated accent, don't I?' Jenny asked Olive.

'Oh, yes,' the reporter agreed.

'But I get paid an extra five dollars if I use what Sterling calls my "Southern mammy voice" or my "gangsta voice." Those are his terms. I'm embarrassed to duplicate what those sound like. It's too demeaning. But I'm just broke enough I need the extra money.'

'And Sterling pays you an extra five dollars an hour,' Olive said.

'An hour!' Jenny looked furious. 'He pays me an extra five dollars a day! A day! That cheap-(bleep) honky (bleep)!'

'Oh, my,' was all Olive could manage.

'And it's just as bad for Suzi Chin. Come here, Suzi.' Jenny grabbed a thin Asian woman with long straight hair out of the scrum of protestors. 'Listen to Suzi tell her story.'

'Like Jenny, I speak educated English,' she said. 'My family has been in this country since the Gold Rush days, when they emigrated from China. That's almost a hundred and seventy-five years. But if I – I hate to use this word, but it's what Mr Chaney says – if I speak "Chinky" – his word for pidgin English – I also get an extra five dollars a day.' Suzi's face glowed pink with shame and she ducked her head. 'I am so embarrassed.'

'You have nothing to be embarrassed about,' Olive said. 'You're trying to make a living. I am so sorry for both of you.'

'It's the same for our friend Juanita Gomez.' Suzi reached out and took the hand of another protestor, a chunky Latina with short, curly hair. Suzi pulled Juanita into the frame with a hug. 'Tell them what you have to do,' Suzi said.

'I have to say things like "I doan theenk so" in an exaggerated Mexican accent,' Juanita said. 'And I'm from Ecuador! All of us are demeaned by these policies. We're forced to cater to men's racist fantasies.'

'This is terrible.' Olive looked genuinely concerned. 'Stand by, please, while we listen to a new report from Valerie Cannata.'

Now Valerie was on the screen, glowing with triumph in a slim dark suit. A heavenly blue shirt framed her face. 'I had no idea that my story about the squalid inner workings of a Chouteau Forest phone sex service would provoke such an angry response,' she said, 'but since my story broke, we have heard from many outraged viewers.

'A group of lawyers has volunteered to sue on behalf of the women for the racist job practices. You heard about those from reporter Olive Nelson. Because the company uses interstate telephone lines, the US Justice Department is investigating. And a number of citizens, who now understand the strange charges on their credit cards, are up in arms.

'One of those is Mrs Janice Monroe. We interviewed her outside her home in Chouteau Forest.'

Mrs Monroe was somewhere in her fifties with short brown hair and a blue tie-dyed T-shirt. Her face was flushed with anger.

'I thought my husband liked to eat steak. That's what his credit card said. And that was bad enough! But after I saw your show last night, Valerie, I realized what he really liked was smut! He spent our mortgage money listening to those ladies talk dirty. Thirteen hundred dollars! Now how am I going to make that payment? I could lose my house. It's all I have.'

She burst into tears while the camera showed her neat gray ranch home with the black shutters and red door. The window boxes were filled with red geraniums.

Oh, man, this was worse than I thought. Sterling was revealed as a racist, a cheapskate, an exploiter of women, and a homewrecker.

I felt sorry for the damage Sterling had caused, and I also felt bad for my friend Camilla, dragged into this mess by her worthless, lying husband. I wanted to call and see how she was doing, but first I called Chris.

'Would you like to come to dinner tonight?' he asked. 'I want to try out a new chicken recipe.'

'Tempting,' I said. Chris was an amazing cook and actually enjoyed working in the kitchen. He delighted in trying out new recipes for me.

'Oh, it's more than tempting. The chicken has a feta cheese filling.'

'Sounds wonderful,' I said. Especially after last night's dinner of cashews. 'What can I bring?'

'Yourself.' I heard the smile in his voice. 'I've made a strawberry torte for dessert and I have a couple of bottles of Malbec.' I winced at the thought of more wine, but maybe I'd feel differently by dinnertime.

'How about a couple of loaves of sourdough?'

'Deal,' he said. 'Seven o'clock OK?'

'It is, but I'm working today. I'll warn you if I get called out.'

'I love you,' he said, and the phone nearly melted in my hand.

'I love you, too.'

I waited a minute for my heart rate to calm down and then called Camilla. 'How are you?' I asked.

'I'm OK.' Her voice was heavy with held-in tears.

'Oh, Angela,' she said between sobs. 'This is so awful.'

'I'll be right there,' I said.

Camilla stopped crying long enough to give me directions to the back entrance to her home, so I could avoid the protestors. I parked my car next to a Forest Repair Service van. The housekeeper, Mrs Ellis, let me inside. She guided me up the stairs to Camilla's bedroom.

'She feels too terrible to get out of bed today, Angela. The poor dear is crushed, absolutely crushed, by that terrible news story. And those protestors! Now the neighbors have called the cops, and they're out front with their lights flashing. Poor Camilla's life has been turned upside down. Your visit will do her a world of good. I'll bring up some tea shortly. Try to encourage her to eat. She hasn't had anything to eat or drink since that TV story.'

'Mrs Ellis?' called a man's voice. 'I have a question.'

'I'll be right there, Phil,' she called back.

'Phil's working on the laundry chute. There's an obstruction on the second floor. I'll be back with the tea as quickly as I can.'

She knocked on the door and said, 'Camilla, dear, Angela is here.'

Camilla's bedroom was vast, and there was no sign of her husband, not even a wedding photo. The room was painted pale rose. Camilla looked lost in an enormous canopy bed with pink velvet hangings.

She also looked even worse than I expected. She was wearing a high-necked, long-sleeved white cotton gown, suitable for a nunnery. It washed out her already pale complexion. Her blonde hair was unwashed and unkempt, and her eyes were red and puffy. On her lap was an open book, but she wasn't reading. She was staring off into space.

'Camilla?' I said, quietly.

'Angela!' she smiled. 'Come sit by me.' She patted the vast bed. A single tear trickled down her face. 'I'm so glad you came to see me.'

I sat on the edge and hugged her. 'Of course I came to see you. That's what friends are for.'

'I don't have any friends anymore,' she said. 'Not after what Sterling did.'

I dismissed her words. 'Of course you do. You've done too much volunteer work.'

'I've been asked to resign from all my committees,' she said. She showed me a handful of note cards, all hand-written on heavy cream-colored stationery. 'These were all hand-delivered this morning. Here, read this one.'

Dear Mrs Chaney,
  Your husband has brought shame and opprobrium upon us all. If you have any self-respect, you will resign from this committee immediately. If you have an ounce

of pride, you will divorce that man as soon as possible.
Too bad your husband didn't die in that crash.
    Sincerely,
    Mrs Potter Du Pres Du Pont

The blue-black ink was bristling with rage.

Camilla held up the other note cards. Anger sparked in her eyes. 'I've been deemed not fit to serve soup to the homeless or sort clothes for the needy. I can't even teach children reading. I'm being totally ostracized.'

'Surely not,' I said.

'Absolutely,' she said. 'Even my money isn't good enough. My latest donation to SOS Hospital has been returned. Ten thousand dollars!'

'I could understand punishing Sterling,' I said, 'but not you. You didn't know anything about his business.'

'How could I be married ten years and not know?' she asked. 'I suspected the way he made his money wasn't totally honest, but I didn't think it was this bad. Now I find out on national television that he exploits the poor. He forces trapped women to use ugly racist stereotypes for five measly dollars. He won't even give them health insurance! I should have known. He refurbished this whole house. I can't even look at it now. It's tainted by the blood, sweat, and tears of those overworked women. And that little girl, the one who might die without treatment. I can't even think about her.'

After the next tear storm dried up, I asked, 'Where is Sterling?'

'He's sleeping in the old chauffeur's quarters, over the garage. I hope the exhaust fumes choke him. I'm never taking him back. Never, ever! I wish he'd died in that car accident! I wish he was dead!'

She was shouting now. 'I want him dead! Oh, God, how could you play such a cruel joke on me?'

I thought I heard a noise outside Camilla's door, but when I looked around, no one was in the hall. Probably Mrs Ellis, the housekeeper.

Still, I thought some caution was called for. Camilla had

collapsed weeping into my arms. I held her and said, 'Sh! Be careful what you say. Sterling has a lot of enemies right now. Someone really could kill him.'

'Good!' she said. 'And not soon enough!'

NINE

Mrs Ellis carried in a tea tray loaded with Limoges china and a small feast. She set the tray on a table by the bed and said, 'I've included all your favorites, Camilla, dear. Strawberries with fresh cream. Cinnamon pound cake. Egg salad sandwiches made with fresh dill from the kitchen herbs, and chocolate chip cookies. Angela, you'll help her eat this, won't you?' She winked at me.

'Definitely.' I promised myself that I would hold back so my friend could get the food she needed.

Boom! The noise made us all jump. 'That's just Phil, fixing the laundry chute down the hall,' the housekeeper said. 'He'll be leaving soon. Enjoy your tea.'

Camilla poured us both cups of tea. 'Lapsang souchong,' she said. 'Smoked tea. If you don't like the taste, I can ask for something else.'

I'm not a big fan of tea, but this was good, and strong enough for a coffee drinker like me.

'Look at all this food,' Camilla said. 'I don't know where to start.'

'How about the strawberries and cream?' I said.

Camilla fixed a heaping bowl for me. I handed it back to her.

'I meant for you,' I said. 'You should eat.'

She sighed. 'I'm not hungry. My life's been overturned. First, my husband is dead, and then he's miraculously alive, and for a brief time I was happy. Then that TV exposé made all his sins public – well, not all his sins, thank goodness – but enough.'

I was surprised how strong Camilla seemed. When I first met her, way back in high school, she wilted at every mean girl's jab.

Camilla set the bowl of strawberries down. To stop my frown of disapproval, she reached for a tiny crustless egg salad square and nibbled it.

'What's wrong?' I stopped myself just in time from adding 'now.'

'I think he's seeing another woman. Already. After he promised our marriage would be different if I took him back.

'I sort his shirts for the laundry because I don't want Mrs Ellis to find something embarrassing. Right before that TV story came out, I found lipstick on his shirt – orange lipstick! And the shirt reeked of perfume. Cheap perfume!'

She took another mouselike bite of the sandwich and said, 'He's also spending a lot of time with that redheaded protestor who's on TV – Erin.'

'He has to see her,' I said. 'He's negotiating with her.'

'Hah!' Camilla bit angrily into the egg salad and downed the entire morsel. I handed her a chocolate chip cookie and took one for myself.

'Any idea who Sterling is seeing?' I asked, and finished off the first cookie.

'I think it's Brenda Burkett, the redhead who works at Solange. On weekdays, she tends bar there and she likes to wear colors that most redheads can't – like orange! I'm sure it was her lipstick on his shirt.'

'I've seen Brenda,' I said. 'She mixes a mean martini. She also has a tattoo on her right arm that says, "I'd rather have a free bottle in front of me than a pre-frontal lobotomy."' I didn't add that the men drinking at Solange thought she was adorable.

'Brenda's good-looking. Why would she be interested in a—'

My words skidded to a stop. Everything I could think of was insulting: 'a drunken blowhard?' 'a married man who runs a sketchy business?' I stuffed another cookie in my mouth so I couldn't say anything awful.

Fortunately, Camilla answered my question before I said something I regretted. 'Because, in her eyes, that pathetic drunk is a star. He's been on national TV. And he's a big tipper.'

I heard a distant rumble, like approaching thunder, and looked up at Camilla. She caught the question in my eyes. 'That's his new drop-top Ferrari 599 SA Aperta. Well, not brand-new. It's a collector's item built in 2011. His hundred-and-fifty-thousand Porsche Carrera wasn't good enough for him. This time he bought a fire-engine red Ferrari. Excuse me,' she said, and the acid dripped from her voice. 'The *exact* color is "Rosso Corsa," one of the fifteen shades of Ferrari red. And the soft top is in "Nero." But I guess when you're paying a million-four for a car, you should have some choice.'

I whistled. 'Is any car worth that?'

'He thinks this one is,' she said. 'It comes with a twelve-cylinder engine, and that's going to give him nothing but trouble. It requires constant tuning. The new car's top speed is two hundred and eight miles an hour. Goes from zero to sixty-two miles an hour in under four seconds.'

'Shouldn't a classic car like that be kept garaged?'

'Sterling says fast cars are meant to be driven, not stuck in a display.'

'You know a lot about cars,' I said.

'My father didn't raise a fool. Not when it came to cars, anyway. He bought me a sweet little Miata when I turned sixteen. But before I could have my first car, I had to learn how to change a tire and how to care for the car. I had to know where the water, oil, and brake fluid went. I can even change my own oil.'

'That's impressive,' I said.

'Not that it does me any good.' Camilla checked the clock on the marble mantel. 'It's almost eleven o'clock. Time for him to leave. That's when the bar opens at Solange. Sterling will sit in the bar drinking and flirting until Brenda gets off work at two. Then they'll shack up at the Four Star Motel.'

'That dump?'

I couldn't keep the disgust out of my voice. The only thing four-star about that motel was its name. It was a no-tell motel out by the edge of town. 'He's taking his girlfriend and a million-dollar car there?'

'No one will see the car, once he parks it,' she said. 'Each sleazy room has its own private garage.'

'Still, I did a death investigation there once, and the bedspreads were disgusting. I'd rather sleep in a dumpster.'

'I hope he catches something,' she said. 'Better yet, I hope he drives this car into a rock face and takes his girlfriend to hell with him. Oh, gawd, I wish he was dead.'

She was shouting again. I heard a small *thunk* and stuck my head into the corridor to investigate the noise. Phil was kneeling by a door at the end of the hall, packing up his tools. 'Hey, Phil.'

'Hi, Angela!' He waved at me.

Rats. He heard me. I waved back and hoped the handyman didn't hear what Camilla had just said. Fast cars, fast women, and booze were a bad combination, and I was sure one of them would be the end of Sterling Chaney.

I stayed with my friend Camilla that afternoon. Mrs Ellis came back once to check on Camilla and encourage her to eat. She also brought fresh tea.

Camilla and I talked, almost like the young girls we used to be. We discussed my romance with Chris Ferretti. 'A man who likes to cook,' she said. 'You're so lucky.'

We moved on to her dreams for the future. 'I've always wanted to be a teacher,' she said. 'I only need a few more hours. I'd like to finish my degree.'

'Where would you teach?' Nowhere in the Forest, I knew.

'I thought I'd teach in the St. Louis suburbs.' She sipped her tea.

'Good idea,' I said. Camilla's plan was realistic.

While we talked, I helped her finish the egg salad sandwiches – that fresh dill was amazing – most of the cookies, two slices of cinnamon cake, and two bowls of strawberries and cream.

Actually, she ate two teeny sandwiches, one strawberry out of her bowl, and a cookie. I ate the rest. I didn't want to hurt Mrs Ellis's feelings.

The longer we talked, the faster Camilla seemed to recover. Soon she had more color in her cheeks and enthusiasm in her voice.

When the mantel clock chimed three, I said, 'Camilla, I need to leave. I have to pick up some bread at the Forest Bakery.'

'And I need to get up, wash my hair, and get dressed.' She held my hand. 'Thank you for coming to visit, Angela. I can't tell you how much it means. No one in the Forest will talk to me.'

'Their loss.' I squeezed her hand and said, 'Stay well, my friend.'

Despite the cheerful afternoon, I felt sad. Camilla didn't deserve to be ostracized by her former acquaintances. The Forest closets were rattling with skeletons.

I headed for the back door in the kitchen, guided by the tantalizing odor of fresh-baked bread. I waved to Mrs Ellis, who was buttering a row of six new loaves.

'Sit down and talk to me, Angela,' she said. 'Just for a minute.'

'I have to go to the Forest Bakery before it closes at five. I'm supposed to bring bread to dinner tonight.'

'You're buying bread at this hour? It will be half-stale – if they even have any left. Take two of these loaves, just out of the oven.'

'Well . . .' I hesitated.

'I really need to talk to you. It won't take long, I promise.'

I sat down at a small wooden table in the kitchen and declined offers of coffee and tea.

Mrs Ellis poured herself a cup of coffee and asked, 'How is she?'

'A little better. She's getting up to take a shower.'

'Thank you for coming. The rest of those . . . witches . . . turned their back on her.'

'I'm glad you're taking care of my friend, Mrs Ellis. She's going through a tough time. You deserve your surname.'

She looked puzzled, then said, 'You know what Ellis means?'

'It's Welsh for "kindly" and you are certainly kind to my friend.'

'That's my pleasure, Angela. I need your expertise. I've disconnected the landline in Camilla's room because of the threats.'

'What kind of threats?'

'Death threats. People are threatening Camilla and her husband.'

'Good heavens! Have you called the police?'

'I don't want to upset her.'

'Camilla needs protection, and so does Sterling. Please call the cops and report this.'

'What if I get the wrong police officer and he laughs at me?'

'No one would . . .' I started to say, and then remembered Ray Greiman. He just might laugh at Mrs Ellis. 'Let me make a call as soon as I leave here. I know a good detective. He can give me the name of the right person to call and I'll get back to you.'

I punched her number into my phone while she wrapped the bread and threw in a dozen chocolate chip cookies. Outside, I stashed all that temptation in my car's trunk, then called Crimes Against Persons detective Jace Budewitz, one of the good guys.

'Angela,' he said. 'You must be psychic. I was just about to call you.'

'Who died?' I asked.

'Well, I'm going to make damn sure it's confirmed this time, but there's been a high-speed accident involving a red Ferrari.'

'Sterling Chaney is dead,' I said.

'I don't know yet, so don't go spreading it around. But the fire department is cutting the bodies out of the car.'

'Bodies, as in two?'

'Yep. The other one is a woman. A redhead.'

TEN

S terling Chaney died half a mile down the road from where car thief Dante Densellante smashed into a rock wall.

If the dead man was Chaney.

All we knew for sure was that a red Ferrari had collided with a bluff of solid rock.

I passed the scene of the first fatal accident on the way to the Ferrari death investigation. The scrapes on the rock face were still visible, along with the tire marks on the blacktop road where the car thief skidded to his death. This section earned its nickname, Dead Man's Curve. The road twisted and turned through the summer woods, with high rock walls on one side and a steep drop on the other.

A little farther down, two patrol cars with flashing lights blocked off the road, while uniforms redirected traffic. Patrol Officer Mike Hannigan let my car through the roadblock.

'Brace yourself, Angela,' Mike said. 'The rookie' – he nodded toward his partner – 'upchucked when he saw the accident. At least he had sense enough not to contaminate the scene.'

I parked behind a scrum of cop cars, a fire truck, and an ambulance with flashing lights. I still couldn't see the accident, but I'd have to face it soon.

I was dragging my DI kit out of the trunk when detective Jace Budewitz jogged over my way. The boyish detective looked upset. He was running his hands through his short brown hair, and his complexion was greenish-gray.

'This is a bad one, Angela,' he said.

'Why is a homicide detective working a traffic accident?' I asked.

'Judging by the expensive car, the dead driver was a bigwig, so the Forest automatically sends a detective to the scene. And we have a witness. From what she says, this might be murder. It sounds like the car may have been tampered with.'

'Where is she?' I asked.

'In the ambulance. She's pretty shaken up.'

'No survivors in the car?'

'They both look like hamburger. The witness said the car came straight at her. She swerved to avoid getting hit. Apparently, so did the Ferrari driver. His car spun out and broadsided that big maple tree over there.' He pointed to a stately old tree with a fresh gouge in the trunk. 'Hitting the tree split the car in two. The front end hit the rock face. The female victim is still in the car, with glass in her hair. The male driver was decapitated, and the car was cut in two.'

My stomach did a backflip. I'd had a decapitation accident a few months ago, when a young motorcyclist ran into a semi, and the memories still haunted me.

'The FD is going to cut out the bodies,' Jace said. 'They said this would be a recovery operation, not a rescue. The FD has already noted the un-deployed airbags and said they'd try not to destroy evidence as they chop and cut with the Jaws of Life.' He rolled his eyes and added, 'Good luck with that one.'

Calling firefighters 'the FD' was pretty restrained for a cop. There was a natural rivalry between firefighters and the police, and unflattering names were traded. 'Hydrant humpers' was one of the nicer cop nicknames for firefighters.

'We've already photographed and videoed the scene,' Jace said. 'The FD is holding off until you take your photos.'

I nodded and pulled on four pairs of nitrile gloves. I'd peel off the layers as the investigation progressed, so I didn't cross-contaminate the scene. I grabbed my point-and-shoot camera out of the DI case. It took better photos than my cell phone camera. I reluctantly went to work.

Now I could see the car wreck. The Ferrari's scarlet front end was accordioned against the gray rock face, and a tree branch speared the windshield. The car had broken into two pieces – three, if you counted the hood, which had flipped off the vehicle and rested upside down near the rock face. The car's rear end had spun off into the woods on the other side of the road. The pricey car looked like a stepped-on insect. Skid marks crisscrossed the road.

A red ball was in the road near the double centerline, one side of the ball strangely flattened. As I got closer, I saw that it was a head – a man's head – soaked in blood. The scene spun before my eyes, and I steeled myself to keep moving toward the two firefighters in turnout gear, waiting to cut out the crushed bodies.

'You OK, ma'am?' asked one of the firefighters. He introduced himself as Scott. His partner was Rick.

'Fine.' My voice sounded too high and shaky.

The driver's headless body appeared to be about the right size for Sterling. The inside of the Ferrari was painted with blood. Broken windshield glass was pebbled across the inside of the car, mingled with green leaves.

The deceased passenger was a youngish woman with fiery red hair. My stomach churned when I saw she was dressed all in black, with a blood-soaked green scarf in her hair. That was the same outfit Erin McBride wore on TV this morning. But bartenders wore black, too, didn't they? Maybe the dead woman was Brenda, the mantrap martini-maker. The dead woman's right arm was hanging out the passenger window. I checked it: no tattoo.

The dead woman's arm was still warm, and I shivered in the hot June sun. Here one minute, I thought, gone the next. My job taught me this lesson again and again.

We'd need dental records to ID both bodies, but I was pretty sure the woman was Erin. She was still wearing her seat belt. Safety glass was pebbled in her hair.

I photographed the crashed car and the two victims, taking dozens of wide, medium, and close-up shots. Sickening close-ups, but I had to document this accident more carefully than usual. The ME's office had made a terrible mistake last time, misidentifying a car thief in place of Sterling Chaney. A mistake like that couldn't happen again.

But, oh, those photos. I never liked Sterling, but he didn't deserve to be turned into steak tartare. And I admired the passionate courage of Erin, who'd fought for herself and her co-workers. I was sickened by their deaths.

'Pull it together,' I kept telling myself, but sometimes my fingers shook when I pressed the camera button for a particularly gruesome photo of the headless driver's bloody hand.

I moved on to photographing the head on the double yellow line. It was lying on its right side.

Next, I concentrated on the nearly faceless dead woman. Her left hand clutched a blood-soaked piece of typing paper.

Viewing the carnage through the camera lens helped distance it, and by the time I finished photographing, I had a grip on my feelings. I backed away from the fatal wreck, then told the firefighters, 'All clear. Thanks for waiting.'

Scott asked, 'How would you like us to handle the bodies? We can lay them out on a fresh plastic sheet, and then hoist the sheet into the body bags.'

I gulped. 'That will work fine. Thank you.'

The firefighters brought out their Jaws of Life machine, which worked like a giant can opener. The noise was fearsome, and I backed away toward the ambulance where the witness was waiting. I could talk to her while I waited for the firefighters to remove the bodies.

Marie Burton was sitting on the back of the ambulance, wrapped in a blanket, sipping hot coffee and shivering as if it was ten degrees outside. She looked to be in her early fifties, with a plump body and short dark hair. She wore pink sweats and yellow sunflower earrings. Her face was pale as paper.

'I'm sorry,' she said. 'I can't stop crying.'

'You saw a terrible accident,' I said. 'Anyone would be upset.'

She nodded and sipped her coffee.

I introduced myself and said, 'Could you tell me what happened?'

'I just told that nice policeman,' she said.

'I understand, but I need to hear your story, too.'

She shifted, then took a deep breath and said, 'I was driving home from yoga class. The warm air felt good, and I had my window rolled down to enjoy the summer day. Then, in my rearview mirror, I saw that Ferrari coming up behind me. The road was twisty, and I only got a glimpse of it. When I rounded the next curve, I saw the red car was moving erratically. I thought the driver was drunk. Dangerously drunk. He was going way too fast for this curving road. Any road, for that matter. I decided I'd call nine-one-one after I passed this big curve up here, but then the red Ferrari blew past my little car like it was standing still. A man was driving with a woman passenger. I could hear screams coming from the car. The woman was shouting, "Slow this down! Slow it down now!" I heard the man yelling, "What the hell do you think I'm trying to do? The damned brakes won't work."'

'You could hear that?' I asked.

'Yes. Even over their engine noise. Something about the rocks along this twisty road amplifies the sound. Didn't you ever come here at night with your friends when you were a teenager and try to scare one another?'

I shook my head no and wondered if the headless Ferrari driver would join the ranks of the local ghost stories.

'Anyway, the man and the woman were screaming at the top of their lungs,' Marie said. 'At first, I thought they were a couple arguing, but then I realized they were scared out of their minds.

'My heart was pounding. Their car was almost past me, and I was trying to stay out of their way. It was hard. I couldn't go as fast as their car, and I didn't want to. Not on this narrow road. There wasn't much room. The big car was wobbling back and forth and I was afraid it would hit mine. I slowed down, then made a quick move to avoid them. The Ferrari moved, too. Then it spun around and around until it hit that big maple old tree. I heard a shriek . . . no, it was a wail, actually – what my Irish grandmother called a banshee wail. Grandmother said it signaled death. Anyway, that poor woman wailed, "Stop! We're going to die!"

'The man shouted, "Oh, shit!" It's terrible those were his last words. But they were. The car cracked in two, and the man . . . the man . . .'

Marie couldn't say 'lost his head.' She just pointed to it in the middle of the road and started crying.

Through her tears, she said, 'The front end hit the rocks. That poor girl was still in the car, along with the rest of the man. There was a terrible silence. Then I heard someone crying. It was me. I'm sorry, I can't stop crying.'

I patted her hand. 'I happens when people are upset.'

'Well, I'm definitely upset. I've never seen two people die before, and I hope I never see anything like it again. The car smashed into the cliff and broke apart. And the head . . . the head . . .' Marie dissolved into more tears, and I patted her back. She leaned into me and cried. 'The nice policeman says it wasn't my fault.'

'No. It definitely wasn't. You did the best you could in a scary situation.'

Finally, she dried her tears and continued. 'I pulled over – that's my silver Toyota over there.' She pointed to her car on the side of the road. 'I called nine-one-one first and then I put on my emergency flashers and got out of my car. I went over to the Ferrari and they were both dead. There was blood everywhere. I sort of blacked out, but then the police showed up and here I am.'

I got her contact information – name, age, address, phone number – and thanked her. The paramedics took her blood pressure and said she was free to go. One strapping young man helped Marie to her car. She drove off slowly. Very slowly.

It was almost four o'clock and I called Chris to tell him I'd have to cancel our dinner. 'It was a horrible accident,' I told him. 'Two fatalities, one decapitated.'

'We can have the chicken another time, but please don't cancel tonight,' he said.

'I won't be much company,' I said.

'I don't care. You can't go home alone. You'll shut down, Angela, and that's not good for you. You push the bad things to the back of your mind and work even harder, trying to block them out. That only makes the stress worse.'

Chris's response echoed my annual department evaluation. I got high marks for my work but scored poorly for self-care. Chris understood burn-out, possibly because he was a cop.

'Promise me you'll come by when you finish the investigation,' he said.

'I promise.'

'I love you,' he said.

'I love you, too.' I felt the glow of his love for just a moment.

Then I rolled my DI case over to the accident site and wondered if Sterling's refurbished casket was ready for him.

ELEVEN

Once the witness departed, I tried to talk to Jace over the roar of the Jaws of Life. We were both getting used to our gruesome duties, and my stomach had stopped flip-flopping.

'What makes you think Sterling – or whoever that is – was murdered?' I asked. 'Besides what the witness said.'

'You took the photos, Angela. The victim died with his foot on the brake, and the car was in neutral.'

'In other words, the deceased was trying to stop the car,' I said.

'Yes. Also, the firefighters said the airbags were disabled.'

'So you think someone tampered with this car?'

'We'll have the wreck towed to the police garage and examined, but that's my guess.'

That's all we had now – guesses. Was the driver Sterling Chaney? Was the dead woman Erin O. McBride? Was the car tampered with? Nothing but guesses.

I couldn't delay my work anymore with chitchat. I called up my Vehicular-Related Death form on my iPad and began the preliminary paperwork. Accidents required stacks of forms, and I was glad our department had switched to iPads. In the old days, these forms were filled out by hand.

Jace gave me the case number and the time the victims were pronounced dead.

Working on these exacting details soothed me. I listed the date, day, time, and location of the accident, the number of lanes, and the speed limit (twenty-five miles per hour, with a flashing light over a yellow warning sign: *Slow! Dangerous Curve*). I noted the clear, sunny weather and the fact that the road was dry and debris-free. The car was southbound.

I wrote down that the headlights were off at the time of the accident. The USB input, HD radio, or other music device was not playing.

One of the eeriest moments of my career was a death investigation where a drunken couple ran into a tree. Both died instantly, but 'Dust in the Wind' by Kansas played endlessly from their car, and I heard the mournful refrain over and over while I worked, reminding me that they really were dust in the wind.

Back to work. The form wanted to know if the driver was using a cell phone. No.

I described the car – its make, model, year, and color. Jace had radioed in the plate number and confirmed the car was registered to Sterling Chaney. We listed the driver as an unknown male.

'What was the estimated speed before the car hit the rock wall?' I asked Jace.

'We'll have to get an accident reconstructionist in here for sure, but I'm guessing the speed was about a hundred and twenty miles an hour.'

Scott, the firefighter, looked so weary as he walked toward us and said, 'We've freed both bodies from the wreckage, Angela. Is the male victim the guy who came back from the dead? It's definitely his car.'

'Can't tell,' I said. 'And we definitely can't say anything. You know the flap we had when the last victim was falsely ID'd by his car. We'll have to wait for dental records.'

'I know one thing for sure,' Scott said. 'Whoever he is, he ain't coming back this time.'

I was in no mood for gallows humor. I rolled my DI case over to the body of the dead man. The firefighters had positioned the head on its left side at the top of the body. Some kind of blunt force trauma had separated it from the body. I was grateful the ants hadn't found the head yet.

I took a deep breath and started with the head, as I'd been taught. The victim had an eight-inch 'cut-like defect' on his forehead, a half-inch from the hairline. Although I'd known Sterling for more than a decade, the face was so damaged I couldn't risk a positive ID. Blood covered most of his injuries, but on the right side of his head he had a four-by-three-inch patch of road rash. I wasn't sure what to call that, so I said it appeared to be a road trauma injury. The head appeared to have separated from the neck at the bones C-4 and C-5.

I estimated his height at six feet and his weight at about two hundred and fifty pounds. Definitely overweight and, judging by the bloody, graying chest hair peeking out near his shirt collar, approaching middle age.

The deceased was wearing a pale-blue shirt with the sleeves rolled up, dark dress pants, and black loafers. On his right wrist was a rose-gold narrow chain bracelet with a large *T* on the clasp and *T & Co.* on a link. Another link said *Makers.* I suspected this was a Tiffany 1837 Makers bracelet, worth nearly eight thousand dollars, but I couldn't say that. I wrote 'pinkish metal bracelet' and described the markings. I wondered if the victim had bought the pricey bracelet when he got the Ferrari. He wore no rings, but there was a pale white line on the ring finger of his left hand.

A Ferrari, a fancy gold bracelet, and a missing wedding ring – this man seemed like a player. More evidence that he might be Sterling Chaney, but no proof.

His wallet was visible in his left front pants pocket. I stripped off a pair of gloves and pulled out the black wallet. It was Gucci and black crocodile. It took some bucks to buy that wallet – about twenty-five hundred dollars. The credit cards, including the American Express Gold card, were Sterling's, and so was the driver's license, but that still wasn't enough for a confirmation. Someone could have stolen his wallet and his car.

Also inside his wallet was a credit card receipt for the Four Star Motel, dated today.

If the dead man really was Sterling Chaney, did my friend Camilla need to know that her wayward husband's last act was to cheat on her?

I could make the receipt disappear. If the dead woman was Erin, that receipt could be explained away as business. Except the only business conducted in that hotel was when one party left money on the dresser. He must have met someone at the hot-sheet motel and then picked up Erin.

I stared at the receipt, tempted to toss it and take away some of Camilla's heartache. I reached for the receipt and then stopped. I couldn't do it. This was evidence. And if Sterling really was cheating on Camilla – and she already suspected he was – this might make it easier for her to recover from his death. His final death.

Instead, I photographed the motel receipt and the contents of the wallet, showed them to Jace, and, finally, bagged them. Anything found on the bodies would go to the ME's office.

The firefighters helped turn the man's body, and I finished documenting the many cut-like defects and measuring the patches of blood. Then the FD helped me hoist the plastic sheet with the decapitated dead man into a black body bag.

The red-haired woman's body was next, and I was grateful she was intact. The tree branch had gone through the windshield and her face was unrecognizable. I documented what I could of her fractured face. The frontal bone that forms the forehead, the bones that formed the wall of the eye orbit, and the mandible and maxilla – the upper and lower jawbones – were broken, along with five upper teeth.

I documented the areas of blood spatter.

From the angle of her neck, I guessed that was broken, too. I hoped she'd died quickly.

She wore a black shirt, black pants, and comfortable black lace-up shoes, suitable for picketing.

Both bloody hands appeared broken, and I documented the many fractures. I suspected she had comminuted fractures of the hands, where the delicate bones were in fragments. Those were common after terrible car accidents.

On the decedent's right ring finger she wore a Claddagh ring, an Irish design of two hands holding a crowned heart that symbolized friendship, loyalty, and love. The crown was pointing toward her body, and if I remembered my Claddagh symbolism, that meant she wasn't in a serious relationship.

In her left hand, she clutched a bloody sheet of white typing paper. I very carefully eased it out of her fingers. It read:

Agreement between Sterling Chaney, CEO of Sterling
Service of Chouteau Forest and Erin O. McBride, repre-
senting the SSCF voice artists.

'Voice artists.' Interesting choice of words. Also respectful, considering the women were reading off-color stories.

I skimmed through the legalese and finally figured it out. Chaney was providing health care for all the 'voice artists,' their spouses, and children, effective immediately.

Also, each voice artist would receive $47.50 per original story.

Hm. The Valerie Cannata exposé revealed that the service currently charged the patrons fifty dollars for a story fee and kept half. Under this new agreement, Sterling, that cheap creep, was keeping two dollars and fifty cents for every story.

If I remembered right, each time the story was used during a call, the company got fifty bucks. One story could be used twenty times or more in one day, bringing in over a thousand dollars. But Sterling insisted on holding back a measly two fifty.

Typical. I'd seen some of the Forest rich go to an expensive restaurant, where the steaks started at fifty bucks, and ask for lemon to go with their glass of water. When the server brought a plate of sliced lemons, these cheapskates would add the free lemon, use the sugar packets on the table, and make their own lemonade, rather than pay five bucks for the beverage.

The agreement was signed and dated today.

I called Jace over and showed him the letter.

'Interesting,' he said. 'Another indication that the dead woman was Erin.'

I photographed the letter and bagged it, then continued documenting her injuries, which included a horrific compound fracture of the right radius and ulna. In other words, both bones in her forearm were broken and sticking out of her skin.

I noted the wounds on the front of the body, a distressing roll call of different kinds of fractures, contusions, and cut-like defects.

When I finished the front of the body, I asked Jace to help me turn her. The woman's long, luxurious red hair was matted with blood. There were no further wounds on the back of the body. I measured the patches of blood, and, finally, I was finished.

It was nearly eight o'clock when Jace and I put the dead woman in a body bag and I called the contractors to convey the decedents to the morgue. Dusk was starting to fall, and the woods were crossed with long shadows. The cooling woods made us both reflective.

While we waited, Jace said, 'Jeez, what a day for those poor people. They started riding in a Ferrari and now they're both in body bags.'

'What happened to the woman's purse?' I asked.

'A uniform found it along the side of the road,' he said. 'The driver's license was for Erin O. McBride.'

We both knew the cardinal rule of body identification: never, ever use a driver's license to identify someone. It could be stolen or forged.

'Do you think the deceased are Erin McBride and Sterling Chaney?' I asked.

'Off the record, yes.'

'Because this is Sterling's car, we're going to have to tell Camilla that her husband might be dead.'

'Again,' Jace said.

'Right. I don't want her to find out on TV.' We could see the tall satellite masts of the news trucks assembling outside the zone. The morgue van arrived, the bodies were loaded inside, and the doors were shut with a terrible finality.

After they left, Jace said, 'I'll go with you when you inform your friend.'

As we headed to our cars, Jace asked, 'Do you think Erin was the killer's target? He tampered with the car because he wanted Erin murdered?'

'Why Erin?' I said.

'When she dies, the protestors will disappear and there will be no more embarrassing exposés about the Forest,' Jace said. 'So that's good, right?'

'Of course, you do know the local one percent consider

Erin a Communist,' I said. 'And Chaney gave in to her demands. He let down the side.'

'This is going to be a tough case,' Jace said, 'if it turns out to be murder. The two most unpopular people in the Forest were killed today.'

TWELVE

I was grateful Jace offered to go with me when I broke the news to Camilla that her husband might be dead. Again. Although we both knew that the headless Ferrari driver was Sterling, we couldn't say so until the identity was officially confirmed by dental records. We couldn't risk another debacle. This was going to be a tricky notification, and I appreciated Jace's help.

It was almost nine o'clock when I followed Jace through the main gates of the Chaney mansion. There were no protestors near the house. I wondered if they were gone for the night or if Erin had told them the good news. If so, they were probably celebrating.

Despite the late hour for visitors, Mrs Ellis let us in and said that Camilla was in the exercise room. We followed the housekeeper through a maze of halls to a room that over-looked the south lawn. The home gym was rubber-floored and furnished with top-line exercise equipment, from a rowing machine to a weight rack. Mrs Ellis closed the door behind us.

A Brittany Spears song was pounding so loud I could almost feel the music. Camilla was running on a treadmill to the tune of 'Womanizer.' The song repeated that word again and again: *womanizer, womanizer, womanizer*. Why did Camilla choose this tune? Was she working off her anger at her unfaithful husband? Or celebrating his final death?

Camilla's blonde hair was in a ponytail. She wore blue sweats and had a towel slung around her neck.

As soon as she saw us, she powered down the machine and turned off the music. Rivers of sweat ran down her face and back. Her ponytail was a wet mess. She grabbed two black folding chairs leaning against a wall and opened them.

'Have a seat,' she said. 'I have water and cold drinks in the fridge by the door. I'm getting myself something. Would you like soda or water?' We both thanked her and said no.

Camilla sat on the weight bench facing us, took a long drink of her water, and asked, 'What brings you both here at this hour?'

I started to tell her that Sterling might be dead, but a picture of that bloody head flashed in front of me, and the words froze on my lips.

Jace jumped in.

'Where's your husband, Mrs Chaney?' he asked.

Her face was suddenly wiped of all expression. 'I threw him out three days ago. We're getting divorced. He's living in the chauffeur's quarters over the garage until he can find a place to stay.'

'I thought he had his own condo,' Jace said.

'He did, but he gave it up after he moved back in with me. When he returned from the Bahamas, we reconciled.'

I tried to study her face for signs that she was hiding something, but she was wiping the sweat off her forehead with the towel. Was that on purpose?

'When did you last see your husband?' Jace asked.

'Like I said, I threw him out three days ago. He came home about midnight and screamed bloody murder about his things being dumped outside.'

'What did you discuss?'

'There was no discussion. I told him that our marriage was over. Period. And if he had any questions, he could contact my lawyer, Montgomery Bryant.'

'What was his demeanor?'

'Demeanor?' Her voice was mocking now. 'He was mad as hell. He hauled his belongings to the chauffeur's quarters. We'd let the chauffeur go when my husband started driving fast cars and I got a BMW. Mrs Ellis had cleaned and prepared the quarters so my husband could move in. It took him more than an hour.'

'Where were you during this time?' Jace asked.

'I was in the upstairs parlor, watching him. I'd dialed nine-one-one on my cell phone and was ready to punch "send" if he became violent.'

'Has your husband ever abused you or threatened you?' Jace asked.

Camilla looked shocked. And I thought that shock was genuine. 'Of course not!'

'What time was it when your husband moved into his new quarters?'

'About one o'clock.'

'What happened then?'

Camilla took a long drink of water. 'By that time, Sterling had calmed down. He stood outside the kitchen door and whined, begging me to take him back. I told him if he had anything more to say to me, he could tell it to my lawyer. That's the last thing I said to him.'

'Have you tried to reach him since then?'

'No.'

'Let's see . . .' Jace said. 'Today is Tuesday. Does your husband have any regular routines on Tuesday?'

'I don't know, Detective. He goes into work about ten most mornings on weekdays, and I don't see him until after seven or eight at night. I have no idea where he goes after work. We rarely have dinner together.'

By this time, I was starting to recover my wits. Enough to wonder what in the heck Jace was doing. This wasn't how you broke the news to a family member.

'Do you think he's in the chauffeur's quarters now?'

'I have no idea, Detective,' Camilla said.

'If he's not home, would you mind if we looked in his quarters?' Jace asked.

'I can't give you permission to enter his home, even if it's a temporary home. You'll have to come back with a warrant.'

'I gather the divorce was your decision,' Jace said.

'Yes.' Camilla's voice was flat.

'Why are you divorcing him?' Jace asked.

She sipped her water so slowly I wondered if Camilla was buying time. 'He was unfaithful, Detective. Repeatedly.' I saw the hurt in her eyes.

'When he took me home from the hospital, after I'd injured my head when I fainted, he promised he would never again cheat on me. Then I found orange lipstick on his shirt, and that same shirt stank of perfume. And it wasn't mine.'

Now she sounded angry. She twisted her gym towel as she spoke. 'Someone – supposedly for my own good – told me he'd taken up with the bartender at Solange. They were meeting in the afternoons at the Four Star Motel. That stinking, lipsticked shirt was my proof. I called my lawyer to file for divorce, and Mrs Ellis helped me drag Sterling's things out to the backyard. Then I changed the locks.'

'Have you worked out the financial arrangements for your divorce?' Jace asked.

'I'm getting the house and half his income,' she said. 'We signed a prenup. We both have the same penalty for infidelity.'

'You said your husband is sleeping in the chauffeur's quarters over the garage,' Jace said. 'If he's not there, what car would he be driving?'

'He's currently driving a Ferrari.'

'Wow,' Jace said. 'Too rich for my blood.'

'Too rich for any sane person,' Camilla said. 'This car cost almost a million and a half bucks.'

Jace whistled. 'Are those cars pretty reliable? I bet repairs cost a fortune, too. Where do you get one of them fixed?'

'Since my husband just bought the car, Detective, it's probably still under warranty and the dealer would handle the repairs.'

'Do you know anything about cars?'

'Of course,' Camilla said. 'My daddy didn't want me to be a helpless female. He taught me all about cars – how to change a tire, change the oil, use cables to charge a dead battery, and more.' She smiled proudly. I bet Camilla was the only upper-crust woman in the Forest with those skills.

'Does your husband have any life insurance?' Jace asked. *What?*

Sure, I was slow-witted from the long day and the shock of the awful accident, but that's when it dawned on me. Jace didn't come along to Camilla's place to support me. He was interrogating her as a suspect, and Camilla was being open with him because she was my friend. I felt a flash of fury. He'd used me and endangered my friend.

Camilla must have wised up about the same time. 'Do you mind telling me why you're asking me all these questions, Detective?' she asked.

This time, I answered. 'I'm very sorry, Camilla, but your husband may have been killed this afternoon. We're not certain, and it will take some time to formally identify him, but I wanted you to know before you heard it on the news.'

There was a long, shocked silence. Finally, Camilla managed one word. 'How?'

'He died in a car crash,' I said. 'His Ferrari hit a rock face on Dead Man's Curve.'

'You're joking,' Camilla said. 'This has to be a joke.' Then she laughed, long and loud. Her jagged laughter came in bitter waves, and she didn't, or couldn't, stop.

I didn't know what to say. Jace just watched her, like she was an exhibit. I thought Camilla was on the edge of hysteria, and put my arm around her. Finally, she stopped laughing and wiped her face again with the towel.

'I guess you expect me to cry.' Her voice was tight with suppressed rage. 'Well, that's not going to happen, folks.'

She paused, and her eyes grew hard and distant. It turned out she was organizing a list of grievances in her head. After a breath, she started in.

'I cried every time I found out he was unfaithful. I lost count of how many times that was. I wept when he cheated on me with my so-called friends. I cried when I couldn't take his tom-catting anymore and we separated. I cried the first time I found out he might be dead. I cried when I picked out that over-the-top casket he wanted. Those were mostly tears of shame, but I was determined to honor his last wishes. I cried on the way to the church in the limousine and at his funeral. And then, thankfully, I fainted dead away and wound up in the hospital.'

Her voice grew higher with each sentence. 'Once I learned he was alive, I cried in the hospital when he begged me to take him back and forgive him. And, stupidly, I did. Then I cried when I learned he was screwing that bartender at Solange. And now you tell me he might – *might!*' – she nearly shrieked that word – 'be dead. Sorry, folks. I'm all out of tears.'

Then she really did cry, but whether those were tears of anger, rage, or even sorrow, I would never know. She cried into that sweaty gym towel until she suddenly stopped and dried her eyes.

I patted her shoulder, but she shrugged off my hand. I felt guilty and confused. I'd betrayed my friend, even though I didn't mean to.

After she stopped sniffling, she asked, 'When will I know if he's really dead?'

'Probably two days at the latest,' Jace said. 'The medical examiner will use dental records to ID the victim.'

'The ME should still have them from last time. Otherwise, our dentist is Doctor John Stone.'

'Just a few more questions,' Jace said.

'No!' she said. 'If you have any other questions, contact my lawyer. I already told you his name. You can look up his phone number. Now I'd like you to leave, Detective. And you, too, Angela.' Her glare seared me. 'Begone! Both of you.'

She waved her hands as if she was casting out demons. Jace and I walked out, neither of us saying anything. Mrs Ellis met us in the hall so quickly that I suspected she'd been listening to the conversation. She guided us through the labyrinth of halls and opened the front door without so much as a goodbye. Now I was sure she'd overheard us. This afternoon, when she gave me the fresh-baked loaves, seemed like a million years ago.

Once the door shut, I turned on Jace, and hissed angrily, 'What the hell were you doing in there?'

'Conducting an investigation,' he said. 'What were you doing?'

'Trying to inform a woman who's been through too much that her husband might really be dead.'

'So you were acting like a friend,' he said.

'And doing my duty as a death investigator.' I sounded self-righteous. 'You said you went there to support me.'

'I did,' Jace said. 'I wanted to help and I didn't want to leave you alone with a killer.'

'Camilla is not a killer.'

'Now you're talking like a friend and not a professional,' Jace said. 'Open your eyes, Angela. Sterling Chaney's wife is the chief suspect. You heard her – she has a truckload of motive, means, and plenty of opportunity. She could have tampered with his Ferrari any time, thanks to dear old Dad's mechanical education. Sterling betrayed her, cheated on her, humiliated her, and trashed her reputation.'

'So what?' I said. 'I can list dozens of people who wanted Sterling dead. What about the women who worked for his company?'

'He'd just brokered a deal with their leader, Erin,' Jace said.

'Did the women know that?' I said. 'And don't forget Larry Perkins, the so-called face of the company, Jace. Did he get to take over the business when Sterling died?'

'I can check that,' Jace said. 'But I also want to know how much life insurance his wife has on him. It must cost a boatload to run this mansion.'

'It does,' I said. 'But Camilla has money in her own right.' At least, she used to.

'So?' Jace said. 'Are you telling me she doesn't need the money?'

'She's not desperate for it. And you're forgetting the hundreds of men who called that answering service to hear dirty stories. Sterling has embarrassing recordings of all of them, and some of them are Forest bigwigs.'

'How do you know that?' Jace asked.

I didn't, but I did know the Forest, and I'd bet my next paycheck at least one of our civic leaders had indulged in phone sex.

'Find out for yourself.' I wasn't helping him frame my friend.

'And last but not least,' I said, 'there's his bartender squeeze he meets at that motel. What about her?'

'I'll interview them all, Angela.' Now Jace sounded weary. 'But this was my chance to interview his wife and get a read on her.'

We reached my car. I chirped open the door and said, 'And what exactly did you conclude, Jace? Is she guilty or innocent?'

'She's guilty as hell,' he said.

'She's innocent,' I said. 'I know my friends.' At least, I thought I did.

I slammed my door and didn't say goodbye.

THIRTEEN

All the way to Chris's condo, I fumed about Jace's treachery. He'd used me to interrogate my unsuspecting friend – if Camilla was still my friend after tonight.

It was ten thirty, and I called Chris to see if it was too late to drop by.

'It's never too late. I told you that.' His deep voice sent shivers through me. I couldn't wait to see him.

Five minutes later, I was in his parking lot. I dragged a comb through my hair and added fresh lipstick, but I still looked ragged. Since I was on call tomorrow, I'd packed an overnight bag with clean work clothes. I also had the bread Mrs Ellis had given me. Its buttery fragrance filled my trunk.

I decided not to mention my disagreement with Jace. That double-dealing detective wasn't going to ruin my evening. Besides, in some small, secret part of me, I knew Chris the cop would side with Jace. The job trumped friendship for them both.

Chris met me at the door with a kiss, and then wrapped his arms around me. I snuggled into his body. He was lean and muscular with broad shoulders. He smelled good and freshly showered. I enjoyed the feel of his slightly scratchy whiskers on my cheek. Then he held me at arms' length, to study me.

'You look like you've had one hell of a day,' he said. 'How are you?'

'I'm fine.' I knew I sounded way too cheerful. So did he, but he was smart enough to avoid that subject for now.

'You must be hungry.'

'Not really,' I said. 'Today ruined my appetite.'

'I heard the accident was unbelievably awful,' he said.

'It was, but I don't want to discuss it while we eat. Can you just make something easy? Maybe a sandwich?'

'I certainly can,' he said. 'How about a grilled chicken Caprese sandwich?'

I should have known. Chris is a foodie. He's not the type to slap a slab of ham and a slice of cheese on bread. For him, eating is an art form.

I followed Chris into the kitchen, since I liked to watch a master at work. I sat on a high stool at his kitchen counter, where he had a cheeseboard with crackers and green grapes laid out.

'Eat,' he said. 'Lay down a base before you have this.' He poured me a glass of my favorite Malbec, a deep red wine from Argentina.

I spread soft, herb-crusted goat cheese on a water cracker. Yum. I was hungrier than I thought.

Meanwhile, Chris was grilling the chicken breasts. 'These have been marinated in olive oil and lemon.'

I munched happily on a thin slice of Cheddar perched on a Triscuit, and nodded. Chris always told me how he cooked his food, as if his lessons would rub off on me. I listened intently because his enthusiasm was adorable, but for me, cooking was a lost cause. I once burned boil-in-the-bag lima beans.

He started slicing fresh cherry tomatoes. 'I grew them myself.' Chris was proud of his container garden.

'May I help?' I asked.

'No!' he said, a little too quickly. He'd once admitted that watching me slice vegetables was painful.

He sprinkled the tomatoes with kosher salt 'to bring out their sweetness.'

The tomatoes were next to a handful of newly picked basil and sliced buffalo mozzarella.

By that time, I'd finished off a slice of creamy Gouda on a Scottish oat biscuit, and a few grapes. I felt sufficiently fortified for my wine.

Jeez, that first sip tasted good after a terrible day. The first glass put me in a mellow fog. As I poured myself another, Chris was cutting Mrs Ellis's fresh-baked bread into thick slices and putting them on the grill. 'Grilling gives the sandwich crunch,' he said.

I giggled a bit too much and set the wine glass aside.

Chris had assembled the open-face sandwiches, layering the chicken, mozzarella, and basil leaves, then topping the magnificent pile with olive oil and 'my very own balsamic reduction.'

'This looks and smells wonderful,' I said.

'Would you like to eat on the balcony, in the living room, or in bed?' he asked.

Suddenly, I was so exhausted I wasn't sure I could make it up the stairs. But Chris didn't mind crumbs in the sheets.

'Bed,' I said.

He carried my suitcase upstairs while I brought the sandwiches, napkins, and silverware. While he made a second trip for the wine and the wine glasses, I plugged in my cell phones, one for work and one for personal calls. I hoped no one would call my work phone for a middle-of-the-night death investigation.

And then we ate. 'This is a banquet,' I said. Chris kissed my ear. He loved being praised for his cooking. 'Everything blends perfectly. Thank you.'

'You know I enjoy cooking for you,' he said.

'How was your day?' I asked him.

He shrugged. 'The usual. You know how it goes.' He told me about a long-standing feud between Detective Ray Greiman and Tessa, an attractive staffer who had the nerve to rebuff him. 'If he doesn't stop harassing her, Tessa's likely to file a lawsuit, and that will be the end of Greiman.'

'Won't make a bit of difference,' I said. 'We'll just lose another good staffer. Greiman is Teflon.' He was also my least-favorite detective. I hated working with him.

Once dinner was over, Chris took me in his arms and stroked my hair. 'Know what I'd like for dessert?' I asked.

'Let me guess,' he said. 'Something sweet, probably with whipped cream.'

'We can skip the whipped cream tonight,' I said, and kissed him long and hard. Soon our clothes were flying everywhere.

After we made love, Chris held me, and I drifted off in his arms. I woke up about half an hour later.

'How are you?' he asked.

I sighed and stretched. 'Much better.'

'Now, tell me what happened today.'

'I'd rather not, but here goes.' Then I described the accident, including all the gory details. I started trembling at the terrible memories. He held me while I talked, and I felt safe.

'That must have been dreadful,' he said.

'It was. I didn't care for Sterling Chaney, but he didn't deserve to die like that – with his head in the road like a deflated beach ball. And Erin. I really admired her. What a courageous woman. Her death was such a waste.'

The scene of the wreck replayed in my mind, and I wondered if I'd ever forget it.

I took a deep breath. My voice sounded shaky, but I said, 'I did it. I got through the death investigation. And you know what? I'm fine. Just fine.'

With that, I burst into tears. I fought hard to stop them, but I couldn't.

Chris held me tighter and rocked me. 'It's OK, Angela love. Those are good tears. Don't hold them back. You need to cry this out.'

And so I did. I cried on Chris's shoulder, while he held me. At last, I fell asleep.

The next morning, the smell of coffee woke me up at about seven o'clock. Chris's side of the bed was empty. He was already awake and cooking downstairs. I checked my work phone – no messages. I was relieved.

I slipped on my robe and started downstairs when I heard Chris come up the stairs, whistling cheerfully out of tune. He was obnoxiously cheerful in the morning, but I forgave him. Especially when I saw the tray he was carrying.

'Room service!' He grinned and set the tray on the bed. 'Eggs Benedict, fresh strawberries, and coffee. Join me, won't you?'

Breakfast in bed with the man I loved was wonderfully luxurious. 'This is perfection,' I said. 'The hollandaise sauce is creamy, and I love the capers. And where did you get this Canadian bacon?'

'The Forest meat shop,' he said. 'Only the best for you.'

We talked about everything and nothing for the next hour, enjoying the decadent start to the day. After we both cleared away the dishes, and I showered and freshened up, he was waiting for me.

He kissed me again and said, 'Do you have to be anywhere this morning?'

'No.' It came out more like a gasp than a word.

We both stumbled backward and landed on the bed. Chris was kissing my neck when my work cell phone rang.

'Rats! I've got to get this, Chris.' I reluctantly answered the phone.

'Angela! We have work to do!' The caller's voice was so cold and harsh that I almost thought it was Greiman.

'Jace, is that you?' I said.

'Of course, it's me.' If I didn't have a grudge against Jace after last night, now I really had one. He'd interrupted me during breathtaking sex.

I recovered enough to hear Jace say, 'There's been a homicide at the headquarters of Sterling's phone service.'

'Who's dead? Is it—'

He cut me off. 'Not on the phone. Meet me there ASAP.'

OK, buddy, I thought. *If you want to play it that way.*

I drove to the dingy headquarters of the phone sex service. Mike, the friendly uniform, met me at the door, handed me booties, and had me sign the scene log. 'Lotta blood in there,' he said. 'Jace is here, but he's in a lousy mood. Never seen him like that. Barking at everyone.'

'Any good news?' I asked.

'Yeah, Nitpicker is working the scene.' That was good news. Sarah 'Nitpicker' Byrne was the Forest PD's best crime scene tech. Wickedly funny, tireless, and thorough, she had a penchant for dyeing her hair unusual colors.

I put on the booties and rolled my suitcase inside, where I was assaulted by the coppery smell of blood and dirty carpet. I could hear someone crying in a back room.

The unlovely Larry, the face of the company with his

fetus head, was lying on the filthy carpet. The manager had been stabbed repeatedly in his scrawny chest. Blood was spattered everywhere – the beat-up desk, the floor, even the ceiling.

'Wow,' I said. 'Someone must have really hated Larry.' I started unpacking my death investigator kit and pulled on multiple pairs of nitrile gloves.

Nitpicker crawled out from behind Larry's beat-up desk and stood up. She dusted off the knees of her white Tyvek suit.

'Look at his chair.' Nitpicker pointed to the red-and-black leather gamer's chair. 'It's sustained fifty-seven stab wounds. The bloody knife is still plunged into the chair back.'

'Is that the murder weapon?' I asked.

'I think so. It's a butcher knife, belongs to a butcher-block set by J.A. Henckels International. Way too common. You can buy it at any Bed Bath and Beyond.

'Besides the dead chair,' Nitpicker said, 'the sixty-five-inch TV is also toast, along with some sweet gaming equipment. Looks like someone beat them to death with a skull.'

Now I was really confused. 'Whose skull?'

'The victim had a metal skull to burn incense. Thing weighs a ton.' She held up an evidence bag with a grinning metal skull the size of a melon.

I fired up my iPad and opened the Death Scene Investigation form. That's when I finally noticed Nitpicker's shoulder-length hair, a complex combination of magenta and hot-pink with gold highlights.

'Cool hair,' I said.

'Thanks. I tried something different.'

Jace entered the room, scowling at both of us. 'When you ladies have finished comparing fashion tips, I'd like this crime scene processed. Angela, here's the case number.' He rattled it off, and I entered it on my iPad.

'And, Nitpicker, you need to go back to work and quit wasting time.'

'What's wrong with you, Jace?' she said. 'You've had a burr under your saddle all morning. This is the first time I've taken a break since I got here at eight.' I'd rarely seen Nitpicker angry at anyone.

'Just do your work, both of you.'

Jace stomped off like a spoiled child. The place was deathly quiet, except for the woman weeping in the other room.

FOURTEEN

'Who's crying?' I whispered to Nitpicker.

'Jenny Brown. She works here. She found the body. Scared her spitless.'

'She's still got plenty of tears,' I said.

'She may be in shock,' Nitpicker said.

If Jace had been himself, I thought, he would have called an ambulance for the distressed Jenny. I had no idea he could be so petty. I'd check her out when I interviewed her for my report.

I glanced over at Jace. The detective was poking his gloved fingers in a battered computer tower near the side wall.

Time to quit stalling. The decedent was blood-soaked, but his death didn't affect me like yesterday's accident. I filled in the form with routine information: date, day, time. Next, I took the room's temperature – seventy-two degrees – and photographed the thermostat. It read seventy.

Nitpicker showed me an in-house directory that had some of Larry's information. His wife's name was Roberta. I copied his phone number and address.

'He lived in Toonerville,' Nitpicker said.

'So he did.' Toonerville was the sneery nickname for the working side of Chouteau Forest. I didn't like to use it.

I'd ask Roberta for the rest of the demographic information when I told her about Larry's death.

I did not smell any alcohol on the deceased and did not see any signs of drug use.

Larry was lying face-up (supine) with his head facing east on the office carpet, next to the mutilated gaming chair.

'Judging by the bloody drag marks in the chair,' Nitpicker said, 'it appears the killer stabbed Larry in his chair. He knew the killer and was surprised when that person knifed him in the chest. Once he lost so much blood that he couldn't fight back, the killer pulled him on to the floor and finished him off, then murdered the chair.'

I started the body inspection – what we called the actualization. Larry was five feet seven, and I estimated his weight at a hundred and twenty pounds. He was on the skinny side, except for that bowling-ball gut.

He was wearing a blue plaid cotton shirt, black cotton pants, and Nike Air VaporMax Plus sneakers, which retailed for a whopping two hundred bucks. Based on the pricey sneakers, I bet when the ME removed Larry's clothes, they'd have designer labels.

I listed his wounds, starting at the head. He had a six-inch cut-like defect on his right cheek. An inch-long slash across his right ear nearly cut off the lobe. An eight-inch cut-like defect crossed his neck but didn't hit any vital arteries. The real damage was to his narrow chest – I counted twenty-six wounds, ranging in length from two inches to eight inches. One cut-like defect was right over his heart area. Was that the fatal wound?

Larry had defensive wounds on both hands and two broken nails on his right hand. He wore a bloody yellow-metal ring on the third finger of his left hand. I covered his hands with brown paper bags and sealed them with evidence tape.

On his left wrist, he wore a Cartier tank watch, spattered with blood. Thanks to working with the Forest's filthy rich, I knew that watch was worth almost seven grand. I described that beauty as a 'steel, oblong-shaped watch with Roman numerals on the white face and a black leather strap. Cartier brand.' Why was a man from the blue-collar side of town wearing such expensive brands? Was he paid that much?

I photographed the watch and left it on his wrist. In the old days, valuables had a habit of disappearing between the crime scene and the coroner's office. Now death investigators made careful note of all jewelry and other valuables. That practice cut down on crime scene 'losses.'

Larry's pants were bathed in blood, but there were no more cut-like defects on his legs or feet.

I took a clean white sheet from a bag in my DI kit and spread it on the floor. Nitpicker helped me turn Larry's body so I could examine the back. I measured the significant areas of blood on his shirt and pants but could find no other injuries.

The body inspection was over.

Jace asked, 'Nitpicker, would you dust this computer tower? I don't know what's in it, but it appears to have been tampered with. After you finish, I'll call the mobile digital forensics lab.'

The MDF, our rolling lab, was the latest addition to the Chouteau Forest PD. Someone had given the force an old ambulance, and it had been turned into a mobile digital forensics lab that could be driven to a crime scene. The cops loved this new toy. It was perfect for cases like this one.

'Yes,' Nitpicker said, her voice flat. She was going to make Jace pay for his rude remarks.

I followed the sounds of quiet weeping to the next room, which turned out to be a staff lounge. The walls contained government-issue safety posters and a giant bulletin board with three weeks of schedules. The cramped room smelled of cheap microwaved dinners and burnt coffee. A battered green fridge groaned in the corner. Three dirty Formica tables were littered with take-out packets of sugar, mustard, and ketchup, and piles of paper napkins.

Jenny was crying at the closest table. She looked to be in her late twenties, with long braids and dark skin. I pulled up a chair. 'Jenny? Jenny Brown?'

Her crying turned into sniffling, and she blew her nose on a nearby napkin and dropped it on the table.

'That's me,' she said, gulping back sobs. Her big brown eyes were red from crying.

'Are you OK? Do you need a doctor?'

'No,' she said. 'I'm just upset. I've never seen a dead body before, except for my auntie, and she was at a funeral home.'

'May I make you some fresh coffee or get you some water?' I asked.

'Water, please. There's a bottle in the fridge.'

The stink hit me as soon as I opened the fridge. It was a penicillin farm: moldy take-out, elderly egg salad sandwiches, and expired yogurt. I grabbed a bottle of water and quickly slammed the door before anything escaped.

'Thanks,' Jenny said, and gulped down half the bottle. She seemed calmer now. I pulled out my iPad, introduced myself, and said I had a couple of questions if she felt well enough to answer them.

Jenny took another long drink and then said, 'Go ahead.'

'You found the body, correct?'

'Yes. I'm on today – well, I was supposed to be – from eight to five. I had a new story. I wanted to show it to Larry and get my bonus, so I came in at seven thirty this morning.'

'Was the building locked?'

'Oh, no,' Jenny said. 'We're open around the clock. Late nights are our busiest times. Five other girls were working.'

'What time does Larry usually come to work?'

'Six in the morning.'

'What happened once you got here?' I asked.

'I knocked on Larry's door and it was open. He didn't answer, so I thought he was playing video games. I came in and found him . . .' Jenny stopped and gulped. 'He was all bloody and stabbed, just lying there on the floor. I didn't touch him. I could tell he was dead. I used my cell phone to call nine-one-one. Lots of police showed up, and after they talked to me, they told me to sit in here. Do you know how long they're going to make me stay here? When can I go back to work?'

'I have no idea, Jenny. Murder investigations take time. When is the last time you talked to Larry?'

'I tried to talk to him last night, to show him my story, but Larry was arguing with some man on the phone.'

'Do you know what the fight was about?'

'Larry had the phone on speaker. I heard the man say, "Who the hell do you think you are, trying to blackmail me? What I did was perfectly legal." Then Larry said, "Does your wife know about your legal activity? You really seemed to be enjoying yourself with Tara." Larry pretended to mimic a woman: "Oh, Potter, you're so big, so strong. I want to touch your big, strong member."'

'Potter Du Pres Du Pont?' I interrupted. 'Was that the man's name?'

'Yes,' Jenny said. 'That's the name. Rich people have such funny names.'

'Did you hear anything else while Larry was trying to blackmail Potter?'

Jenny nodded. 'Larry said, "Maybe you do have an understanding wife, Potter, but what about the men at your club? What if I sent that audio file there? You'd be the talk of the town." This made Potter furious. He made a choking sound and then screamed, "You'll never see a nickel of mine, you slime wad. I'll see you dead first!" Larry laughed. He looked up, saw me, and waved me away, mouthing "go home." As I left, I heard Larry say, "Cut the crap, Potter. You've got one more day to pay up or I'll make you sorry you ever lived." Then Larry slammed down the phone.'

'Did you like Larry?' I asked.

'Hell, no,' Jenny said. 'None of us do. I mean, did. He was lazy. The TV reporter may have believed his excuse about trying to find the best health insurance, but we knew better. Larry spent his day playing video games. We also suspected he was cheating us, and I'm not surprised he was blackmailing customers. We have a lot of regulars who live in the Forest. Larry would look up information about them, mostly in the *Forest Gazette*, or on Facebook. He gave us a list of regulars and told us to make our stories "more personal for our special customers" – his words. For instance, Potter called us at least once a week. He just bought a Bentley Continental GTC. It was a silver convertible – a used one, but he still dropped more than a hundred grand for that car. When Potter called, we had to automatically add something to our stories like, "I'd love to be in your Bentley with the top down and feel the wind in my hair. Better yet, I'd like to be in the back seat and feel you!"'

Yuck, I thought, but I didn't say it. I wasn't much of a poker player. Jenny saw the disgust on my face.

'We're here because we're trapped,' she said. 'I was arrested for shoplifting at an expensive store. I stole a Gucci silk scarf worth six hundred and thirty-eight dollars. Anything over five hundred dollars is a felony in Missouri. The law-and-order judge sentenced me to the max – seven years in prison and a five-thousand-dollar fine. I'm still paying off the fine and, thanks to my record, I'm basically unemployable.

'One way or another, we all have similar stories. We're here because we can't work anywhere else. As far as I'm concerned, I might as well be in jail.'

FIFTEEN

As soon as Jace got his search warrant, the techs from the MDF lab shut down the phone sex service and went to work on the computers. Camilla Chaney, on the advice of her lawyer, Montgomery Bryant, gave written permission for the warrant and the shutdown.

Monty said he wanted to make an announcement at his office at two o'clock this afternoon. He asked Jace if the employees at the crime scene would be free to meet him there. Jace said that he was finishing his interviews with the staff, and they could attend the meeting.

Was Camilla going to make the shutdown permanent? In that case, what would happen to people like Jenny Brown, who believed they were unemployable?

I'd finally finished my death investigation and was waiting to hand over Larry Perkins' body to the morgue van. First, I called Chris to see if he could go with me for the notification.

Next I called my lawyer friend Monty Bryant and asked if I could attend the meeting at his office. 'No problem, Angela,' he said. 'You're working the case, aren't you? I'm going to announce Erin McBride's death and then tell the women about their job status.'

'Is Camilla closing the business, Monty?'

'Just between us, yes. Don't say anything until I announce it.'

'Those poor women.'

'They'll be hard hit by the loss of Erin,' he said, 'but the job news is not all bad. You'll see. After the meeting, I'll make an announcement to the media. See you soon.'

Once the van arrived to take the decedent to the morgue, I stopped by to report to Jace. I was matter-of-fact, if not downright cold.

'Larry Perkins' body is being transported to the ME's office.

I'll notify Larry's wife that her husband is dead, and then attend the meeting at Monty's at two o'clock.'

'I'll go with you for the next-of-kin notification,' Jace said.

'No, thanks. Chris Ferretti is on duty. I've asked him to go with me.'

'Be that way,' Jace snapped.

It looked like our war would continue, but at least I had an excuse to see Chris. He was parked on the street around the corner from the new widow's home. I parked behind him and he greeted me with a quick kiss.

Roberta and Larry owned a neat two-story home with white vinyl siding and green shutters. In the center of the velvety green lawn was a tall green urn bursting with red geraniums and trailing ivy.

A new dark-blue BMW glowed in the driveway. Chris whistled softly when he saw it. 'That's a series 840i Gran Coupe,' he said. 'Costs almost as much as this house. What car did Larry drive?'

'No idea. I'll have to check. But I'm glad you're here.'

'Me, too.' Chris's goofy grin was irresistible, and I kissed him lightly on the cheek.

'OK,' I said. 'Time to get professional.'

We both put on somber faces and knocked on the front door. A trim woman of about fifty answered, flaunting designer labels from her Givenchy glasses to her Tory Burch sandals. Her Versace top clashed with her Gucci pants.

'There you are,' she said, as if we were pets who'd run away. 'Finally!'

'Mrs Perkins—' I tried to get a word in edgewise but failed. Roberta talked right over me.

'It's about time someone got here to take a missing person's report on my husband. I reported him missing last night.'

She sounded angry – at the police – but not the least bit worried about her absent husband.

Under the heavy layer of make-up (I was pretty sure she was wearing the latest shade of Chanel lipstick, much too red for her complexion), she was pretty, with small, neat features and brown eyes.

Now those eyes flashed fury at both of us. 'So? Are you going to come in or stand on the doorstep all day?'

Chris and I walked into a living room that was overwhelmed by a faux Louis XV couch and matching ottoman. The long champagne leather sofa was tufted with fat rhinestones, and everything else – the lamp tables, lamps, and coffee table – was white trimmed with gold.

The white wall-to-wall carpet dared us to walk on it, but we did. Chris and I sat on the huge couch.

Roberta sat across from us in a tufted, gold-trimmed wing chair. She sat stiffly, like a headmistress confronting a wayward pupil. 'Well?' she said. 'What do you have for me?'

'What time did you report your husband missing last night?' I asked.

'Midnight,' she said. 'Larry is always home by ten at the latest. I called his cell phone repeatedly, but he didn't answer. That's not like Larry. He always answers. The officer on duty didn't take my call seriously. He suggested that Larry might be having a beer with the boys at some tavern and wasn't answering his phone, but my husband would never do that. He might get lost in his video games, but he is a good man.'

And a blackmailer, I thought.

I introduced us, and Roberta's mind skipped right over my title. 'Death investigator' didn't register. She kept talking a mile a minute.

'Anyway, I'm glad you're taking my call seriously. Have you found Larry?'

Delivering bad news is always difficult. I believe it's better to rip the Band-Aid off quickly.

'We did find your husband,' I said. 'But we have bad news. Larry is dead.'

The color drained from Roberta's face. Now the heavy make-up looked clownlike. Roberta was at a loss for words.

Finally, she said, 'Dead? How? Who?'

'Larry was found dead in his office,' I said.

'Did he have a heart attack? I tried to get him off red meat, but he insisted on eating hamburgers and fries.'

'No, we believe Larry was murdered,' I said.

'Murdered! It was one of those crazy bitches at his office.'

Now Roberta was angry again. 'Always wanting something. Some of them had prison records, you know.'

'Yes,' I said. 'Did your husband have any run-ins with the women at the telephone service?'

'Yes, all of them. Especially that Erin.' She added extra venom to her voice. 'Have you talked to her yet?' Roberta asked.

'Uh, no,' I said.

'Well, if anyone would hurt Larry, it's Erin. Prancing around on TV with the other no-goods who worked at that place, carrying picket signs for attention. They were out to ruin Larry's good name. He was getting death threats, you know.'

'From whom?' I asked.

'I don't know. They used those voice-disguiser thingies. He got two calls this week. Both callers said Larry had better get off his lazy ass – sorry about that word, but that's what they said – and give the employees health insurance.'

'Did you call the police?' I said.

'No, Larry said he didn't want the police involved.'

I bet. He couldn't risk having the cops poking around in his financial records.

'I warned Larry that he needed to be careful,' Roberta said, 'but did he listen to me? I wanted him to take a gun to the office, but he refused. And now look. This couldn't come at a worse time!'

'Why?' Was there ever a good time to be murdered?

'We're about to close on a new house in the Chouteau Forest Estates.'

I raised one eyebrow. 'Those houses cost millions.'

'We were looking at a small home for a little over a million.'

'And you could afford that?'

'Yes, Larry made good money at the answering service. He did all the work, you know. Sterling Chaney didn't like to get his hands dirty.'

I wondered if Roberta knew just how dirty Larry's hands were.

'He promised me he'd get me out of Toonerville. We were just about to escape, and now this. How could he do this to me? The timing couldn't be worse!'

I was shocked by her heartless response to her husband's death.

'I'm sure Larry agrees the timing is bad,' I said.

'You must think I'm a bit cold-hearted,' she said.

'People grieve in different ways,' I said.

'I loved Larry, in my own way,' she said. 'But the physical side of our marriage was over years ago. We were good friends. Very, very good friends. We had a modern arrangement, but it worked for us.'

'Like an open marriage?' I asked.

'Sort of. Larry was asexual – I guess that's the right word. As for me, once I found out I couldn't have children, I wanted an end to that messy stuff. Everything is sex, sex, sex these days. There's way more to life than rolling around in bed.'

I didn't dare look at Chris.

I saw a single tear slide down her face, and then Roberta was weeping harsh, noisy tears. Chris handed her the gold box of tissues from the lamp table.

'Mrs Perkins, may I get you some coffee or tea?' I asked.

'Coffee, please. Black. I just made a fresh pot. It's Hawaiian Kona coffee. Help yourselves to a cup, if you want.'

Chris shook his head no. I was eager to get a look at her kitchen knives, to see if she had a butcher-block set by J.A. Henckels International, the knife used by the killer. She was definitely cold-blooded enough to murder her husband.

Roberta had the knives – right next to the coffee pot on the countertop. Too bad all the knives were in their correct slots. None were missing.

Speaking of coffee, it was Volcanica Hawaiian Kona Extra Fancy Coffee, and the price on the red-and-black bag said it cost $124.99 for a pound.

Wow. No wonder Roberta drank that coffee in Hermes twenty-four-carat gold-patterned mugs. I took two mugs, filled them with hot coffee, and carefully carried them into the living room.

Roberta had turned off the waterworks and accepted the coffee with thanks.

After she took a drink, she said, 'Have a sip and tell me what you think.'

What the hell was this? Her husband was dead, and she was conducting a coffee tasting?

I obediently took a sip. My first thought was *not worth the money*. But maybe my taste was off after spending the morning with a bloody body. I remembered what the coffee said on the label and repeated it.

'It has a smooth body, superb aroma, and a buttery richness with cinnamon and clove overtones,' I said. 'It's the real deal, not a Kona blend.'

Chris looked at me like I had two heads, but Roberta was delighted.

'Perfect! You really know your coffee,' she said.

Roberta not only wore labels, she drank them.

'I need some more demographic information for my report,' I said. 'Will you help?'

Roberta nodded, took another sip from her gold cup, and answered all my questions. She rattled off Larry's birth date, Social Security number, and age – fifty-six.

'We would have been married twenty-five years in two more weeks,' she said. 'On the twenty-fourth. The new house was Larry's anniversary present to me. Now I'll never get it.'

Another tear slipped down her cheek. If she expected me to feel sorry for her, she'd better think again.

'Do you have life insurance on your husband?' I took another sip of that coffee. It was growing on me, but I didn't pick up any trace of cinnamon or cloves.

'Not much,' she said. 'Only ten thousand. I could use that for his burial expenses, and I'm not sure that money will cover them. I really need Larry's salary to make the payments.'

Plus whatever the dearly departed could earn skimming from the women's story fees and blackmailing the men who listened to them.

'Any other questions?' I asked.

'Like what?' She looked baffled.

I could think of lots of questions any caring wife would ask: *What killed Larry? Did my husband suffer? Was he in pain?*

I drank more coffee to give her time to think. Finally, she said, 'When can I get the corpse?'

Not 'my husband,' not 'Larry,' but 'the corpse.'

'After the autopsy is conducted and the ME releases it,' I said. 'I'll make sure you get an email with the details. And here's my card if you have any other questions.'

'So that's it?' Roberta's torrent of words had dried up. She stood. Chris and I were dismissed.

I didn't even ask my standard question when someone experiences a sudden death: *Do you want to call a friend or relative to stay with you?*

I couldn't imagine this cold woman had anyone or anything that could comfort her. And there sure weren't any glaciers nearby.

SIXTEEN

A s we walked back to our cars, Chris said, 'Are all your death notifications like that?'

'No, Mrs Perkins is especially cold-blooded, even for the Forest. I swear, that woman should be exhibited as a two-legged reptile.'

'She didn't give a plugged nickel about her dead husband.'

'I figured she could have murdered him – even if she lost her precious million-dollar house. I checked her butcher-block set, but all her kitchen knives were there. Nothing was missing.'

'That doesn't mean she didn't kill him,' Chris said. 'She could have had another butcher knife in a drawer somewhere.'

'I'm glad she didn't procreate,' I said.

Chris tried to mimic Roberta's voice with a wonky falsetto: 'There's way more to life than rolling around in bed.'

I started giggling, and he laughed, and soon we were leaning against my car, kissing.

'Whoa there, boy,' I said, pulling away. I was still panting. 'You're in uniform and I'm working. Let's get it under control.'

'Until tonight,' he said.

It was one o'clock, so we grabbed a quick burger and headed for Monty's law office.

The parking lot alongside the office was nearly full, and several TV news vans were camped outside the front. Monty's efficient red-haired office manager, Jinny Gender, opened the side door for us, wearing a stylish green summer dress. Smart, organized, and efficient, Jinny managed the law office – and Monty.

'Come on downstairs to the big conference room,' Jinny said. 'The meeting's about to start.'

We followed Jinny to the lower level. The paneled conference room featured a table as long as a bowling alley, surrounded by leather executive chairs. Each chair held a woman who worked at the Sterling Service. They were an eclectic group of black, brown, Asian, and Caucasian women. I recognized Jenny Brown, the witness I'd interviewed this morning. She looked a lot less teary-eyed.

Suzi Chin, Juanita Gomez, Linda, the very pregnant Sheila, and some of the other women I'd seen in the news reports were also seated at the table. Erin was not there, of course, and neither was my newly widowed friend, Camilla Chaney.

In the center of the table was a buffet of sandwiches, fruit, pastries, coffee, and bottled water. Monty knew these women needed a free meal. The attendees were chattering as if they were at a party.

Chris and I took seats against the wall at the back of the room, and Chris helped himself to a brownie and coffee. Several women eyed him appraisingly. Two or three looked uneasily at his police uniform.

Monty stood behind a podium, next to a table piled with papers. He looked quite dashing with his dark hair, muscular shoulders, and bespoke suit.

Promptly at two o'clock, he tapped the mic and said, 'Good afternoon, everyone, and thank you for attending this meeting. I'm attorney Montgomery Bryant, and I represent Mrs Camilla Chaney, now the owner of the Sterling Service of Chouteau Forest. Mrs Chaney is unable to attend today, and I am speaking on her behalf.

'First, I'm very sorry to tell you that Ms Erin McBride died in the car crash with Mr Sterling Chaney.'

'Noooooo!' someone shrieked. 'Not Erin!' The other women were crying and shouting their denials.

'How did she die?' Suzi asked over the din.

'As I said, she died in the car crash with Sterling Chaney,' Monty said.

'Why didn't we find out sooner?'

'Her name was withheld while we tried to find her next of kin.'

'You could have asked us.' Juanita sounded angry. 'The poor girl was an orphan.'

Monty waited for the commotion to die down. When the room was quieter, he said, 'As you know, Erin was working on a deal for health insurance for the voice artists at the answering service. The afternoon she died, they'd reached an agreement. Thanks to Erin, you will all be getting health insurance as of today.'

'Yay!' cried Jenny, while the other women wept again for Erin. Jenny looked abashed, then raised her hand. Monty nodded at her.

'Is there going to be a funeral for Erin?'

'Yes, there will be,' Monty said. 'Mrs Chaney will arrange for a service and burial at the Chouteau Forest Cemetery.'

'That was really nice of Camilla,' I whispered to Chris. 'She couldn't be more different from the reptilian Mrs Perkins.' He nodded agreement.

Only one person wasn't smiling through their tears. Diana Dunn, the mother of eight-year-old Abigail, was crying as if her heart would break.

Monty went over to the weeping mother. 'Ms Dunn.' His voice was soft. 'What's wrong? What can I do for you?'

'Nothing. These are happy tears. With health insurance, my Abby can finally get the treatment she needs.'

That set off another round of crying. Monty waited until the tears stopped, then said, 'Mrs Chaney is a compassionate and sympathetic woman. So I don't want you to get too upset when I tell you the next part of my announcement:

'Mrs Chaney is closing the Sterling Service, effective immediately.'

There were gasps and horrified cries of 'No!'

Monty held up his hand for silence. 'Mrs Chaney had no knowledge of how her husband's business was run, but now that she has learned a little about it, she wants to help you.'

When the voices died down to murmurs, Monty continued. 'First, Mrs Chaney will give all the women voice artists a check for twenty thousand dollars in severance pay.'

Now there were cheers and cries of delight.

'Second, Mrs Chaney will pay for four years of college or for technical training at any local institution. You have six months to make your decision about continuing your education.'

'Incredible,' someone whispered reverently. I thought so, too.

'And last but not least, Mrs Chaney will give you that free health insurance for one year.'

'What's the catch?' someone asked. I couldn't see who it was, but I bet she never used that streetwise voice when she read her phone stories.

'No catch,' Monty said. 'My office manager, Ms Gender, will pass out some forms now. Read them carefully and talk them over. Take them to your lawyer. As soon as you sign, you'll receive your check for twenty thousand dollars and an application to apply for your education payment.'

Jinny Gender handed Chris and me each a document, ten pages of dense legalese. I skimmed through it until I came to this:

> While admitting no wrongdoing, Mrs Sterling Chaney agrees to pay the employees the one-time sum of twenty-thousand dollars ($20,000). The recipients agree to defend, hold harmless, and indemnify . . .

There was a lot more, but from what I could figure out, the women could collect the twenty grand if they promised not to sue Mrs Chaney.

'Can we sign right now?' Jenny asked.

'Certainly,' Monty said. 'You'll find pens in the containers on the table. Just raise your hand and either Ms Gender or I will help you. I've brought in a notary, Mrs Frances Adams, with the Notary Services of Chouteau Forest. She will witness your signature, and once the agreement is completed, you can collect your check before you leave today.'

Almost everyone's hand shot up immediately. Monty went from one woman to another, saying, 'OK, initial each page on the bottom. Now don't sign it yet. Mrs Adams will complete the process at that desk in the corner. You can sign and date it in front of the notary. Then look for Ms Gender. She'll give you your check.'

Mrs Adams, a gray-haired woman in a severe black suit, was seated at a small desk with her notary equipment at the ready, an old-fashioned, long-handled metal stamper and her 'Journal of Notorial Acts.'

Once the women initialed each page of the contract, they lined up in front of the notary.

'Monty's playing it safe bringing in an outside notary,' I whispered to Chris. 'A lawyer can't use his in-house notary if his name is mentioned in the agreement.'

'He's a slick,' Chris said, 'and I mean that in a good way.'

Monty made another statement. 'I've called the media, and when we finish here, I'll make the same announcement to them. They'll be here at four o'clock.'

'Just in time for the evening news,' I whispered to Chris, and took a moment to admire his ears. He had cute ears.

Monty was still talking. 'You're welcome to stay and talk to the press, if you'd like.'

Only two women left without signing the contract. Everyone else seemed happy to take the money. Once the women signed the contracts and collected their checks, many of them made plans to celebrate their good fortune. A handful stayed behind to talk to the media. Erin seemed forgotten in the general jubilation.

At three thirty, the conference room had settled down. Chris had to leave. I promised to drop by his house about eight o'clock.

The hard-working Jinny Gender was tidying up the table, throwing out used paper plates and napkins, filling the urn with fresh coffee, and putting out more water and pastries.

Monty was behind the podium, checking his notes.

'Do you have time to talk?' I asked.

'About fifteen minutes. Is this about Camilla?'

'Yes, I'm worried about her.'

'Come on up to my office, Angela. Do you want some coffee?'

'No, thanks.'

I followed him up the stairs to his office, which smelled of old books and leather. It looked like a men's club with its dark-green walls, leather wing chairs, and horse prints. One wall was devoted to leather-bound law books, and another was all-glass with a view of the summer Missouri woods, the green leaves lightly wrapped in a heat haze.

Monty sat behind his desk, and I claimed one of the leather client chairs.

'That was very kind, what Camilla did for those women,' I said.

'She's a kind woman, Angela, and when she found out how her late husband and his now-deceased manager were running that business, she was horrified. She's determined to help make amends for how they exploited those women.'

Monty leaned forward on his desk and said, 'What's going on, Angela? Why do you want to talk to me?'

'Is Camilla OK?' I asked. 'She was upset with me the last time I saw her.'

'Upset doesn't begin to describe it, Angela. She was livid.'

'I know. Jace Budewitz went with me when I notified Camilla about Sterling's final death, and I was too dumb to realize that the detective was interrogating Camilla as a suspect until it was too late.'

'She told me about that, Angela. She felt hurt and betrayed, as well as angry. She should not have talked with that detective at all. I explained to her how the police operate and that Detective Budewitz was just doing his duty, and it wasn't your fault.'

'Oh, good.' I was relieved.

'Sort of good,' he said. 'She's still angry with you, but if you want to see her, I think she'd like that.'

'Me, too. I'll apologize in person.'

'If you see her, go soon, Angela. I'm afraid she's going to be arrested for murder.'

'Why? She didn't kill her husband.'

'I know that and so do you, but you have to think like a prosecutor. The evidence against her looks bad. Can I tell you this information in confidence?'

'Of course.' Monty knew he could trust me.

'First, the cliché is true: the wife is always the chief suspect. It doesn't help that Camilla threw her husband out of the house for being unfaithful and filed for divorce. A source inside the police told me that the investigators concluded the Ferrari's brakes were tampered with, along with the airbags. Sterling and an innocent passenger were both killed.

'Camilla loves cars. She told me she examined the car because she wanted to see why it cost more than a million bucks. Her fingerprints are on that car. She lifted the hood and looked in from the side, so her prints are on the hood and pointed inward on the horizontal surface of the fender above a front tire.'

'That makes sense,' I said.

'But her prints were also found on the side at the wheel, as if she was holding on as she reached under the car. And there were prints at more than one wheel.'

'She's thorough,' I said.

Monty frowned at me. 'The master brake cylinder was tampered with, and her prints were found near it.'

'Oh.'

'Camilla told me she wears coveralls when she works on her car, and her coveralls were hanging in the garage. There was grease on one knee, as if she'd knelt down in the garage. She also has her prints in grease on the tools.'

'But that's normal, isn't it?' I said.

'Sterling Chaney installed a security camera at the entrance to the garage. He was living above it, remember. The video for the night before he was killed shows Camilla entering the garage late, at two seventeen in the morning.'

'Maybe she couldn't sleep,' I said.

'She told the detective that she thought she was in the garage about twenty or thirty minutes. The garage video has her leaving at twelve minutes after four.'

'So? She lost track of the time.'

'Jace thinks she's lying, Angela. It doesn't help that she'll make millions from the insurance.'

'Don't rich people always have lots of insurance?' I asked.

Monty ignored me and laid out more damning evidence.

'A repairman in her house said he overheard Camilla talking to you, and she said she hated her husband and wished he was dead.'

'I thought he was lurking around while Camilla and I were having a private conversation.'

'The repairman says he'll testify.'

'Good. That will ruin him in the Forest. When word gets out that he's eavesdropping on his customers, he'll be banned.'

'Look, Angela, you're not getting it. Camilla is in big trouble.

Jace wants to arrest her. I've tried to get him to agree to call me, so she doesn't have to do the walk of shame through the media scrum.'

'Why is Jace behaving this way?' This didn't seem like the man I'd worked with for so long.

'He told me he's sick of the rich getting special privileges in this town,' Monty said, 'and everyone covering up for them.'

'I'm sick of it, too,' I said. 'All their friends either get amnesia and can't remember anything or they cover up vital evidence. Jace has a point.'

'A point!' Monty was close to shouting. 'Jace says you're part of the problem. You're hiding information to save your friend, Camilla.'

SEVENTEEN

I stayed at Monty's law office for part of the press conference. The room was crammed with print and TV reporters. I could pick out the TV reporters easily – they were as groomed and polished as show dogs. The print reporters and photographers were a scruffier tribe, but they did the dirty work of digging for news.

Before the press conference, everyone but the TV 'talent' was chowing down on muffins and brownies.

Promptly at four o'clock, Monty came out and made almost the same announcement he'd given the voice artists.

When he finished, the reporters exploded into questions:

'Why is Camilla Chaney doing this?'

'How many voice artists are there?'

'When will the phone sex women get their money?'

Standard questions and expected. Monty handled them well. Until Bill Russell, a reporter for one of the rowdier free papers, asked, 'Why are you painting Camilla Chaney as Mother Teresa? Is it because she's about to be arrested for murder?'

'Are you so cynical, Bill, that you can't believe someone could be kind?' Monty said.

I didn't wait for Bill's answer. I couldn't. I knew the reporter had good contacts at the cop shop. If he said Camilla was going to be arrested, Jace was dusting off his handcuffs. There was no deal, after all. Jace wasn't going to call Monty so his client could avoid the perp walk. The angry detective was going to make sure Camilla was completely humiliated. I'd better get to Camilla's if I wanted to talk to my friend before she was behind bars.

I slipped out of the room, then hightailed it out of there. Fifteen minutes later, I was at the wrought-iron gates to Camilla's home. No TV vans were in front of the place. So far, so good.

Mrs Ellis answered the front door. 'Ms Richman.' The

housekeeper's voice was as cool as a January morning. 'I'll see if Mrs Chaney is at home.'

'No time for formalities, Mrs Ellis. I have to see Camilla before the cops come and arrest her.'

'Oh, my lord. She's in her study. Upstairs, second door on the right.'

I blew past the housekeeper and ran up the stairs. Camilla was sitting at a carved antique desk, a pair of glasses perched on her nose, reading through a thick stack of paperwork. She looked up when I barged into her room.

'Angela? What are you doing here?' The frost in her voice should have flash-frozen me.

'Listen, Camilla. We don't have much time. The police are coming to arrest you.'

The blood drained from Camilla's already pale face, leaving her whiter than the papers she was reading.

'No! Monty said it wouldn't happen yet.'

'Well, it's happening. He's holding his press conference now. Remember, don't say anything when the police arrive except "I want my lawyer." Just keep repeating it. Promise?'

'Yes, of course. That's what Monty told me to say.'

'Also, I'm very sorry that Jace interrogated you during what was supposed to be a death notification.'

'That's not your fault, Angela. Monty told me that. I understand. You've always been a good friend to me.'

She stood up and wrapped me in a hug.

'I'm so sorry this happened to you,' I told her.

She smelled of lavender and roses, and her features were as delicate as carved ivory. Sterling was a fool for chasing other women. Now a dead fool.

'Oh, Angela, I thought my life would be so much better once Sterling was gone. Instead, it's infinitely worse.' She burst into sobs, and I held her and patted her back.

'It's going to be rough for a bit,' I said. 'But you'll get through it. I promise. You have a real advantage – one of the best lawyers in the Midwest.'

Mrs Ellis entered the room carrying a tray. 'I've brought you some food, Camilla dear.'

'I'm not hungry.'

'Please eat, Camilla,' I said. 'If the police show up, you're looking at an unpleasant couple of hours. You need to eat to keep your mind sharp.'

'It's chicken stew – your favorite,' Mrs Ellis said, as if she was talking to a small child. 'Have some to please me.'

The chicken stew smelled delicious. My stomach gurgled. I ignored it.

'I brought you some coffee and cakes, Angela.' Mrs Ellis poured fragrant coffee into a bone china cup and handed me a plate of tiny iced cakes and a silver fork. I helped myself to a chocolate cake with a pink sugar rose.

While I sipped my coffee, I studied my friend. Camilla didn't look good. She seemed frail and even thinner than she had the day of Sterling's first funeral. (Jeez, I couldn't believe I'd thought that, but this situation was downright strange.) Even her pink blouse didn't give her much color.

Camilla sat at her desk and ate about half the stew, drank some tea, and nibbled on a tiny iced cake. 'Sorry, that's all I can eat,' she said.

'Well, it's better than nothing. But I wish you'd eaten more. You're too thin.' Mrs Ellis piled the dishes on the tray and left the room.

'Should I pack a bag for jail?' Camilla said.

Oh, boy. She really wasn't getting this.

'I don't think you're allowed any personal items in jail,' I said.

'Not even a toothbrush?'

'They use fingertip toothbrushes. You have to buy them at the commissary.'

Camilla looked confused. 'What's a fingertip toothbrush?'

'It's a toothbrush that fits on the end of your finger,' I said.

'Ew. Why would they do that?'

'Because a regular toothbrush can be turned into a shank, a deadly weapon.'

'Oh.'

'What about my reading glasses? Can I take my tranquilizers and blood pressure medicine?'

'Ask Mrs Ellis to deliver them to the staff after you're,

uh . . .' I couldn't bring myself to say 'booked.' I finished with, 'after you're settled in.'

I grabbed a nearby chair and pulled it over to her desk, then took her soft, manicured hands. 'I'm so sorry, Camilla, but these next few days will be difficult. Jail will be way different from the life you're used to.'

'I'll be in with women only, right?'

'Yes.'

'How am I going to handle jail? Some of those inmates will be murderers. They can't even have a toothbrush because it could be turned into a weapon.'

I didn't have the heart to tell her she'd probably be booked for two counts of murder.

'And some of the women might be innocent, like you,' I said.

'I'm new to this, Angela. Tell me what I need to know to survive there. How do I handle the guilty ones?'

'Well, a police officer I know said the trick is to carry yourself in a confident manner. That's your protection. Don't permit your fear and anxiety to be obvious.'

'Look at me, Angela. Do I look confident?'

She looked like a Dresden shepherdess with her white skin and blonde hair. A lost shepherdess.

'In your own way, you do.' She had the confidence of the privileged.

'Here's another tip. Whatever you do, do not accept gifts or favors from anyone. Most come with strings attached.'

'That's what Monty told me. He said I should talk to no one. Do you think I can get a job in the prison library?'

'I don't know. I do know you're expected to clean your room every day. And you'll be charged a fee for your laundry, uniform, and board.'

'You're joking. I have to pay to stay in jail?'

'Yes. It's not a lot of money. It's called a daily subsistence fee. They won't give you a bill like you'd get after a stay at the Ritz. But you'll have to pay a little each day.'

'Should I bring some money?'

'Any cash you have on you when you're booked will go into your special inmate account.'

'How much should I bring? A thousand dollars?'

'Way too much,' I said. 'Seventy or eighty in cash will do.'

Reality was setting in. Camilla started sniffling, struggling to hold off her tears. I put my arm around her. 'You're a strong woman. I know you can get through this.'

My comment sounded inane, and I knew it. 'I wish I could do more to help you.'

'There's nothing, Angela. I'll just have to get through this. Should I wear this for my arrest?' She indicated her white linen pants, Egyptian cotton blouse, and pink scarf.

'If I were you, I'd change out of that expensive blouse and designer pants and put on something old. Same for those Tory Burch flats.'

She tore off the scarf and dropped it on her desk. 'Let's go to my closet and look for something to wear, Angela.' Now Camilla sounded giddy. 'Remember when we went looking for bridesmaids' dresses for my wedding, and the saleswoman at the shop kept bringing out those horrible ruffled dresses? I still have nightmares about that green satin number.'

'It looked like an explosion in a salad factory,' I said.

Camilla laughed, too long and too loud.

'Let's go.' I guided her down the hall to her bedroom.

'My clothes are in a guest room,' she said. 'It was too small for our guests, so we broke through the wall to connect it to my room. I had it redone as a closet.'

The dressing room looked like an upscale boutique. I saw sections for evening gowns, all bagged in plastic, as well as suits, dresses, blouses, skirts, pants, and purses. There were racks for shoes and boots. Sweaters and tops were folded in glass-fronted drawers and arranged by color. That section was a rainbow: I counted six shades of blue and fifteen shades of pink, ranging from shell pink to a dramatic fuchsia.

'Those two cabinets have socks and underwear,' she said.

One wall had a full-length three-piece mirror surrounding a carpeted platform so Camilla could view her complete outfit or get alterations. Next to it was a make-up table with a lighted mirror.

'Amazing,' I said. 'Now, what are your oldest clothes?'

'I guess my favorite Levi's,' she said, 'and my blue sweatshirt.' She pulled them out to show me.

'Perfect. Put them on.'

While she turned her back to begin dressing, I asked, 'What about shoes?'

'I have some plain white Keds.'

'Another good choice.' None of those items would make her look rich and privileged. She combed her hair at the dressing table and put on light-pink lipstick.

Dressed like that, she looked ten years younger.

'What about cash?' I asked.

She pulled a roll of bills out of another drawer, counted out eighty dollars, and shoved the money in her pants pocket.

'Now take off your rings,' I said. 'Especially your engagement ring.' She slipped off both her rings and dropped them in her jewelry chest.

She held out her hands in front of her and tried a wobbly smile. 'This is what the well-dressed woman wears for her Murder One arrest.'

Her careless bravery nearly made me cry.

EIGHTEEN

C amilla and I were in her sitting room, drinking coffee and waiting for her arrest. As waiting rooms go, it was topnotch. The rose-trellis wallpaper made me feel like I was sitting in a garden. The pink silk chairs were cushy and I had a view of that verdant side lawn. The more I admired the room's luxury, the more I worried about Camilla. She was as delicate as the vase of roses on the table. How would she survive surrounded by gray steel and streetwise criminals?

Camilla and I made meaningless small talk – if you put a gun to my head, I couldn't tell you a word we said. Mrs Ellis kept running up the stairs to check on us, then back down to look out the front window that had a view of the main gates. She made that trip so often, Camilla and I worried about her health.

'You should rest, Mrs Ellis,' Camilla said. 'Come have coffee with us.'

'I'll rest when I'm dead,' she said. 'Besides, I'm too nervous.' And she clattered back down the stairs.

Finally, the housekeeper came running into the room. 'They're here! They're here! That detective and a bunch of police officers. What are we going to do?' Her eyes were frantic, and she was wringing her hands.

I could hear loud knocking at the front door and the bell was buzzing like an angry hornet.

'Open the front door, please, and I'll call my attorney.' Camilla's voice was alarmingly calm, almost robotic. She walked over and kissed Mrs Ellis's cheek. 'It will be OK. I promise.'

Mrs Ellis burst into tears, wiped her eyes with her apron, then rushed downstairs again.

I recognized Jace's voice before he introduced himself. 'Is Mrs Camilla Chaney home?' he asked. No, he *demanded*.

Mrs Ellis burst into noisy tears but managed to say that Camilla was upstairs in her study.

We heard heavy feet pounding up the stairs. Camilla calmly took a last swallow of her tea and smoothed her hair.

Jace was first through the door, followed by two burly uniforms. The detective had not dressed with his usual care. His beige shirt was coming untucked, and he had grease spots on his brown tie. His short brown hair stuck out in comical spikes, but there was nothing funny about his next speech. He ignored me and walked over to Camilla.

'Camilla Chaney, I'm arresting you for murder in the first degree for the deaths of your husband, Sterling Chaney, and Erin O. McBride, both killed in a car accident. I have evidence that you premeditated these murders and tampered with Mr Chaney's car. You have the right to remain silent . . .'

The way Jace chanted the Miranda warning, it sounded like an ancient curse. When he finished, Camilla stood and said, 'I've called my attorney.' That's all she said. I admired her dignity.

Jace produced handcuffs from his back pocket and said, 'Hold out your hands.'

Camilla still said nothing, but that was too much for me. Her grace and his surly attitude enraged me. I'd never seen Jace being deliberately cruel. I had to speak up.

I got right in his face. 'Really, Jace?' I said. 'Handcuffs? Do you think this woman is going to attack you and your beef brigade?'

He turned his pent-up anger on me. 'You should talk, Angela! I thought you were different. You were one of the few people I could trust here. You didn't kowtow to this town's rich people. You stood up on your hind legs. You went after the guilty, no matter how much money they had. And I was proud of you.

'But now . . . now I can't believe how you've changed. One of *your* friends is accused of murder, and what do you do? Start kissing rich butt. You couldn't wait to head out here and smooch Camilla's over-privileged ass.'

What? I was so angry I could hardly speak. 'Shame on you, Jace. Camilla doesn't deserve that kind of talk. And for the record, she's one of my oldest friends. We were friends in high school. I never cared how much money she had. And I'm not kissing Camilla's ass, Jace. I'm comforting a friend in trouble. An innocent friend.'

'That's not what the evidence says.' Jace's boyish face was twisted into a ridiculous snarl.

'Then you're reading it wrong. I agree – a lot of the rich people in this town are stuck-up jerks. But Camilla's never been like that. You're wrong about her, Jace. You're prejudiced.'

'You're right, Angela, I am. I'm sick and tired of the fat cats getting away with murder – and it's not going to happen this time.'

He stuck a thick finger in my face. 'Now butt out, or I'll charge you with obstruction of justice and file a complaint with the medical examiner's office that you're interfering in a police investigation and concealing vital evidence.'

'What evidence?' I said.

'You didn't tell me that Mrs Chaney wanted her husband dead. I had to hear that from the repairman.'

'So what if she said it, Jace? There isn't a wife alive who hasn't said that at least once in her marriage. Do you want to lock up all the married women in the Forest?'

'No, just the ones with dead husbands. Keep interfering and I'll have you fired, Angela.'

'You're wrong, Jace,' I said. 'Camilla is innocent. And I'm going to prove it.'

He grabbed the handcuffed Camilla by the elbow and was steering her toward the door when Mrs Ellis rushed in. 'The TV reporters are out front, Detective. Would you like to use the back entrance?'

Jace bristled and turned on the housekeeper. 'No, I would not. Rich or poor, they all do the perp walk. She's going out the front door.'

As Camilla passed me, head held high, I grabbed the pink linen scarf she'd tossed on her desk and threw it around her neck. It was long enough to cover her cuffed hands. She gave me a grateful smile.

Jace glared at me.

Mrs Ellis and I followed the awkward group downstairs and

watched from the window. At least a dozen reporters were camped outside the gate. Camilla kept her head up as the press hurled hurtful questions:

'Are you glad your husband is finally dead?'

'How much money will you get from his life insurance?'

'Was he having an affair with Erin McBride?'

Finally, Camilla made it to the cop car. Jace opened the door and Camilla slid on to the backseat. The press kept shouting questions as the car drove down the street.

Mrs Ellis stood at the window until she could no longer see the police car. Then she said, 'Did you hear those reporters, Angela? Asking if Erin had an affair with Mr Chaney. Isn't that terrible? Now the media has managed to sully that poor woman's name. Erin was fighting for her co-workers. She never engaged in any funny business.'

'How do you know?' I asked her.

'I changed the sheets on Mr Chaney's bed.' The house-keeper's round face showed her disgust.

'The things that man did.' She shook her head. 'His bedroom was a shambles after he brought a woman here. Liquor bottles tipped over, lamps knocked off the tables, scented oils spilled on the sheets and the rug, lipstick on the wallpaper – even chocolate syrup on the sheets.'

'Chocolate?'

'Yes. Plain old Hershey's syrup. Scared the stuffing out of me, first time I saw it. I thought it was dried blood and that he'd killed somebody. But no, it was chocolate syrup, and I had to throw those sheets away.

'I was forced to turn a blind eye for poor Mrs Chaney's sake, but I could tell you some stories. I don't know how Mrs Chaney stood it. I'm glad she slept in her own room on the other side of the house, so she wouldn't know about most of his shenanigans. Rich people like to sleep in separate bedrooms. I don't know why. They miss a lot of cuddling with their husband that way.'

'That's what I thought,' I said. 'I was a bridesmaid at the Chaney wedding, and Camilla was crazy about him.'

'She still is, even now that he's dead,' Mrs Ellis said. 'And Sterling loved Mrs Chaney. In his own way. He couldn't stop himself from taking up with other women. Sterling Chaney had some kind of sickness when it came to women.'

'Was it a sex addiction?' I asked.

'I'm no doctor, but something was wrong. He couldn't quit chasing them, even after he promised his wife he'd be faithful. But I'll tell you this. The only time he had Erin here was when they were negotiating for health insurance. They sat in the downstairs parlor, and I brought them coffee. There was no funny business – and if you've ever sat on that horsehair sofa in the parlor, you know I'm telling the truth.'

'I do,' I said. 'And I'll never forget that torture. Is that thing stuffed with concrete blocks?'

Mrs Ellis managed a small smile. 'Come back to the kitchen and have coffee with me.'

I checked my watch. It was five thirty. I had a little time before I needed to get ready for my date with Chris.

Cozy was the only way to describe Mrs Ellis's kitchen, despite its huge size and shiny steel appliances. Cheerful blue café curtains let in the sunshine. Houseplants in colorful Mexican pots were everywhere. On the window sills, kitchen herbs grew in clay pots sporting their names: basil, thyme, parsley, dill, and rosemary.

We sat at a blue-painted table by a window. Mrs Ellis poured us both mugs of fragrant coffee. I turned down the offer of cake, since I was having dinner with Chris.

'So you believe Camilla is innocent,' she said.

'Yes.'

'And did you mean it when you said you wanted to find the real killer?'

'Definitely.'

'So how are you going to do that,' she said, 'without getting fired? That policeman was madder than a wet hen. He's going to come after you, and the way he was acting, he will get you fired.'

We both sipped our coffee. After a while, I said, 'I thought Detective Jace was my friend. We've worked together for a long time. I don't know why he turned against me because I disagreed with him about Camilla.'

'Did you always agree with him before?' she asked.

'Not always, but usually,' I said. 'I helped him, though I wasn't supposed to. My job is supposed to end when the body goes to the morgue and I turn in my report. But he didn't mind my help. Jace is from Chicago and doesn't know the ways of the Forest.'

'Sounds like he's fed up with rich people.'

'He is, and sometimes I can't blame him. My parents worked for the Du Pres family, so I have an easier time handling them.'

'I met your mother years ago,' Mrs Ellis said. 'She's passed, hasn't she?'

I felt a small pang of sadness for that loss. 'Yes, she and my father are both gone. I live in their house on the Du Pres estate.'

'To get back to your detective,' Mrs Ellis said, 'maybe the problem is he's used to having you as his yes-woman. I don't mean any offense, Angela, but men can be bullheaded some-times, especially when they're catered to. This detective thought he had an easy answer, and you interfered with his plans to close the case. I'm guessing he's taking your refusal to go along as a betrayal.'

'Well, that's just too darn bad. I'm not letting Jace Budewitz railroad my friend.'

'And I'm thankful for that,' Mrs Ellis said. 'Now, what can I tell you?'

'Who hated Sterling Chaney?'

'Just about everybody disliked the man, except his bar buddies, and they were a bunch of drunks. Bums, all of them.'

'I met some of them at the funeral. Let me rephrase that. Who hated Sterling enough to kill him?'

'That would be a shorter list. I suppose some of the women who worked for him at that dirty stories answering service.'

'Any idea who? Did any of them ever come to the house?'

'Yes, the Asian woman – the pretty one. Suzi something. What was her name? She was on TV.'

'Suzi Chin?'

'That's her. She came here once or twice and started talking about how she was falling in love with him. She left love notes on his pillow – which I found – and wrote "SC + SC = LOVE" on the bathroom mirror in a lipstick heart. Took all morning to scrub that nonsense off. In her love notes, Suzi said their "love was fated."

'Sterling never saw her again. The foolish girl scared him away – not that he would have ever left Camilla for the likes of her. When he quit seeing her, Suzi called here a couple of times and started spewing foul language. I told her if she ever called again, I'd call the police. I'm surprised she has the nerve to still work there.'

'OK, Suzi has a good reason. Anyone else? Didn't one of Camilla's society friends threaten her?'

'Oh, you mean Henrietta Du Pres Du Pont. She ordered Mrs Chaney to resign from the Young Readers committee. I told Camilla to ignore that awful woman. But here's the best part. Henrietta's note ended with, "Too bad your husband didn't die in that crash."'

NINETEEN

'I remember seeing that death threat,' I told Mrs Ellis. 'The note followed all Miss Manners' guidelines for genteel communication, right down to the blue-black ink on cream-colored stationery. Henrietta actually put that death threat in writing. Does Camilla still have it?'

'She threw it away, but I fished it out of the wastebasket,' Mrs Ellis said, proud of her detective work. 'That detective never asked Mrs Chaney about any death threats she may have gotten, but I knew that note would come in handy.'

'Do you think Henrietta is capable of murder?'

'Hah.' Mrs Ellis snorted. 'That stiff-necked snob is capable of anything.'

'What does she know about cars?'

'Not much, but they call her husband "the chauffeur."' Mrs Ellis took a sip of her coffee.

'Wait. A Du Pont is a chauffeur?' I couldn't believe what I was hearing.

'No, Du Pont and Du Pres are both *her* names, from her snooty ancestors. She made Potter P. Miles change his name when he married her. He went to the ceremony Potter Miles and came out Potter Du Pres Du Pont.'

'Du Pres Du Pont sounds like a bouncing basketball,' I said. 'And why would a rich woman marry her chauffeur?'

'He wasn't really her chauffeur. He worked in a pit crew for a Formula One race team. That's just the snarky name the Forest has for him. You know how they treat outsiders.

'Henrietta met Potter when she was in college and was infatuated with him. He was young, good-looking, and had money to burn. His life seemed glamorous. He was a tire changer. They can make about three hundred and fifty thousand dollars a year, plus bonuses when their team wins.'

'So she married him?'

'Where have you been?' Mrs Ellis looked at me in surprise. 'That shotgun marriage was the talk of the Forest.'

'When did it happen?'

I was usually up to date on Forest gossip, but when Mrs Ellis mentioned the date, I knew why I'd missed this tale. 'That's when my mother was dying of cancer. I went around in a fog for months.'

'Of course you did, dear.'

The oven timer dinged. 'Have some more coffee and I'll tell you what I know.'

She poured me a fresh cup. I was grateful for the coffee. Mrs Ellis opened the oven and a few minutes later set a warm cinnamon coffee cake on the table. I broke down and helped myself to a slice. Even a strong woman has her limits.

Mrs Ellis sat down, cut herself a slice of cake, and leaned in. 'Well, let me tell you what I know about that marriage.' She lowered her voice, indicating this was Grade-A gossip. 'You know Henrietta is the daughter of Wynonna Du Pres Du Pont.'

'Not Weeping Wynonna, the woman in black who used to spend all day praying in St Philomena Church?'

'That's her. You know how Wynonna got that way, don't you?'

'I heard she caught her husband, Luke, in the saddle, and he dropped dead.'

'That's the one.' Mrs Ellis said. 'Luke was with the upstairs maid when Wynonna caught them going at it in her bed. She blames herself, because when she surprised them, Luke croaked and – worse – he died in the state of mortal sin. At least according to her. She devoted the rest of her days to prayer for the repose and redemption of her husband's soul.'

'It sounds like old Luke died happy.'

'You couldn't tell Wynonna that. She was convinced her man was broiling in hell. Her priest and even the bishop himself tried to convince the poor woman that God is merciful. When that didn't work, they suggested she get counseling. But Wynonna kept on wearing out her knees until she went to her reward.'

'What does that have to do with her daughter Henrietta

marrying this man they call the chauffeur?' I took another bite
of cake. It melted in my mouth.

Mrs Ellis gave me a mischievous grin. 'Wynonna surprised
her daughter having a little afternoon delight with Potter in
her room.'

'Wynonna had a bad habit of lurking around bedrooms,' I
said.

'She was a Peeping Tom, if you ask me,' Mrs Ellis said,
'looking to spot sin everywhere. But I bet she was really sorry
when she surprised Henrietta with that man. She insisted the
pair get married "to save Henrietta's soul."'

'Didn't high-and-mighty Henrietta object to marrying a
nobody?' I asked.

'She threw a fit,' Mrs Ellis said. 'And Wynonna wasn't happy
that her daughter was diluting the precious family bloodlines
with a commoner. But Wynonna thought her daughter's soul
was more important, and I give her credit for that. She stood
her ground. She said she'd disinherit Henrietta if she didn't
marry Potter Miles immediately. A week later, they married
quietly in the family garden.'

'How did that work out?' I asked.

Mrs Ellis shrugged. 'About like you'd expect. Wynonna
insisted on an unbreakable prenup, and Potter bears the burden
of the restrictions: if he divorces Henrietta, he doesn't get a
penny. If he engages in any "unseemly conduct," Henrietta
can dump him and he won't get anything. Same if he's
unfaithful in any way. If Henrietta wants rid of him, all he'll
get is a hundred thousand dollars.

'Henrietta inherited tons of money, along with lots of Forest
real estate, when her mother died two years later. She also
inherited her father's wandering eye. The couple live separate
lives. Potter gets a big allowance and does what he wants. Mostly,
he races Porsches at a private racetrack and crashes them.'

'Sounds like Henrietta could be a widow soon,' I said.

'Not sure she wants to be,' Mrs Ellis said. 'Being a married
woman makes it easier for her to conduct her affairs – her
partners know there are no strings. She's not going to fall in
love with them and want to get married. And she sure doesn't
want to get pregnant.

'Also, Potter makes a presentable escort at charity functions. Henrietta fancies herself a great lady and meddles in every important committee. She's the one who made sure poor Camilla was banished from the charity work she loves, even though Mrs Chaney did nothing wrong.'

'This is interesting, Mrs Ellis, but where are you getting this information?' I took another bite of cake.

'I'm best friends with Henrietta's housekeeper, Millie Webber. I won't say Millie listens at doors, but she has an amazing knack for absorbing information. And I think she might be able to help you.'

'When can we meet?'

'Tomorrow just happens to be Millie's day off, and I suggest you take her out to lunch and ask her about Henrietta and Potter. I guarantee she'll have useful information.'

'How do I get in touch with Millie?'

'I'll set it up for you. Where do you want to go to lunch?'

'Solange,' I said.

Mrs Ellis raised an eyebrow. 'You're going to take Millie to the best restaurant in the Forest. Are you sure you want to be seen there with a housekeeper?'

Snobbery existed at all levels in the Forest. 'My mother was a housekeeper,' I reminded her. Mrs Ellis had the grace to look embarrassed.

'Solange is expensive,' she said. 'Lunch for two could cost twenty-five dollars.'

More like seventy-five, but she didn't need to know that. 'If Millie has useful information, it will be worth it,' I said. 'If she doesn't, we'll both have a nice lunch.'

'I'll make my call in the breakfast room,' she said.

By the time I'd finished my cake and drunk the last of my coffee, Mrs Ellis was back.

'Millie is really excited to go to lunch at Solange. She wants to meet at one o'clock, if that's OK.'

'Perfect,' I said, and called Solange for reservations.

I thanked Mrs Ellis and went home to prepare for my date with Chris. I was looking forward to seeing my lover.

I missed his loving, his kisses, and his caring. He always listened to me and offered thoughtful opinions and comfort when my day went wrong. I hummed happily as I showered and blow-dried my long brown hair. I slipped into my lacy black underwear, looking forward to the time when he removed it – or, better yet, when we left our clothes in a frenzied trail up the stairs to his bedroom.

I came on duty at midnight, so I packed a small overnight bag with my DI uniform and added my office cell phone charger. Then I took a bottle of Malbec, fired up my black Charger, and drove the short distance to Chris's condo. It was a pleasant trip. The setting summer sun was casting long shadows, and the day was cooling. Green lawns were wrapped in a soft haze.

Best of all, Chris was waiting for me when I got to the condo parking lot. I parked the car and ran to him, enveloped in the smell of his aftershave. We kissed in the parking lot, then ran inside holding hands. I was so happily distracted that I forgot everything in my car.

Once inside, I sniffed the air. 'Let me guess,' I said. 'That's your soon-to-be famous feta-stuffed chicken.'

'It is,' he said. 'And it will be ready in a bit, but in the meantime, I'm hungry for something sweeter.'

He kissed me again, and we both ran upstairs giggling, leaving a trail of clothes behind us. Then we fell into bed, and Chris's inspired and enthusiastic lovemaking made me forget the day's troubles.

Sometime later, we were lying in each other's arms, sweaty and pleasantly exhausted. We sat up and he poured me a glass of Malbec.

'I have a bottle of this in my car,' I said.

'I know it's your favorite,' he said. 'I opened a bottle before you showed up and kept it on my nightstand so it could breathe.'

'Good idea,' I said. 'Now that *I* can breathe again.' I stretched, enjoying the afterglow.

We clinked glasses, and he said, 'So what's this I hear about you fighting with Jace Budewitz?'

'What?' The afterglow vanished. 'What do you mean?'

'I heard you insulted him when he arrested Camilla Chaney and called the two uniforms he had with him the "beef brigade." It's the talk of the station, Angela.'

'Wait a minute. I insulted Jace? He insulted me, and the woman he was arresting. He told me I was smooching Camilla's "over-privileged ass." Those were his words.'

'Well, she did kill her husband.' Chris looked at me over his wine glass.

Now I was furious. 'You don't know that. I think she's innocent.'

'The evidence says she's guilty.'

'Then you're all looking at it wrong. Do you know that Camilla actually had death threats from a Forest fat cat, Henrietta Du Pres Du Pont? Henrietta said – in writing – that Sterling should be dead. And her husband used to be part of a Formula One pit crew. He knows cars and he could have tinkered with the Ferrari.'

'Well, if he did, then why aren't his fingerprints on the car?' Now Chris had raised his voice.

'Because Potter is a slick. He could have worn gloves. He tampered with the car that night. Then Camilla wanted to look at her husband's super-expensive car. And since she's innocent, she didn't worry about leaving her fingerprints all over the car.'

'Oh, yeah? What's this about you covering up the fact that Mrs Chaney wanted her husband dead?'

'I didn't.'

'Well, a repairman at the house said Mrs Chaney told you, "I want him dead! Oh, God, how could you play such a cruel joke on me?"!'

'So what? She was upset that Sterling was cheating on her.'

'And you didn't see fit to mention that to Jace?'

'No, it was a private conversation. Surely we can talk without the police monitoring our every word.'

'Look, Angela, you have to decide whose side you're on: the police or the killer.'

'I told you. Camilla isn't a killer.'

Damn that man. He didn't even ask for my side of the story. I wasn't about to stalk out of his bedroom naked, so I yanked the sheet off us and wrapped myself in it. Then I started gathering my clothes on the stairs.

When I had them all, I marched downstairs and dressed in

his guest bathroom. All the while I was getting ready, he stood outside my door, pleading with me. 'Angela, look, I'm sorry I upset you. Please stay. I don't know what I did wrong, but I apologize.'

He didn't know what he did wrong? That was even worse.

I was dressed now. I threw open the door. He was standing there in his robe. He tried to kiss me, but I brushed past him.

'Angela, please! I'm sorry. I love you. Please stay.'

I turned to face him. 'No.'

'But what did I do wrong?'

'You never asked me what happened. Not once! You just assumed Jace was right.'

'But Jace is one of the good guys, Angela.'

'Usually. But this time he's wrong.' I reached for the doorknob.

'Please don't go, Angela,' he said. 'What will I do with the chicken?'

As I walked out, I said, 'You can take your chicken and stuff it.'

TWENTY

As I drove away from Chris's condo, I told myself I wasn't going to cry. No man was worth that.

And I didn't.

I made it all the way to my house before the tears started. I ran upstairs, threw myself on the bed, and cried myself to sleep.

When I woke up the next day, I was furious at Chris – and myself. I was wrong to get so attached to a man. I did perfectly fine as a widow. I had my work, and that was enough.

Speaking of work, I checked the clock. It was noon. Oh, lord, I'd left my office cell phone in my purse, uncharged. I pulled it out in a panic, praying I didn't have any calls in the middle of the night.

Whew! I didn't. What a relief. I had less than an hour to get dressed for my lunch with Mrs Webber, the housekeeper who could help me with my investigation. I hauled my unopened overnight case out of my car, along with the untouched bottle of Malbec. After I put my office and personal phones on to charge, I dressed in my DI suit, just in case I was called into work.

When I looked in the mirror, my black work suit seemed a bit severe for a casual lunch, so I added a colorful scarf and silver earrings. Much better.

Solange was about fifteen minutes away. I left my car with the restaurant's valet and went inside. I checked in at the front desk and asked that the server give Mrs Webber a guest menu without prices. I didn't want her to be shocked at the cost.

By that time, Mrs Webber had arrived, dressed in a summery powder-blue A-line dress with a matching jacket. Pinned on the jacket was a pink flower brooch that matched her earrings. She was barely five feet tall, with a sweet, open face and a comfortable figure. She reminded me of my mother, right down to the permed gray hair.

I introduced myself and said, 'Thank you for joining me on your day off, Mrs Webber.'

'It's my pleasure.' Her smile lit up her face. 'Please, call me Millie.'

The hostess was ready to take us to our table. Millie admired the restaurant's pink-and-black decor, which flattered the women lunching there.

When we were seated in a booth, a server in a sleek black dress introduced herself as Isabella and took our drink orders. Millie asked for a glass of white wine, and I wanted a club soda with lime. If I was called out to work, I couldn't have alcohol on my breath.

Millie sat primly, with her purse on her lap.

Once the server left, Millie said, 'I've never been to this restaurant before, but I understand all the important people eat here. Is that Mrs Du Pres in the corner booth?'

'Yes,' I said. 'She's Reggie Du Pres' sister-in-law.' We both knew Reggie ran the Forest.

'Oh, my. I've seen her in the society pages.' Millie was impressed. 'I believe she's wearing a real Chanel suit. And that looks like the mayor coming out of the bar.'

'I'm not surprised,' I said.

Millie looked at me oddly. Clearly, she didn't know His Honor was usually plastered by noon. 'He dines here often,' I said. 'What would you like for lunch?'

We studied the menu, but Millie kept quiet. I wondered if she was waiting to see what I ordered. 'I'm having the grilled sole. It's very good if you like fish. Otherwise, I recommend the petite filet mignon.'

'I'll have the filet,' she said.

'How about a salad? They have a delicious spinach and avocado salad, but it's too big for one person. Would you split one with me?'

'Oh, yes. That would be lovely.'

'And more wine?'

'No, thank you. One glass is more than enough for me.'

I put my work phone on the table and said, 'Excuse the phone, but I'm on call today. If it rings, I'll have to leave.'

We talked about my job as a death investigator until the

server arrived. I ordered for both of us. 'And how would you like your filet, ma'am?' Isabella asked Millie.

'Well done,' Millie said. 'I don't want to see a speck of blood in that meat.'

The server fought to contain her disapproval of Millie's request. 'As you wish, ma'am.' Isabella headed for the kitchen.

'Now, how can I help you?' Millie asked.

'Mrs Ellis said you could tell me about Henrietta and Potter's strange marriage.'

'Strange doesn't begin to describe it. I was housekeeper when her mother forced that poor young woman to marry Potter. They never loved one another. It was just a fling. She wanted to see what it would be like to bed a hairy-chested working man, and he wanted to try it on with a rich girl. If Mrs Du Pont hadn't caught them, they would have stopped once their curiosity was satisfied.

'But catch them she did, and now they were stuck with each other. Fortunately, there's enough money that they can do what they want. They both go their own way.'

'Do they do anything together?'

'A little. They sometimes have a meal together, though they rarely say two words. And he's required to take Henrietta to those endless social events. Potter's a good-looking man, and she likes having arm candy. They make a handsome couple. She's very pretty, if you can overlook her haughty ways.'

'Potter's a hunk,' I said. 'Women must hit on him.'

'They do,' Millie said. 'Married ones, too. They chase him shamelessly, even calling his home.'

'How does Henrietta like that?'

'She likes the idea that other women find her husband attractive. She likes it even more that he can't do anything about it. If a woman calls too often, Henrietta will read Potter's part of their prenup – that he can't engage in "unseemly behavior" or be unfaithful or he'll be tossed out on his ear.'

'Does Henrietta have sex with her husband?'

'Sometimes. She has a lot of boyfriends – she calls them "my little distractions" – but when she gets tired of a boyfriend, or the man tires of her, she seeks comfort in the arms of Potter.

'Lately, she's hardly been interested in him, and that's how I think he got into trouble.'

'What kind of trouble?'

'He was being blackmailed. I heard him on the phone—'

With that, our server rolled over a cart covered with a pink linen cloth. Isabella was ready to prepare our salad. Millie watched fascinated while the server mixed the ingredients in a large glass bowl, then added the dressing and tossed the salad. Meanwhile, I was dying to know who was blackmailing Potter.

At last, Isabella divided the salad into two wooden bowls and said, 'Would you like fresh pepper on your salad?'

'No, thanks,' I said.

Millie piped up. 'I'd like some.' The wooden pepper grinder was nearly the size of a baseball bat. It took an eternity for Isabella to grind the pepper on Millie's salad. When she finished, the server said, 'Anything else you'd like?'

For you to go away, I thought. Instead, I said, 'No, thank you.'

'I'm fine,' Millie said.

Now I had to wait while the housekeeper savored her salad. She held up a single spinach leaf on her fork. 'This is perfection, don't you think? Each spinach leaf is coated with dressing.'

'I'm glad you're enjoying it.'

'It's so nice to be waited on.' Millie sighed happily. 'I wonder what the secret is to this dressing? I think it has lemon in it.'

'And a touch of garlic,' I said.

'And the avocados are perfectly ripe. That's hard to do, you know – get avocados at their peak.'

I munched on my salad, hoping it would encourage Millie to eat. Finally, she dug into her salad, too. At last, Isabella took our empty bowls. Now I could ask Millie who was blackmailing Potter.

As soon as I opened my mouth, the server wheeled out our main course on a cart. She deboned my fish at the table, artfully removing the backbone in one piece.

'That's amazing, how you took the bones out of that fish, dear,' Millie said.

'You're very skilled.'

'Thank you,' Isabella said. 'And here's your filet, ma'am – well done.' She handed Millie a steak knife.

The housekeeper cut into the meat. 'Just the way I like it. Cooked all the way through.'

'Would you like some Béarnaise sauce on your filet?' Isabella asked.

'Yes, please,' Millie said.

The server ladled the rich sauce from a silver sauceboat. Millie looked like she'd died and gone to heaven.

'This is just lovely.' She smiled at me. 'Real silver, a pink linen tablecloth and napkins, and a pink rose in a crystal vase on the table. And me, being treated like a queen.'

I resolved then that I would control my impatience for the information about who was blackmailing Potter. Millie would savor her meal.

And she did, enjoying each bite of the Béarnaise-smothered steak, the new potatoes, and asparagus. My fish was good, too. I'd forgotten I'd missed dinner last night until the server placed my food in front of me.

'That's a pretty brooch you're wearing,' I said.

She positively glowed with pride. 'Thank you. My two grandkids gave me these earrings and matching pin for Mother's Day. They bought them with their own money from their allowance, too.'

For the next half-hour, I heard about Gillian, the soccer star, and Charlie, the next big-league baseball player. I didn't have to pretend interest. Millie was a good storyteller.

Isabella quietly took our plates when we finished and brought us both coffee. 'May I tell you about our desserts?'

'Oh, yes,' I said.

'We have warm peach cobbler, chocolate soufflé, homemade sorbet, and fresh berries with cream.'

'How about chocolate soufflé?' I asked.

'It will take a while to prepare,' Isabella said.

'That's fine with me,' I said. 'Millie, do you mind waiting for dessert?'

'Not for a soufflé.'

Isabella poured us more coffee and disappeared into the kitchen. Now we could talk.

'So, tell me about Potter being blackmailed.'

'Well, he's been really jumpy these last few weeks, and he asked for an advance on his allowance. He gets five thousand dollars a week and still goes through it. Henrietta gave him the money. She doesn't care how much he spends.

'Anyway, Potter started getting these calls on our landline at odd hours. I'm supposed to answer the house phone, but he always picked it up first. Then one night, about eleven o'clock, the phone rang. I picked up the house extension at the same time as Potter, and he answered first. I heard him say, "I told you not to call me at my home number, Larry. Use my cell phone."

'This Larry sounded threatening. He said, "I only use your landline when you're not answering your cell phone, Potter. Where's my money?"

'Potter sounded scared. His voice shook. He said, "I'll have it for you tomorrow."

'"You'd better," Larry said. "Otherwise, your wife and her society friends will get to listen to you enjoying our services. Here. I'll play you a sample to jog your memory."

'Then I heard a woman with a sexy voice say, "I bet you're hard listening to me describe my smooth, full-breasted body. I can't wait to take you in my luscious . . ." The rest of her talking was drowned out by a man's heavy breathing. He was moaning and groaning. Suddenly, he stopped. It was Potter.

'This Larry said, "Think hoity-toity Henrietta will enjoy that bedtime story as much as you did, Potter?"

'"I said I'd pay!" Potter was pleading now.

'"You've got till ten a.m. tomorrow," Larry said. Then he hung up.'

'Potter didn't actually have sex with that woman,' I said.

'I know, but it could be considered unseemly behavior. Especially if that Larry sent copies to Henrietta's friends.'

'When was this?' I asked.

'Right before that rich man – Sterling Chaney – was killed

in a car crash for good. Then Larry was murdered, and Potter seemed much happier. He was going around the house whistling.'

Isabella brought our chocolate soufflé. Our dishes of the fragrant chocolate treat were dusted with powdered sugar.

'Would you like whipped cream on your soufflé?' the server asked.

'No, thank you,' I said, virtuously.

'I would,' Millie said. Isabella piled the whipped cream on Millie's soufflé and poured us both more coffee.

The soufflé was amazing: light and slightly bittersweet. Millie and I scarfed down our treat as if we'd been starving. I'd just finished my last bite when my work phone rang.

'Sorry,' I said. 'I have to take this.'

I hurried outside and answered the phone. 'Took you long enough,' Greiman said.

Terrific. After that splendid lunch, I'd have to work with that jerk. 'I'm at the Avalon,' he said. 'Some geezer dropped dead. Get over here now.'

'On my way.'

Back inside, I settled up the check at the front desk. Behind the desk, I saw a row of crystal vases under a sign that said, *Take home a memory of your special meal.*

'May I have one of those vases for my guest?' I asked. 'And could you put a rose in it?'

'Certainly,' said the woman. I settled the check and added a twenty-five percent tip for Isabella. The bill was a hundred and twenty bucks. Worth every penny.

I carried the vase with the rose back to our table and presented it to Millie.

'Oh, my dear, you didn't have to do this.'

'But I wanted to,' I said. 'I'm sorry that I have to run, but I've been called into work. Take your time and finish your coffee.'

'I think I will. And thank you for a lovely lunch, dear. I'll always remember it.' She stood up and hugged me. 'I hope I was a help.'

'More than you know.'

TWENTY-ONE

T he Avalon was a 1930s movie theater made into an art house. It showed foreign films that almost nobody in the Forest watched. What really saved the old theater was the afternoon Dollar Deal. Older people, priced out of the first-run cinemas, went for the one-buck movies. So did younger people if the Avalon showed a classic.

This afternoon, the place was packed. The show was Hitchcock's *Strangers on a Train*.

I found a parking spot two blocks away from the theater, pulled my hair back into a practical ponytail, ditched the scarf and earrings, and dragged my DI case out of the car trunk.

I rolled it past the police cars and emergency vehicles, including an ambulance. A paramedic was standing around, looking grumpy. What was that about? Why weren't the paramedics going to the hospital – or on their next run?

Mike, the cheerful uniform, let me through the yellow crime scene tape and gave me the lowdown.

'An old man collapsed in the theater just before the end of the movie,' Mike said. 'His wife started screaming and the movie stopped rolling. Everybody was running around trying to call nine-one-one, but they couldn't.

'I think the movie house was using one of those phone jammers, where you can't make calls in the theater. They're illegal, but the guy running this place has enough problems surviving. I'm not going to say anything.

'The lights went up, and somebody yelled, "Is there a doctor in the house?" There wasn't, but an off-duty ER nurse came forward. She helped move the old man out into the center aisle, took off his tie and suit jacket, and unbuttoned his shirt. She tried giving him CPR, but it didn't work.

'Somebody finally got through to nine-one-one. The police showed up, shut down the show, and told everyone to clear out. Boy, was the audience ticked! The manager gave them all rainchecks but some wanted their money back – a measly dollar!

'By the time the paramedics showed up, the poor guy was already dead. They have his body and can't leave until you do your death investigation. They rolled the stretcher into the ladies' room. It has a big area where the women can chat and comb their hair. The women can't use their bathroom, so they're pissed.' He looked at me. 'Excuse my language.'

'And the pun,' I said. Mike blushed.

'Anyway, there's a long line of people – men and women – using the one remaining public john, and it only has two stalls. Plus the women won't go in when the guys are using it. The manager is trying to keep a riot from breaking out.'

'Looks like I'd better get to work. Where's Greiman?'

'He's in the lobby, trying to put the moves on the girl selling popcorn at the concession stand,' Mike said.

'Of course he is,' I said.

'He's wasting his time. Jemima is only sixteen and her father will shoot that detective if he so much as looks sideways at his daughter. I'd hate to see her dad go to jail for killing that worthless—'

'I'll handle it,' I said.

Inside, the theater smelled of popcorn and mold. It was clearly running on a shoestring. The black tile floor was cracked. The hot-pink walls were covered with movie posters, but the posters couldn't hide the water damage bubbling through the plaster.

To the right were two black restroom doors. A paramedic and a uniform guarded the ladies' room. There was an angry mob in front of the men's room, with a harried manager trying to calm and apologize to the furious crowd at the same time.

On the other side was a vast glass concession stand. Sure enough, Greiman was leaning over the counter, trying to charm a buxom blonde teen. He wasn't looking at her sideways. He was staring straight down the front of her striped uniform. What a sleaze.

I rolled my suitcase over and said, 'Hi, Jemima. It's Angela Richman. I heard your sixteenth birthday was so cool. Your party was the talk of the Forest.'

'Were you there?' she asked. 'We had more than a hundred people.'

'No, I had to work that day. But people are still talking about it.'

'It was amazing.' Jemima's blue eyes lit with enthusiasm. 'We had a real DJ, and a Sweet Sixteen candy bar, where my friends could have all the best candy, and the coolest mocktail bar, with margaritas, piña coladas, and mai tais – all with no alcohol.'

'Sounds like fun,' I said. 'Were you there, Detective?'

Greiman straightened up, suddenly losing interest in the underage girl. I started to walk away when Jemima called my name. 'Ms Richman, could I talk to you a minute?'

She moved to the opposite end of the concession counter, behind the soda machine. She dropped her voice to a whisper and asked, 'Are you with the police?'

'I'm a death investigator, Jemima. I work for the medical examiner's office, but I know some police officers.'

'I need to talk to you before you go. Something bad is happening here – and I don't mean the man who died. I think the owner was involved in a murder. My dad says it's none of my business, but it *is* my business. This is my first grown-up job, and I don't want to lose it.'

Jemima's eyes were wide with fear.

'Tell you what,' I said. 'Why don't I talk to you after I finish my work here?'

'Promise?'

'Definitely.'

When I got back to Greiman, his face was red with anger. Naturally, he turned on me.

'Where the hell have you been?' he said. 'I've been waiting for you.'

I could see why he turned the head of an inexperienced girl. He was superficially handsome with his thick black hair, and he dressed to impress in a gray Armani suit and light blue shirt.

I rolled my DI suitcase to the middle of the lobby and asked Greiman, 'So what happened?'

'Some old geezer collapsed in a seat. Dropped his glasses

and went looking for them, but never sat back up. The wife started screaming and they stopped the picture. The EMTs were here and declared him dead at two thirty-six this afternoon. Probably a heart attack.'

'Where is his wife?'

'That old biddy there, "Miss Chouteau Forest 1923." She can't stop crying.'

The older woman was dressed in a festive blue party dress, sparkly earrings, and impossibly high heels. She had a pert figure, though the thick beige support stockings somewhat spoiled the effect.

She was seated in a chair in the lobby, wrapped in a blanket. A kindly paramedic was patting her hand and talking to her.

I'd forgotten just how mean Greiman could be. Yes, I was mad at Jace, but dealing with a jerk like Greiman took all my self-control. I'd only been here five minutes and already I wanted to slug him.

'Where's the decedent?' I asked.

'In the women's bathroom.' He pointed across the vast lobby. 'The paramedics can't leave till you do your thing. They're mad because they're stuck here.'

No surprise. Paramedics are adrenaline junkies. They hate waiting. 'I'll go there right away, and then interview the wife. Any other witnesses?'

'None. They were all watching the movie. In the movie, the cops were closing in on one of the bad guys, and nobody noticed anything was wrong, except the dead man's wife.'

I rolled my DI case toward the paramedic outside the restroom, who was now pacing up and down. I recognized Dave, a burr-headed hulk with a nice smile.

'I'll do my job as quickly as I can, Dave, and set you free.'

'I understand, Angela,' Dave said. 'I'm just no good at standing around.'

I gloved up with four pairs. Dave followed me into the restroom, which must have been opulent ninety years ago. The first section had mirrored Art Deco vanities and worn pink velvet chaise longues. The stalls were behind another black door.

In the center of the room was a stretcher with an old man

in black pants. His white shirt was open, and his chest was dotted with EKG stickers.

I opened my iPad, called up the Death Scene Investigation form, and wrote down the case number, date, day, and time.

'The decedent's name is Richard Henley.' Dave spelled the man's last name for me. 'His wife's name is Virginia.'

I'd get the other demographic information from Mrs Henley.

The deceased was lying supine, on his back. I noted in my report that the body had been moved after the discovery, and the decedent was currently on a stretcher. I photographed him with my point-and-shoot camera, then began a detailed examination.

The Body Inspection form started with several ghoulish but necessary questions: 'Is the body fresh? Beginning to break down? Decomposed? Insects present?'

I answered 'yes' to the first question and no to the others. That made my job easier.

Mr Henley was tall. I measured him at six feet and one inch, and estimated his age as late seventies. He had a full head of thick white hair, and he was slender. I guessed his weight to be about one hundred and eighty pounds. The ME would weigh him to get an exact figure.

The decedent was wearing suit pants that were too big for him. He'd cinched them tightly with a black leather belt. The notches on the belt showed that he'd lost weight, possibly as much as thirty pounds. He was wearing black socks and well-polished black shoes with laces. The shoes had been re-soled. His shirt was heavily starched, and the cuffs and collar were worn. It looked like Mr Henley had fallen on hard times.

There was no damage to his craggy face. He was a handsome old man.

'The ME might find some cracked ribs,' Dave said. 'We tried hard to resuscitate him, but I think he was gone before we arrived. That's how I want to go – quick.'

'Thanks, Dave. Knowing he didn't suffer may help comfort his widow.'

Mr Henley's pale skin was age-spotted. The shirt sleeve on his left arm was rolled up. He had good muscle tone for an older man, but big bruises on his forearm. One wine-colored bruise was seven inches long. A smaller one was two inches. I would ask his widow about those.

His nails were well tended and unbroken, but the backs of both hands were crisscrossed with scratches. The three on his right hand ranged from one inch to three inches long. He had four two-inch scratches on his left hand. I made a note to question Mrs Henley about those, too.

I documented the jewelry. Mr Henley wore a yellow-metal watch with a silver-metal dial and the brand name *Caravelle*. The black leather watchband needed to be replaced. On the decedent's ring finger on his left hand was a yellow-metal wedding ring. In his right shirt cuff was an oval yellow-metal cufflink with the initials *RH*.

'Dave, I know you were busy trying to save Mr Henley's life, but do you know what happened to his other cufflink?'

'I think Mrs Henley picked it up when the nurse who gave him CPR tore open his shirt. His wife also has her husband's suit jacket and tie. His wallet was in her purse. She found his movie-watching specs on the floor and took them.'

I wrote down those facts.

Dave helped me turn the body. There was nothing else to note, except that he had soiled his pants when he died, and the pants had sticky spots from whatever was spilled on the theater floor. A wad of gum stuck to the left pant leg just below the back of the knee.

Dave helped me wrestle the decedent into a black body bag and zip it up. That zipping sound always had a sense of finality.

'I need the stretcher back,' Dave said. 'Can we put him on that chaise longue?'

We quickly transferred the body bag to the chaise. I held the door while Dave rolled the stretcher out.

'It's about time.' A young woman in ripped jeans and a tight T-shirt tried to barge past me.

'Oh, no.' I blocked her entry. 'This restroom is closed.'

'Why?'

It was a rude demand, and I decided she needed an answer. I opened the door wider. 'See that black body bag? No one is coming in here until that man goes to the morgue.'

'Ew,' she said, backing away. 'Gross!'

The uniform agreed to stand guard until the morgue van arrived. 'May I get you a soda or anything from the concession stand?' I asked the cop.

'I'm fine, thanks,' he said. 'This beats writing speeding tickets on Gravois Road.'

The Forest PD denied it, but they had monthly ticket quotas, and cops hated working the speed traps.

Back in the lobby, another paramedic, Dick, was holding Mrs Henley's hand and talking softly to her. She kept dabbing at her eyes with a big pocket handkerchief.

'Mrs Henley,' I said. 'May I speak to you?'

'Certainly, dear.' Mrs Henley was about seventy-five, a petite woman who weighed less than a hundred pounds. Her long, sparkly earrings swung like chandeliers in an earthquake when she moved her head.

The paramedic gently squeezed her hand and said, 'I have to go back to work now. Will you be OK?'

'Yes, my sister Bernice is coming.'

The paramedic stood up. 'I'm very sorry for your loss, ma'am.'

As he turned to leave, Mrs Henley said, 'Wait! What about your handkerchief?'

'You keep it,' he said. 'And the blanket.' He waved goodbye.

'What a nice young man,' she said.

I introduced myself and asked, 'Do you feel well enough to tell me what happened, Mrs Henley?'

'Call me Virginia. Richard and I have been married fifty-six years. Today was our anniversary.'

'I'm so sorry.'

'We've been a little short of cash, but we can always afford the Dollar Deal movies, and we both like Hitchcock. We dressed up for our date. I know I'm overdressed for an afternoon movie, but Richard liked this dress, and it was fun to look pretty. I'm old and wrinkled, dear, but in his eyes, I'm still the girl he married.'

A huge lump formed in my throat, and I tried to swallow it.

'Did your husband say he didn't feel well?' I asked.

'No, he was in a good mood. We got here early and had good seats. We were watching the movie, and I jumped when the police were about to get Robert Walker. At least, I think that's when it happened. I must have brushed Richard's glasses off, because we both started searching for them. He was looking on that sticky, nasty floor, and I was checking our seats.

"'I didn't find them,' I whispered to Richard, but he didn't answer. I called his name, but he didn't move. Then I screamed, real loud, and kept screaming until the lights came on and someone said, "Is there a doctor in the house?" There wasn't, but Sandy, this real nice ER nurse, came forward.' Virginia told the same story as Mike the uniform, ending with, 'Then the paramedics told me my Richard was gone.'

Virginia made a mighty effort to hold back her tears, but she broke down when she said, 'He was the love of my life.'

I fought to keep from crying myself. I kept patting her hand until she stopped. 'Did your husband have any health problems?' I asked.

'Oh, yes. He had a bad heart. I mean, he had a loving heart, but the physical heart was sick.'

'I understand,' I said. 'Did he take any medications?'

'A slew of them. He took an adult-size aspirin. The rest had long names, but I knew them all: benazepril, carvedilol, atorvastatin, and furosemide.'

Virginia gave me her husband's birth date and Social Security number, the name of his physician, and her husband's occupation. 'Richard is a retired TV repairman. He was forced to retire. No one gets anything fixed anymore.

'We have two beautiful daughters and four grandchildren, but they live in Chicago and Atlanta.'

'Your husband had some very bad bruises on his left arm.'

'Yes, he did. Richard was a strong man, but as he got older, his skin became thin, and even bumping into a doorjamb could cause a bruise.'

'What about the scratches on his hands?'

Virginia managed a small smile. 'Those are from our cat, Elsah. She's a young calico and she likes to play.'

Virginia had answered all my questions. I wanted to stay with the new widow until her sister Bernice arrived.

'May I ask you a question?' Virginia's voice was small and timid, and she seemed embarrassed. 'I need my husband's suit pants. He wanted to be buried in that suit – it's his only good one. The pants got kind of messed up, but if they're dry-cleaned, they should be OK.'

'I can't remove any clothing or jewelry. The medical examiner has to do that. But I'll make sure that the ME takes good care of your husband's pants and returns them to you.'

She gave me a relieved smile. 'Thank you,' she said. 'Money is a little tight right now.'

We sat in silence for a few minutes until she said again, 'He was my whole life, you know.'

I did. Painful memories of my own husband and his untimely death came flooding back. I was grateful when Bernice burst through the door and enveloped her sister in a warm hug.

I pulled Bernice into a corner and asked her to take Virginia inside the theater. The morgue van had arrived. After the women left the lobby, I handed over the paperwork and body to the van driver. Dave, the cop who'd guarded the restroom door, was free to go. So was I.

I was heading out the door when Jemima, the concession girl called out, 'Ms Richman, you promised to talk to me, remember? It's important.'

TWENTY-TWO

Yikes! I'd completely forgotten about Jemima after the emotional interview with Virginia Henley, and I had almost walked out the door.

I made a U-turn toward the concession stand. Jemima slapped a *Closed* sign on the counter and ran toward me. She pointed to a door marked *Private* and said, 'We can go in there.'

We entered a storeroom perfumed with chocolate. Its shelves were a treasure trove of movie candy, and more supplies were stacked on the floor. I sat on a sturdy carton of Milk Duds and parked my DI case next to me. I wondered if I could inhale calories. Jemima pulled over a big carton of Junior Mints for a chair.

'Sorry,' I said. 'I was interviewing Mrs Henley. She lost her husband of fifty-six years.'

'That's so sad.' Jemima looked sympathetic. 'I can't imagine even being fifty-six, much less being married that long.' She looked at me wide-eyed.

'You'll be surprised how fast it happens,' I said, and then realized I sounded like my mother. I quickly switched course.

'How can I help you, Jemima?'

'It's my boss, Eldon, Eldon McIntyre. Do you know him?'

'Just to say hello.'

'I think Eldon may be in big trouble, Ms Richman. He owns this place, and it's been in his family since his great-grandfather Floyd started it almost a hundred years ago. The theater's just barely hanging on. You can look around and see it's hard up for money.'

'I saw the water damage in the plaster,' I said.

'And that's just the start,' she said. 'Eldon is a good guy. He pays me ten dollars an hour, even though he can't afford it. I don't want to lose this job, Ms Richman. I'd have to go back to babysitting, and I hate watching screaming kids, even if it pays more.' Jemima was picking at the label on the Junior Mints carton with a blue-painted fingernail.

'So, what's going on?'

'Eldon is being blackmailed. I heard the phone call. His office is right next door. I didn't mean to listen, but I needed more candy, and Eldon was yelling into the phone.' Pick, pick. She kept picking at the label.

'He said, "I don't care if you do want money, Larry. I'm not married, so I'm not afraid how my wife will react. I don't have to give you one red cent." Eldon was quiet for a moment, and then he screamed, "You'll what? You'll play the recording for my mother?"

'Now he sounded scared – and desperate. "You can't do that, Larry. My mother is ninety-two. That recording would kill her. I don't have that much money and there's no way I can get it." By now Jemima had ruined her manicure trying to pull off that label.

'Eldon listened again. Then he sounded threatening. "If you send my mother that recording, Larry, I'll kill you. You're a dead man, do you understand? Dead!" He slammed down the phone.'

'When was this?' I asked.

'About two weeks ago.' She pulled off the box's label and rolled it into a ball.

'Do you know who this Larry is?' I asked her.

'I didn't at the time. But a day or two later, I came back for more Kit Kats and heard Eldon screaming into the phone, "Ten thousand dollars! Where the hell am I going to get that much money? No, I can't borrow from my mother! She took out a second mortgage on her house to keep this place going. And I'm tapped out. You're trying to ruin me!"

'Then Eldon hung up the phone and I heard him crying. I ran out of the storeroom and went back to work. He seemed real sad the next few days, and then I saw the story on the news about that Larry guy, the one who ran the phone sex company, getting murdered. The police arrested that woman, the rich lady married to the company's owner.' Jemima was rolling the balled-up sticky label around in her hand.

'Camilla Chaney,' I said.

'That's her,' Jemima said. 'Since Mrs Chaney was arrested, Eldon's been happier, but jumpy. He nearly had a heart attack when the cops came running in here. He locked himself in his office and made me go out and talk to the cops. I went to Eldon's office and told him why the cops were here. I saw him do a little happy dance when I told him that a man had died in the theater.'

I was ready to do a happy dance of my own, but I had to remain calm and try to distance myself. *Think like a detective*, I told myself. What would Jace – the Jace I knew – say next?

'So you saw Eldon celebrating a customer's death,' I said, hoping to keep Jemima talking.

'Yes, and Eldon's not like that, Ms Richman. He's a kind man. Normally, he'd be devastated that someone died in his theater. But like I said, he's not been the same since he got that blackmail phone call from Larry.'

Now she was twisting her uniform skirt and crying. 'I think Eldon killed Larry. And he let that poor woman, Camilla, go to jail for his crime. I don't want Eldon to go to jail, but that other lady shouldn't be there if she's not guilty. I can't call the police and I don't know what to do.'

Jemima was a good kid. I felt like a total rat when I said, 'The murdered man was Larry Perkins. He's not the only Larry in Chouteau Forest. It could be some other Larry.'

Jemima quit torturing her uniform skirt and looked at me with hopeful eyes.

'Do you really think so, Ms Richman?'

'Yes, I do.' I hated myself for lying to the poor girl, but she had given me a good lead. 'We have to be very careful about accusing Eldon. And you need to be careful yourself. If Eldon really did kill Larry Perkins, he might be desperate.'

'You're scaring me, Ms Richman.' Jemima was back to twisting her uniform.

'That's what I want to do,' I said. 'You need to watch out. Don't get caught poking around where you shouldn't. But if you should happen to hear anything, call my number. Here's my card. And if you feel threatened, call nine-one-one. Understand?'

Jemima nodded again and asked, 'Should I get a gun?'

Guns, the all-American solution. I sighed, then said, 'No, you're not old enough to buy a gun.' I was going by federal law. Illegal guns were everywhere.

'And guns are only a good idea if you train at a gun range every week. You have to know how to use them.'

'What about pepper spray?' she asked.

'You can't buy that, either. You have to be eighteen. Do you have any hairspray?'

'Hairspray is so eighties.' Jemima rolled her eyes. 'I bought some when I went to the Harvest Dance and wore my hair up.'

'Good. Carry that. Bug spray works, too. If anyone tries to hurt you, spray them right in the eyes.'

My work cell phone chimed, and I said, 'Excuse me, Jemima, I have to take this call.'

I ran outside the building. Katie, the assistant ME, was calling. 'Can you meet me in my office in half an hour?' she asked. 'I have the autopsy reports for the car accident and for Larry Perkins.'

'On my way,' I said.

Jemima was cleaning the concession counter when I came back in. I warned her again to be careful.

And this time, I really did leave the building.

On the way to Katie's office, I stopped for coffee at Supreme Bean and picked up two extra-large black Supremos, one for Katie and one for me. Usually, I bought three, but Katie didn't say that Jace would be there.

OK, it was petty, but so what?

Katie's office door had something new – a shiny metal hasp so that it could be padlocked. I wondered if she was having problems with someone stealing her sensitive files. Morgue workers had done that before, and I suspected a photo of Sterling Chaney's head sitting in the road like a deflated soccer ball would fetch a high price from the trashy tabloids. Still, the staff here had been vetted, and I'd never known them to pull a stunt like that. Well, that was Katie's problem, and she was smart enough to solve it.

The assistant ME was sitting behind her desk, pounding her

computer keys. She wore a starched white lab coat, a matronly brown suit, and a frown of concentration. Somehow, she managed to look cute.

'I brought you coffee.'

Katie's face lit with a grateful smile until she saw I only had two cups.

'Where is Jace's coffee?' she said.

'I didn't know he'd be here this afternoon.'

Katie stood up and spoke with what I can only call a towering rage. 'Bull! Jace comes to every autopsy. Every single one. You know that. What the hell is going on with you two? Are the rumors true, that you're feuding?'

'Not feuding exactly,' I said. 'Just not getting along.'

'That's not what I heard. Your fight is all anyone can talk about in the Forest, especially around the cop shop. You know what gossips cops are. Did you really scream at Jace when he put handcuffs on the suspect during an arrest?'

'The suspect is Camilla Chaney, and she weighs about a hundred pounds,' I said. 'She didn't need them.'

'Small female suspects can do real damage to cops,' Katie said. 'Women stab police officers with scissors, knives, knitting needles, and worse. And it doesn't matter what she weighs if she has a gun.'

'But I was with Camilla,' I began.

Katie interrupted me. 'And Jace is supposed to take it on faith that she was unarmed? A trusting cop is a dead cop.' I thought she was finished with the lecture, but Katie was only warming up.

'Did you really call the uniforms with Jace the "beef brigade"?'

'They looked ridiculous, intimidating that fragile woman.'

'The only person who looked ridiculous was you.' Katie paused to take a breath, but she wasn't ready to stop.

'Next, I hear that you walked out on your boyfriend, Chris.'

'I didn't walk out. I left early.'

'Before dinner? That's definitely not like you, Angela. Chris brought in chicken sandwiches the next day. They were delicious.'

'Did he rat me out?'

'No. Chris isn't like that,' Katie said. 'But I know you. And I'd already heard about the Jace feud. Now you have Jace and Chris both angry at you – two good cops. You're fighting a war on two fronts, Angela.' Sparks seemed to fly from her brown eyes.

'It's not a feud.' Jace Budewitz was leaning against the doorjamb, holding a huge go-cup of coffee. 'Angela tried to interfere with a police investigation. She withheld valuable information.'

Now Jace's face was flaming red with fury. I had no idea how long he'd been standing at the entrance to Katie's office, or what he'd heard.

'Get in here, Jace,' Katie said, and the huge detective meekly entered her office and sat on the edge of her desk. I scooted to the far end of the room by the filing cabinet to avoid him. Since Katie's office wasn't much bigger than a minivan, it was a pointless move.

Katie walked over to the door, checked the hallway for eavesdroppers, and shut her door.

She also dropped her voice to an angry hiss. 'Both of you. It's time to end this. Now.'

'But he—' I said at the same time as Jace said, 'No, she—'

Katie interrupted us both. 'I'm not going to listen to a he-said, she-said fight. The two of you make an unbeatable team, and now you're fighting each other. That's wrong. And bad for the people you're supposed to protect and serve.'

'But I've made an arrest,' Jace said.

'He arrested the wrong person,' I said.

'No, I didn't. Camilla killed her husband,' Jace said. 'Her fingerprints—'

'Shut up! Both of you!' Katie didn't yell exactly, but her voice got the attention of both of us.

Heavy silence overwhelmed the small room. Katie glared at us.

'You two are going to work this out. Right here. Right now. The pair of you are terrific. Together. But right now, you're acting like second-graders. No, that's an insult to school-children. You're acting like two-year-olds. When you work together, you're a kick-ass team. You are going to fix this, or

I'll kick both your asses up between your shoulder blades. You will solve this issue. Now. Without coffee.'

Katie grabbed Jace's cup of coffee and one of the coffees I'd brought and poured both cups into her metal wastebasket.

'Hey!' Jace and I shouted together.

'I have to get back to work,' Jace said.

'I have paperwork,' I said.

'Tough.' Katie snagged a heavy padlock off her desk and picked up her large coffee. 'I'm locking my door, and you two are not getting out of here until you shake hands and make up. I want you to apologize to each other.'

'Like hell!' I said.

'No freakin' way,' Jace said.

Jace and I glared at each other, lower lips stuck out like petulant children.

'It's three o'clock. You have half an hour,' Katie said. 'I'll check back on you then.'

'And what if we don't make up?' Jace said.

'Then you're stuck in this room until you do. And don't get any funny ideas about calling for help. I promise I'll make up a story that will turn the two of you into the biggest laughing stocks in the Forest.'

She paused at the door. 'Wait! No. I can't do that. You two have already made yourself into laughing stocks. See you in thirty minutes.' She gave us a mocking grin and slammed the office door. We both heard the padlock click. We were trapped.

The thunderous silence was matched only by Jace's thunderous expression. Rather than watch Jace glower at me, I leaned against Katie's filing cabinet and scrolled through my cell phone. No messages from Chris, but I didn't expect him to see reason. And I wasn't selling my soul for a lousy chicken.

Today had started bad and gone downhill. Poor Mrs Henley. I was sorry that her husband died, but I envied the fifty-six years she got to spend with the man she loved. I didn't get that luxury. Now Donegan was gone. I missed him terribly. What the hell was I thinking, taking up with another man? I didn't need that heartache. Once was enough.

Right now, I was sick of the entire male species.

I could hear the wall clock ticking. Only eight minutes had passed, unless the clock was broken. I checked my phone for the time. Yep, three-oh-eight.

I sneaked a look at Jace. He was looking at his phone, too, and pacing. He had so little room that he walked in a tight circle.

We continued in silent deadlock until we had seven minutes left. Jace finally spoke. 'Angela, I've gotta get home soon. My boy has a flag football game tonight.'

'So?'

'Don't take out your anger at me on my son. He doesn't deserve that.'

'OK.' I liked Jace's kid. I didn't know what to say next.

I was grateful when Jace shattered the silence. 'I'll start. Why didn't you believe me when I presented the evidence that Camilla Chaney was guilty? I had a witness who heard her say she was glad her husband was dead.'

'Not glad he was dead,' I said. 'More like relieved.'

'OK,' he said. 'Relieved. I can accept that.'

Progress, I thought.

'And we were having a heart-to-heart talk. Why should I tell you?'

'Because it has a bearing on the case,' he said.

'I didn't think her statement did. It was my judgment call, not the opinion of some eavesdropping repairman halfway down the hall.'

'OK. But why did you dismiss the physical evidence? Camilla's prints were all over that Ferrari.'

'Too obvious,' I said.

'Too obvious?' Jace's voice was etched with acid. 'Angela, most killers are stupid. That's how we catch them. And we're talking about a sheltered rich lady without an ounce of street smarts.'

'Who liked to put on coveralls and play mechanic,' I said.

'Oh, she played mechanic, all right. She fixed that car so her husband would die – along with his innocent passenger.'

'No,' I said. 'You've got it wrong. I've known Camilla since high school. She's my friend.'

Now his anger flared up. His face was stroke red. 'Everybody in the Forest is either friends with or related to someone else. They're so inbred their family trees don't fork.'

Jace gave a bad imitation of an upper-crust dowager's reedy voice. '"But, Detective, you can't charge Muffy Moneybags with murder. Her Grandmamma Gotrocks and mine took tea together in 1898. I know her family. I'm sure the butler did it.'"

I almost laughed but stopped just in time.

'Look, Jace, I've found new information, and that's why I don't think Camilla killed her husband. Eldon McIntyre, the owner of the Avalon Theater, was being blackmailed by Larry, the phone sex company manager. Larry promised to send a tape of Eldon's rather enthusiastic response to a phone call to Eldon's ninety-something mother, and Eldon was afraid it would kill the poor woman. Eldon said he would murder Larry – and I have a witness.'

'What's that got to do with Sterling Chaney's death?' he asked.

I knew the answer. *Nothing*. 'The two men are connected by the same company.'

It sounded lame when I said it out loud. I needed a stronger argument.

'How about this? Henrietta Du Pres Du Pont's husband, Potter, was also being blackmailed by Larry. Potter has a prenup that says if he engages in – and I quote – "unseemly behavior," he'll get dumped with almost nothing. Plus, his socialite wife wrote a note to Camilla that said, "Too bad your husband didn't die in that crash." I can get you that note. Potter used to be part of a Formula One pit crew, so he definitely could tinker with Sterling's car.'

Jace seemed to consider my statement. 'So you think this Potter guy could have killed Larry?'

'Yes. Or he and Henrietta could be working together, and killed both Larry and Sterling. Besides, we still haven't investigated the women who worked for the company. Any of them could have a good reason to want Sterling and Larry dead.'

'I agree, Angela, with that. You've come up with some good theories, but I can't continue to look for Sterling's killer when I've already made an arrest. You understand why, right?'

'I do.'

'And you understand why I arrested Camilla Chaney?'

'Yes, but—'

'Hold on.' Jace held up his hand. 'I didn't say you had to agree with me. I just asked if you understood.'

'OK, I can agree with that.' We were cautiously inching toward an agreement.

'I still have to find out who killed Larry, and since you know the Forest better than I do, I'll need your help.'

'You've got it,' I said.

'One last thing, Angela. Go easy on Chris Ferretti. He's a good guy.'

'I know that.'

'OK, our half-hour is up. I'll tell Katie.'

He banged on the door, and we heard Katie remove the padlock. She poked her head in the door.

'Did you two make up?'

We shook hands.

'And what did you learn, Jace?'

'That the Forest is overrun with jerk-offs.'

Katie handed us each a Supremo-size coffee. 'Get out of here, both of you.'

TWENTY-THREE

As I walked away from the morgue, I felt better – and not just because I was leaving the house of death. Katie's coffee had revived me, and, thanks to her, I was once again back on good terms with Jace. Chris was still a problem, but I'd sort that out later.

Meanwhile, I needed to see my friend Camilla. I hoped she'd been released on bail, but when I called her cell phone from my car, there was no answer.

Uh-oh.

I called Monty, her lawyer, and got the bad news. 'Bail was denied, Angela. She's considered a flight risk.'

'No! That's terrible.'

'It is, but bail is rarely given in murder cases, and this one is high-profile. Camilla's being held in the Chouteau County women's jail.'

'When can I see her?' I asked.

'She wants to see you as soon as possible. Visiting hours start at eight o'clock tomorrow morning. Camilla is only allowed one visitor a week, and she needs to see Mrs Ellis. From the way she was talking, I don't think she can wait two weeks to see you.'

'Oh.' Anyone who thought prisoners were coddled didn't know anything about the rules.

'However,' Monty said, 'she can have unlimited lawyer visits, and you can come along as my assistant.'

'When?'

'Right now. Can you do that?'

'Sure. I'm leaving the ME's office as we speak.'

'OK. I'll meet you in the visitors' parking lot at the county jail.'

I got to the Chouteau County Women's Correctional Facility before Monty, and parked way in the back. From the outside, the plain beige building looked like a junior college – except for the razor wire coiling on top the fences.

Monty's car entered the visitors' lot and parked in a special lawyers' section near the sidewalk. I ran to meet him.

'Thanks for coming, Angela.'

'Anything for Camilla.' We walked together up the sidewalk.

'I have to brace myself mentally to enter this place,' I said.

'The inside has been remodeled,' Monty said. 'But it's just as dismal as ever.'

'I'm worried about Camilla.'

'Me, too,' Monty said. 'I don't know what kind of coping skills she has.'

Once inside, it took nearly ten minutes to clear security. We waited another half-hour before we were taken to a small windowless room with just enough space for a table and two chairs. Monty pulled out a chair for me and said, 'I'll stand. You sit down and talk to Camilla.'

Before I could protest, an enormous woman guard arrived with Camilla.

'Take off those handcuffs,' Monty ordered the guard, and she did, grudgingly.

I was shocked by my friend's appearance. She looked shell-shocked and seemed to have lost weight overnight. Camilla was shrunken and her pale face was lined. She moved like an old woman. I quickly checked for obvious bruises and injuries but didn't see any.

'Angela!' She smiled, and I caught a glimpse of the Camilla I knew. 'I'm so glad to see you.'

I held her hands. 'How are you doing?'

'Like my new jumpsuit?' She made a feeble joke. 'Beige is the new orange.'

'Stylish,' I said. 'But a little too big.' The oversized jumpsuit made her seem even smaller.

'Baggy clothes are in now,' she said.

She was avoiding my questions. 'Camilla. Look at me. Are you OK? Is anyone hurting you?'

'Oh, no. The ladies here are very nice.'

I relaxed a little. She seemed sincere.

'Most of the women in here are innocent, like me. Shauna accidentally killed her husband when he came home drunk late at night. She shot him because she thought the man stumbling around in their apartment was a burglar.'

Right, I thought. Obviously, the jury didn't buy that story.

'And Tina grabbed the wrong bottle when she was making a hot toddy for her baby daddy.'

'Her what?' I couldn't help myself. No one in the Forest talked like that, especially not a woman like Camilla.

'Her baby daddy,' Camilla said. 'I just learned that. It means he's the father of their child, but they aren't married. Isn't that cute?'

'Adorable,' I said. 'What happened to Tina's baby daddy?'

'He died. It turned out the bottle was antifreeze and Tina accidentally poisoned him.'

Sure. I always keep antifreeze in my liquor cabinet.

Camilla looked at Monty. 'Many of these women are innocent, Monty, and I told them you'd look into their cases.'

So that's how Camilla was staying safe. By pimping out her lawyer.

Monty's voice was stern – and exasperated. 'First of all, Camilla, I warned you not to talk to anyone in jail about your case.'

'I didn't have to say anything, Monty. Everyone already knew I was the wife of the headless Ferrari driver. That's what they're calling Sterling. They also knew that I like to work with cars. They call me "badass." That's a compliment, and I like it.'

She straightened up and looked proud. 'Can you help these innocent women, Monty? I don't expect you to do it for free. I have money. I can pay you.'

'I'll look into their cases for you, Camilla. But I'm asking you to please be careful. In jail, many people will claim to be innocent, but they're guilty.'

'Oh, I know that,' she said. 'Dilma stalked her boyfriend and found out he was seeing another woman. She shot them both – in bed! I don't believe that she's innocent and I stay away from her.'

'Good,' Monty said. 'Now, why did you want to see Angela?'

'Sorry, Angela, I didn't mean to ignore you. I'm hoping you'll help Mrs Ellis plan Sterling's funeral. It's in less than a week. I had the casket refurbished and delivered to the Forest Funeral Home. It has a new red velvet lining. There will be no viewing, just a church service, graveside prayers, and a reception afterward at the Forest Inn. Monty thinks he can get me out of here for the funeral, but I can't check the details when I'm behind bars.'

I took out my iPad to make notes.

'First, Sterling wanted to be buried in his black Tom Ford suit,' Camilla said. 'Make sure the undertaker does that. The last time they just wrapped that poor car thief's body in a sheet, but I want Sterling fully dressed, right down to his shoes.'

I nodded. 'I'll make sure.'

'I want twelve dozen red roses. Three dozen for the arrangement on his casket, and the rest to be distributed in vases around the altar.'

Camilla said 'vah-ses.' The same woman who thought 'baby daddy' was cute.

'Got it,' I said.

'I've asked Father Win to officiate at the funeral and the graveside service. You're not Episcopalian, so you didn't know that Father Win made some changes in the traditional service for my sake. There will be no speakers at the funeral service, and no one will be invited up to make any extra remarks.'

'Too risky,' I said. 'What about the Forest Inn reception?'

'It's booked,' she said. 'I've already discussed and approved the menu. I won't have an open bar.'

'Good idea,' I said. 'Some of Sterling's friends can get too exuberant after a few drinks.'

'Exuberant? They're a bunch of barflies, Angela, and giving them free booze is asking for trouble. If anyone wants a drink, they can buy one in the lobby bar.

'I've also hired security to keep the press out of the church and away from the graveside.'

'Very smart,' I said.

'Oh, if you need any contact information, Mrs Ellis will have it.'

'Sounds like you've thought of everything.'

'I tried to.' Camilla squeezed my hand. 'I can't believe you helped me plan our wedding, and now you're helping with Sterling's funeral.'

And with that, she started crying, terrible tears of regret. When she stopped, she said, 'I'm sorry.'

'Why?'

'I thought I was all cried out.' She wiped her eyes.

'Hey, you've got a lot to cry about,' I told her. 'You're being very brave, and you seem to be doing well in jail.'

She shrugged. 'I'm doing OK, Angela, but I have to tell you, some of those women are big and scary.'

'Yes, they are. You be careful.'

'It's time for me to go back now,' she said. 'Thanks for coming.'

I gave her a goodbye hug, and Monty signaled to the guard. Camilla was handcuffed again to go back to her cell.

In the parking lot, I thanked Monty and we promised to keep in touch. As I walked to my car at the far end of the lot, I saw a man leaning against it. I felt in my purse for my pepper spray, but as I got closer, I saw it was Chris. My Chris. Holding a big bouquet of stargazer lilies, my favorite flower.

I ran toward him. I'd forgotten how much I missed him.

As I got closer, he put the lilies on my car hood and gathered me into his arms. 'I missed you so much, Angela,' he said between kisses.

He was wearing my favorite blue shirt, rolled up at the sleeves, and smelled like coffee and citrus aftershave.

'I missed you, too, Chris. I'm so sorry.'

'No, I'm the one who should be sorry.' His kiss was long and lingering.

'Hey, get a room!'

I wasn't sure who shouted that, but I felt myself blush.

'Come to my place,' Chris said. 'Let's talk this over.'

'Yes.' I kissed him again. 'See you there.'

I gently placed my bouquet on the passenger seat and soon my car was filled with the lilies' sweet perfume.

Ten minutes later, I was at Chris's condo. He was waiting for me in the parking lot. I gathered my bouquet and carried it up the stairs. Once inside, Chris kissed me so passionately that I dropped the lilies on his hall table.

'We can talk later,' I said as we ran upstairs, tossing our clothes everywhere.

Our lovemaking was urgent and hungry the first time, then slower and more satisfying the second time. When we finished the third time, Chris said, 'I'm hungry.'

'Me, too.'

'I don't have any food,' he said. 'Want to go out to dinner?'

I was wrapped around him, running my fingers through his chest hair and kissing his ear.

'No, I want to stay here with you in bed. That's why God created pizza delivery. I'd like pepperoni and mushroom.'

Chris called the Forest Pizza, and I put on a robe from his closet and went downstairs to put my bouquet in water. By the time I'd cut the lilies' stems, put them in a vase, and carried them upstairs, our pizza had arrived.

Chris found a couple of bottles of good Chianti and two glasses, and I carried both pizzas and a pile of napkins upstairs to the bedroom. We wolfed down the pizzas like we hadn't eaten in a week. We also finished most of the wine.

I was drowsy with contentment.

That's when Chris said, 'Angela, I am so sorry. I should have listened.'

'I understand. You're a cop.'

'But I'm also a man. A man who loves you very much. I should have listened to you. Why do you think Camilla is innocent?'

So I told him everything, and this time he did listen. 'OK, if you think she's innocent, then who killed Sterling? And Larry? Was it two different people or one?'

'I think it was one. It could be someone who wanted both men dead because it would put the company out of business. Which is what happened. It's closed for good, and Camilla has promised to destroy the recordings. The question is, who killed both men? Was it Eldon, worried about his aging mother? Or Potter, who could lose his cushy life?'

'Maybe Sterling's squeeze has some information,' Chris said.

'And there are the women voice artists who worked for Sterling and Larry,' I said. 'They all had reasons to hate him.'

'Looks like your work is cut out for you,' Chris said. 'And let me remind you again, messing around in an investigation can get you fired.'

'And let me remind you, I need to save my friend. If I'm fired, I can move somewhere else and get a job.'

'That's what I love about you,' he said. 'You're fearless and loyal.'

I kissed him again. Eventually, I fell asleep, content and satisfied.

TWENTY-FOUR

I kept a few things at Chris's place, including a fresh blouse, to avoid the walk of shame. I changed, but I knew my huge bouquet of stargazer lilies would give me away.

Besides, I suspected most of the Forest already knew where I spent last night. Chris and I had been seen kissing in the jail parking lot. The local gossips would put two and two – or, in this case, one and one – together.

This morning, I didn't care. All was right in my world.

Chris had to leave for work today at seven a.m., but he fixed French toast, bacon and coffee for breakfast, and his good-bye left me walking on a cloud. A man who was good in bed and the kitchen – what more could a woman want?

After he left, I loaded the dishwasher with the breakfast dishes, made the bed, and vacuumed. I carried the pizza boxes out to the trash, along with the empty wine bottles, and waved to Mrs McGonagle, the old woman who lived next door. She was the unofficial head of the neighborhood watch program.

Yep, I bet Mrs M was on her phone now, reporting everything. She seemed to find our romance fascinating, poor old gal.

Back home, I sat in the living room and admired my bouquet. The lilies' sweet perfume lingered, like the memories of last night.

I was on call tomorrow, so I needed to quit acting like a love-struck teenager and find Sterling's killer. Eldon, the owner of the Avalon, seemed like a good person to start with. It was already after nine o'clock. I checked online. The Avalon had an eleven o'clock movie, and I suspected Eldon would be at the movie house. I dressed in a new hot-pink sleeveless dress and black strappy sandals, and thought I looked pretty good.

Eldon must have thought so, too. He dropped his broom and ran over to the locked theater doors.

'Ms Richman.' Tall and stringy, Eldon wasn't a handsome man, but his craggy face had character when it was lit with a smile. He quickly unlocked the doors and said, 'I remember you. You were the death investigator when poor Mr Henley died. I'm sorry I didn't get to meet you, but, well, things were busy.'

'I saw you trying to stop a riot by the restroom.'

'I was so glad the police were there. People can be so unreasonable.'

'They behaved very badly that day.'

Eldon picked up his abandoned broom and started sweeping the cracked tile floor. 'How can I help you?'

'I have a couple of questions. May I talk to you somewhere private?'

He leaned against his broom. 'Sure, sure. Come into my office.'

I followed Eldon through a black door next to the storeroom. His office was small and musty, with a massive V of cracked and blistered plaster on the wall behind his desk. He saw me staring at the damage. 'Water leak. Nothing serious.'

'Right.'

We both knew it was only a matter of time before the wall caved in. He settled into a black leather office chair patched with duct tape. I sat gingerly on the edge of a musty yellow club chair.

'So, how can I help you?' He leaned forward on his desk, a landfill of paper, dotted with candy wrappers and the occasional banana peel. There was barely room for his elbows.

'I'm looking into the death of Sterling Chaney and his manager, Larry Perkins.'

'I thought the police arrested Mrs Chaney for her husband's death.'

'They did. But I believe she's innocent. And no one has been arrested for Larry's murder.'

'Well, whoever killed Larry should be given a medal and a parade.'

Interesting.

'Why, Eldon? Because Larry was blackmailing you?'

Eldon sat straight up, and his arm hit a massive pile of papers. A landslide of documents slid off his desk. His face was five shades whiter.

'How did you know?'

'You just told me. Larry was threatening to send a copy of your phone sex session to your mother, wasn't he?'

'So what? He's dead and he can't hurt Mother now. And – *and* – you shouldn't be investigating a murder, Ms Richman.' His face turned sly and unpleasant. 'What if I called my friend Evarts Evans at the Medical Examiner's office and told him what you're doing?'

'You're going to play the "I've got important friends" game, Eldon? Bad move. Because I can call my friend, Camilla Chaney, and tell her not to destroy your recording. I have the pull to do that. I was her bridesmaid and now I'm helping plan her husband's funeral. What would it do to your business if your customers found out what a perv you are?'

Eldon crumbled quickly. I could watch the process. First, his face went white with shock. Then, red with fury. Next, fear intruded around the edges. Soon, he was crying. Like his wall, he was a pathetic, damp mess.

'Don't. Please don't hurt Mother. I'm just trying to save the theater. What do you want?'

I gave him props for thinking of his mother first.

'Information.' I looked him in the eye. 'Did you kill Larry Perkins?'

'No! I don't even know how to shoot a gun.'

Since Larry had been stabbed, I figured Eldon was off the hook for the man's murder. I didn't think he was that good an actor to try to lie his way out.

'Look, I was happy when he was killed,' Eldon said. 'It was the first good luck I've had in years. He had my recording and he wanted ten thousand dollars. This place is falling down around us. You can see I don't have that kind of money. That's what I told him. But he was relentless, calling constantly. And then the calls stopped. When I heard on the news that he was dead, I thanked my lucky stars. I actually went to church for the first time in ages.'

'So, who do you think killed Larry?'

'Any man who was on those recordings. That's all I know, Ms Richman. Would you like a free ticket to today's show?'

'No, thanks, Eldon. Good luck.'

I slithered out of the theater, feeling lower than a gopher's basement for threatening Eldon. On the other hand, I did get what I needed.

It was ten forty. Time for my next stop. Brenda, the red-haired bartender at Solange, came on duty at eleven. She might know something.

At Solange, the old guys in the bar were eyeing me. There were only two of them, sitting at the far end, scarfing down free peanuts and expensive scotch.

The bartender was rinsing glasses. She had long, flaming-red hair and a hot-pink dress that was way tighter than mine. My friend Camilla was right: Brenda liked to wear colors that most redheads couldn't, and they looked good on her. The green eyes didn't hurt, either.

Sure enough, she had a tattoo on her right arm, one that said, *I'd rather have a free bottle in front of me than a pre-frontal lobotomy*. That tattoo confirmed this was Brenda. So did her name tag.

The bartender looked up and saw me. 'What can I get you?' she asked.

I put a twenty down on the bar and said, 'A dry Boodles martini with three olives.'

She slapped a cocktail napkin down on the bar, and I watched Brenda build the drink. She took a chilled martini glass from a fridge, then filled a cocktail shaker with ice cubes, added Boodles gin and a whisper of Noilly Prat vermouth. She stirred the cocktail shaker with a long-handled bar spoon for a good half a minute and poured the drink into the chilled glass through a cocktail strainer. Brenda topped the frosty glass with a three-olive garnish and set it in front of me without spilling a drop.

'Beautiful.' I took a small sip. The cold gin made my tongue do a tango and my eyes pop open. 'This is perfect. You stirred this martini. You didn't shake it. You're a classicist.'

She smiled and put a bowl of peanuts in front of me. 'I learned early on from my daddy that shaking won't get cocktails

colder. If I take the time to stir the drink correctly, it creates
an icy, silky cocktail. Good gin deserves good treatment. I
always stir martinis, unless the customer asks me not to.'

'So James Bond was wrong?' I asked, taking another sip
of that martini.

'I'm afraid so. A good martini should be ice-cold, but
shaking it with ice adds tiny ice particles to the final cocktail.
The martini is cloudy and diluted. Stirring with large ice cubes
makes it cold and crystal clear.'

I could see why she was popular. She made good drinks
and good conversation.

Brenda took my twenty, and deftly fanned the remaining
change: a five and three ones. I pushed all the money toward
her.

'Anything else I can get you?' She gave me a practiced,
professional smile that never reached those green eyes.

I put a fifty-dollar bill on the bar top. 'Information.' I took
another drink. A long one, this time.

'What kind of information?' Brenda looked wary.

'Information about Sterling Chaney.'

'He's dead. He was killed in a car crash.' She tried to grab
the fifty, but I hung on to it.

'I know that,' I said. 'I also know that you were seeing him
at the Four Star Motel.' I ate the first alcohol-soaked olive.

Brenda's green eyes were hard as bottle glass. 'So?'

'So . . . do you know who wanted to kill him?'

'No. He wasn't a bad guy. Decent tipper. Treated me right.'

'At the Four Star?' I didn't hide my disbelief.

'Yeah, it was a dive. But we drove there in a Ferrari. And
the way he talked about his wife, I was sure he was going to
dump her. He said she didn't understand him.'

'And you believed that? Seriously?' I chomped the other
two olives.

'OK, I was stupid. But look around this room.' It was rapidly
filling up with well-heeled businessmen, mostly between forty
and seventy.

'One of these dudes is gonna be my ticket out of here. I'm
not bad to look at and I make a mean martini.'

She was still gripping the fifty, but I refused to let go. 'Nope, you can't have it. You haven't answered my question yet. Who wanted Sterling Chaney dead?'

'Try the girls who worked at his phone sex place. He'd bring some here to impress them. Most were starry-eyed at being in the Forest's most expensive hot spot. He was all over them like an octopus. The valet said he'd bang them in the parking lot. One visit here and he never brought them back again. So you wanna know who could have killed him? Every woman who worked for him.'

Brenda tried again to grab the fifty, but I still wouldn't let her touch it.

'Not yet. Tell me about the women he brought here.'

She looked up at the ceiling, pretending to search her memory. 'Let's see. One was the cutest little Chink. Long hair and good tits. Most Chinks are flat as a board.'

'What!' I was outraged by her insulting language.

'Hey, she's not here, so her feelings can't be hurt.'

'It's not her. I don't want to hear talk like that.'

'Relax. You're in the Forest. This is a PC-free zone, my little snowflake.'

'Apologize, if you want to see that fifty.'

She sighed and gave me a fake pout. 'OK. I'm sorry. The other one was a colored girl. Is that OK?'

'No. Try "person of color." Anyone else?'

'The third one was strange. A white lady. Looked like a cracker, if you ask me. Can I say that?'

I glared at her.

Her voice was mocking. 'So it's OK to insult white people? Well, in case it isn't, she looked like someone who lived in Toonerville. Sterling wasn't playing grab-ass with her. She was trying to convince him of something, but I don't think it worked. She left here angry. That's all I remember.'

'Any names?'

'Yeah, Girl One, Girl Two, and Girl Three. And if I insulted you or your diverse friends, I'm very sorry. Now may I have my money?'

I let her have the fifty, and she tucked it in her bra.

'One more thing,' Brenda said. 'You're friends with Mrs Chaney, right?'

'Yes, I am.'

Brenda's voice was as silky as her martini. 'Please tell her how terribly sorry I am about the accident. I was just devastated. That Ferrari was one sweet ride.'

Her laughter followed me out of the bar.

TWENTY-FIVE

I left the bar seething. I didn't care how good Brenda's martinis were – I never wanted to see that creature again. I was mad at her – and furious with myself for letting her mock me. As I stepped outside, the summer heat walloped me, and I felt woozy.

Those three gin-soaked olives left me a bit fried. Not to mention the martini. I drove straight home and made my default meal: scrambled eggs and toast. Plus a pot of strong coffee.

The food and coffee helped. I was ready to work. I had to find out who killed Sterling and Larry, and soon. First, I wanted to talk to the voice artists – the women who told racy stories. The easiest way to get information about them was to look up the TV coverage of their protest online.

That's when Monty called. The lawyer's voice was quick and concerned. 'It's Camilla. She was attacked in jail. She was rushed to Sisters of Sorrow Hospital.'

'Oh, my lord. How bad are her injuries?'

'Bad. She was beaten unconscious and she's bruised. She has a black eye, two broken ribs, and her left arm is fractured. She'll need surgery for the broken arm later. It gets worse. She has a severe concussion and needed an MRI. Luckily, there's no brain bleed.'

'That's good.'

'She's not out of the woods yet. With a concussion that bad, she's been vomiting, has trouble talking, and is seeing stars. Do you want to come to SOS with me and see her?'

'Of course. I'm happy to be your legal assistant again.'

It was a fifteen-minute drive to SOS. I met Monty in the hospital lobby. He was his usual dapper self, but now he looked worried.

'I blame myself, Angela. Camilla told me she was doing fine, but she's too fragile to survive in a women's jail. First thing I want to do is take photos to document her wounds.'

I followed him to the elevator and then to room 315, at the end of the hall. I could see a bored sheriff's deputy sitting outside the door of her private room.

I whispered to Monty, 'She needs a guard? Really?'

'It's the law.' He shrugged. 'I'm glad they brought her to the hospital and didn't try to treat her in the jail's infirmary.' Monty showed the guard his credentials, and he let us in. He never asked who I was or why I was there.

Camilla looked overwhelmed in the hospital bed. Her face was bedsheet-white, and her blonde hair stuck up in unruly tufts. From the orange Betadine on her head, it looked like someone had pulled out clumps of her hair. She wore a dingy blue hospital gown. On her left forearm was a white plastic splint with velcro straps. Her right hand was handcuffed to the railing.

Ugly bruises were blossoming on her jaw and both arms. She had a necklace of bruises around her neck and one swollen eye was nearly closed. She was going to have a spectacular black eye.

'Camilla, sweetheart, I'm so sorry.'

Before I could say anything else, Monty interrupted. 'Camilla, I need to photograph you so we can document how badly you were beaten. Is that OK?'

'My head hurts, but it's OK.'

Monty's photos were a bit like the ones I take as a death investigator. He started with Camilla's hair and the wounds in her scalp, then her face, focusing on her black eye, then the bruises on her neck. I helped remove the covers and lift her gown so he could photograph the bruises on her chest and stomach. Monty photographed her from head to toe.

When he finished and Camilla was comfortably settled again, I asked, 'What happened?'

Camilla started crying. Monty gently petted her broken left arm. Actually, her plastic splint. I dried her tears with a tissue, since her right hand was cuffed, and then asked, 'Would you like some water?'

'Yes, please. I have to ring for the nurse when I'm thirsty, and they're very busy.'

I poured her a glass of cold water from the foam pitcher on her tray and directed the straw to her mouth. She drank thirstily.

'Oh, that tastes so good.'

I blotted her lips with another tissue and then sat in the chair by her bed.

'Thank you.' Camilla laid her head down on the pillow.

'Now, tell me what happened.' Monty's voice was soft with sympathy.

'In jail, we only get fifteen minutes to make a call on the payphone, and I was careful not to go over my time. I'm a newbie, and hogging the phone is really bad.

'When I hung up, this woman, Earlene, was mad at me. She said I talked for twenty minutes. She's a big bully – she looks like a sumo wrestler with bleached blonde hair. I politely told her she was mistaken, and I only talked for fifteen minutes. She called me a liar. I backed away from her. It didn't do any good. Earlene started punching me, all the while screaming that I was a "country club bitch" and using other words I'd never repeat.

'She kept getting madder and madder. I tried to hit her, and she broke my arm. I heard the bone crack.' Camilla shuddered. 'She started choking me, and I bit down hard on the fat part of her hand, under the thumb. I tore out a big chunk but didn't swallow it.'

'Good for you,' Monty said.

'That didn't stop her. Earlene pushed me down on the floor and started kicking me. Now I was really scared. She kicked me in the head, the legs, and my arms – even the broken one. She yelled, "You dumb bitch. My husband spent more than two thousand dollars on that phone sex service of yours and maxed out my credit card."

'"That's not my fault," I said. "I didn't know anything about my husband's business."

'That's when she really got really mad and shouted, "Oh, yeah? Well, you're living in a damn mansion. I saw it on TV. So you may not know where that money was coming from, but you were definitely spending it. Meanwhile, I have to pay off his credit card."

'She jumped on top of me, punched me in the eye, and started pulling out my hair and pounding my head on the concrete floor. That's when I passed out. The next thing I knew, I was in here.'

'Where were the guards when Earlene attacked you?' Monty asked.

'They were standing around watching. Everyone is afraid of Earlene, even the guards. She beat a man to death with her fists in a bar fight. That's why she's in jail for murder. Besides, the guards usually don't intervene in a fight unless it's serious.'

'Putting you in the hospital is definitely serious,' Monty said. 'We can sue for compensation and hospital bills. When you go back, I'll have you placed in protective custody.'

'No!' Camilla sounded frightened. 'Don't do that. Please! Protective custody is really bad. I heard from the other girls that protective custody means I'd be locked inside a six-by-nine cement box twenty-three hours a day. I'd only get a shower twice a week.'

So Camilla was wising up a bit, I thought. Suddenly, she turned even whiter and started breathing funny.

'What's wrong?' Monty said.

'I'm gonna throw up. Can you hold my barf bag for me?' She pointed to a bright blue plastic bag on her tray table.

I held the bag for her while she vomited. When she finished, she laid her head back on her pillow, exhausted. I wiped her mouth with a tissue.

'The doctor said throwing up was one of the symptoms of concussion.' Her voice was weak. 'I'm so sorry, Angela. I'm embarrassed to subject you to that.'

'No big deal,' I said, though my stomach was churning. My nose would short out when I was at a crime scene that had decomposition, but this was different. I pretended I was fine, walking across her room on wobbly legs. I dumped the barf bag in the bathroom trash and washed my hands.

When I returned, Monty said, 'Whose idea was it to cuff your good hand, so you can't even get a drink of water?'

'The guard did that,' she said.

'I'm going to have a word with him,' Monty said. 'I'll also talk to your doctor. Angela, can I see you for a moment?'

I followed him to the bathroom. He said, 'I may be gone for an hour or more. Can you stay with her?'

'Yes, of course.'

He left with a goodbye wave. As I went back to my seat, I noticed Camilla had smears of blood on her face, neck, and arms.

'Would you like me to clean off some of that blood?'

'Yes, please. The ER nurses tried, but they couldn't get all of it.'

I found a washcloth and one of those flimsy plastic wash basins hospitals issue patients. In the bathroom, I filled the basin with warm soapy water. The washcloth was rough as sandpaper. I gently dabbed at the blood spots on Camilla. She winced occasionally, but never complained.

'What are they giving you for pain?' I asked.

'Not much. Tylenol.'

'Why can't you have something stronger?'

'When Earlene hit me, I blacked out for more than five minutes. The doctor says that's a really bad concussion. It's a grade, uh . . . I can't think of the word.'

'Grade three?' I said.

'That's it. I can't have anything stronger until they do the surgery on my arm. This splint is temporary.'

She held up her arm. 'They have to wait a day or so. I can't have anesthesia yet because of the concussion.'

'Do you remember what kind of fracture it is?'

'They told me. Let me think. It's a community, communal . . . something like that.'

'A comminuted fracture?' I guessed.

'Yes! That's it! How do you know so much?'

'I don't, but I spend time with my doctor friend, Katie.' At the morgue, I thought. Looking at dead people's injuries.

'So what's a comminuted fracture?' Camilla asked.

'It means the bone is broken in at least three pieces. They have to do surgery to repair it.'

That was the short version. The longer version was that the doctors might need to use wire, screws, and metal plates to stabilize the break. But Camilla had enough to worry about right now.

I'd finished cleaning her up. After I dumped the soapy water, I found the hospital-issued mouthwash, toothpaste, and a toothbrush and brought them back to her.

'Here. Let me help you brush your teeth and use the mouthwash to get rid of the taste of Earlene.'

She started to laugh. 'Ouch. Don't make me laugh. Those ribs hurt.'

'What are they doing for them?'

'Nothing. They don't tape or strap ribs anymore. I just have to put up with it.'

After I finished cleaning her teeth, I emptied the basin again. 'Where were your friends when you were being beaten to a pulp?'

'Standing there, yelling at Earlene to stop. She didn't. It's not their fault, Angela. Earlene is a killer. They can't take her on.'

A short, compact nurse bustled in and said, 'I have to take your vitals, dear.' I got up while the nurse took Camilla's blood pressure and temperature and shined a small light to check her eyes.

'OK,' she said, her voice cheerful. 'Now get some sleep.' She turned to me. 'I'm glad she has a visitor, but she needs to rest.'

After the nurse left, I said, 'Go to sleep, Camilla. I'll catch up on my emails while you rest.'

'I can't, Angela. This is all my fault.'

'What's all your fault? And why?'

'Sterling's dead and so is Erin. And the men who used that phone service suffered so much misery. So did their families. That's my fault. I suspected my husband's money came from a bad source, but I never looked into it, Angela. He was spending so much to restore my grandparents' home. He fixed the dry rot in the windowsills and bought new storm windows. He re-sodded the lawn, painted the siding, and re-shingled the roof. Inside, he painted or wallpapered the whole house and I got to decorate the rooms. And in some secret part of me, I knew that money was dirty. But I let him keep working on the house.'

Now she was crying, hard, bitter tears. I tried to comfort her, but she was too bruised to hug. All I could do was hold her cuffed hand and wipe her eyes while she wept. At last, Monty came back with the guard. Camilla sat up, and I dried her eyes. The guard, a silent, pale slip of a man, unlocked Camilla's cuffed right wrist and cuffed her left foot.

After he left, Monty said, 'The doctor wouldn't let him cuff her left hand. Too risky.

'Camilla, I went to see Butch Klaven, the jail director, and told him your incident needed to be investigated and that Earlene, the bully, should be in isolation and charged with first-degree assault. I also said the two guards who stood by while you were beaten should be arrested and charged with negligence.'

'That's wonderful, Monty. What did he say?' Camilla said.

'He wasn't too happy with me. He said he'd run his jail the way he wanted, and a lot more. Director Klaven said the only way he can guarantee your safety is to put you in isolation.'

'No!'

'Easy there,' Monty said. 'There are still some things we can do. I can petition the court to have you released because the jail can't keep you safe. I can have the court order Director Klaven to investigate. If we can show the corrections officers were negligent, then they could be charged, disciplined, or terminated. If I sue the jail, Camilla, do you think your friends will testify?'

Camilla looked doubtful. 'Most of them would be afraid of retaliation, Monty. Wait! One might. Shauna, the one who shot her husband because she thought he was a burglar. She only has three weeks left before she's released. Shauna might testify after she's free, especially if you look into her case.'

'OK.' Monty sounded dubious. 'I have some good news. Your doctor has agreed to keep you here until your husband's funeral.'

'What happens after that?' Camilla asked.

'Then we'll see. We have a lot of options.'

But the exhausted Camilla was already asleep. I let go of her hand and kissed her forehead.

I left more frightened than ever. Time was running out for Camilla.

TWENTY-SIX

I t was about five o'clock when Monty and I slipped out of Camilla's hospital room. I could see the massive dinner carts rolling down the hall, and the air was filled with the flat, greasy scent of hospital food.

'Smells like mystery meat day at my school cafeteria,' I said.

'It's still better than jail slop,' Monty said.

I caught a glimpse of a dinner as a uniformed attendant walked by with an uncovered tray. A patient must have rejected the gray meat with muck-colored gravy, the gluey snowball of mashed potatoes, and limp boiled green beans. The tray was a grim reminder of the many hospital meals I'd had when I was in SOS recovering from brain surgery and strokes, and I started to gag at the smell. I swayed slightly and nearly lost my balance. I thought I might pass out.

Monty pulled me into the elevator alcove and sat me down on a hard gray couch. 'What's wrong?' he asked. 'Are you sick?'

I choked back the bile in my throat. 'No, no, it's just that hospital meals bring back bad memories.'

'Have you had lunch?' he asked.

'I made some scrambled eggs right before you called.'

'And then you sat here with Camilla, cleaned the blood off her, and held her barf bag while she threw up. We're going to get dinner.'

'Ugh, after that description, I'm definitely not hungry.'

Monty gave me a fierce glare. 'You're going to eat, and that's an order. Follow me to the new restaurant, Lettuce Eat. I promise you, there's no mystery meat there. In fact, there's no meat at all.'

'But I need to help—'

Monty finished my sentence for me. 'Camilla. And that's what we'll talk about, over dinner.'

In my car, I checked my phone. I had a call from Chris asking me to dinner. I texted that I'd call him tomorrow. Then I followed Monty to the restaurant. We were both looking a bit wilted. I parked in the lot and put on fresh lipstick, but I couldn't do anything about my wrinkled dress. Monty had stripped off his tie and coat and rolled up his shirt sleeves. He looked much better.

Lettuce Eat was a new vegetarian/vegan restaurant in the Forest, located in a long-empty building. The restaurant's wooden tables and chairs were upcycled from charity shops and the city dump, but clever use of paint and decoration made them colorful and comfortable. Usually, the diners were young and hip, but we arrived during the early-bird special time. Two older couples sat at a table in the far corner.

Our server, bearded and man-bunned, recommended the gazpacho and the veggie power salad with green goddess dressing. I ordered both. Monty wanted the chilled soup and meatless tacos.

While we waited for our meal, our server brought us coffee and warm wheat bread with honey butter. One bite banished the bad memories of the afternoon.

'You're worried about Camilla's safety,' I said, between bites of sweetly buttered bread.

'Yes. I told Camilla I had a lot of options, but I don't,' Monty said. 'Not really. After her husband's funeral, she'll have to go back to that jail. The best option is protective custody, and you know what that means.'

'She'll be stuck in a box twenty-three hours a day, with only two showers a week during the summer.' I felt like I was passing sentence on my friend.

'I can use the photos I took of her injuries to petition the court that the jail can't protect her,' Monty said, 'and ask that she be sent home with an ankle monitor, but if the judge says no, Camilla's life will be even worse.'

Monty leaned forward and said, 'She doesn't know this, but the Missouri prison system has a terrible reputation. Prisoners have been beaten and even killed by guards, and little was done to help the inmates. The system has been plagued with rapes and drug use. The ACLU says Missouri has the nation's fastest-growing female prisoner population. There have been some reforms, but not nearly enough, in my opinion.'

'And you think Camilla is going to wind up back in prison,' I said.

'I hope not, but that's my fear. If we get the wrong jury, they may decide that the "country club bitch," as Earlene so elegantly put it, should be locked up permanently for killing her husband.'

'Don't you have a detective on retainer with your firm who can help Camilla?'

'He's a good man, but he's an outsider. You have a much better understanding of the tricky ways of the Forest.'

Our gazpacho arrived. The fresh, cool tomato soup was perfect for a hot summer day. We ate in respectful silence until our server brought our main courses.

'How's your salad?' Monty asked.

I took a taste and said, 'Fabulous. That dressing was definitely made by a kitchen goddess.'

He laughed.

'What's in your meatless taco?'

He poked it with a fork. 'Refried beans, avocado, shredded cabbage, pickled onions, and feta cheese.'

'Sounds good.'

'It is.' Monty smiled, but I saw the weariness around his eyes. Camilla's case had taken a toll on him.

We quickly cleaned up our plates and let the server talk us into carrot cake. He came back with two large pieces and more coffee.

After the first bite, I said, 'This cake is swoon-worthy.'

'Please, don't try fainting again.' He grinned at me. 'Once was enough.'

'Monty, why does Camilla get to attend the funeral of the man she's accused of murdering?'

'First, Sterling has no relatives to object to her presence,' he said. 'Second, Missouri law allows her to attend. She'll have to pay for some sheriff's deputies to guard her while she's at the funeral. Of course, it doesn't hurt that she's rich, white, and well connected – and she has me as her lawyer.'

Monty's flash of humor cut the pompous edge of his remark. We both drank our coffee and savored our carrot cake.

'I talked with two people yesterday when I started looking into Sterling's murder,' I told him. 'The first was Eldon McIntyre. He was being blackmailed by Larry Perkins about his sex tapes.'

'Why in the world would Eldon care if anyone found out he used a phone sex service?' Monty asked. 'He's single.'

'He is, but that lowlife Larry threatened to send the tapes to Eldon's ninety-two-year-old mother.'

'Larry was even worse than I thought.' Monty sighed. 'Personally, I can't believe anyone would care about phone sex tapes in this day and age.'

'But it's not 2022 in the Forest, Monty. You know that. We're trapped here in a fifties time warp.'

He sipped his coffee. 'I know. I know. Who else did you talk to?'

'Brenda, the redheaded bartender at Solange.'

'Oh, her. Brenda makes an impeccable martini, but she's a real piece of work.'

Monty's tone implied there was more going on than a man ordering a martini from a bartending master. 'Brenda tried to get her hooks in you, didn't she?'

'Uh.' Monty hesitated. 'How did you know?'

'It's not much of a leap. You're a single, rich, handsome lawyer. I bet she chased you around that bar with a butterfly net.'

I saw the color rise in Monty's face. I'd hit a nerve. 'She asked you out, didn't she?'

'Several times. I made it clear I wasn't interested. Katie is the only one for me. Jinny, my office manager, screened Brenda's calls, and when she couldn't reach me at my office, she somehow got my personal cell phone number. I told her if she didn't quit calling, I'd get a restraining order. I also changed my cell phone number and I've never gone back to that bar when she's on duty in the afternoon. It was a narrow escape.'

'Closer than you know,' I said. 'Stalkers rarely give up easily when they're fixated on a subject. Brenda told me she's hunting for a husband at the bar.'

'If the coke doesn't kill her first,' Monty said.

'She uses coke? I didn't peg her as a druggie.'

'She didn't use it around me. But I heard she got hooked on it partying with one of her so-called potential husbands.'

'That may be why she dropped you, Monty. Cocaine is a powerful distraction.'

'I doubt Brenda will ever marry, Angela. She's close to forty. That's too old to be a trophy wife, and she knows it. She's desperate. She's getting to be known as the kind of woman who'll do anything for a couple of lines.'

'So she's a coke whore.'

Monty gave me a strange look. Was it disappointment? 'I don't use that word, Angela, and I don't think you should, either. What do you call the men who take advantage of her addiction?'

'Uh.'

'Right. There isn't any word for them. But in our society, we're always quick to label the women.'

Somehow, the way he said that didn't sound self-righteous. I felt mean and embarrassed. 'I'm sorry, Monty. I promise to never use that phrase again.'

'Good. End of lecture.'

'Wait!' I said. 'How do you know Brenda is using coke? It could just be Forest gossip.'

'What time did you see her at the bar, Angela?'

'About eleven,' I said. 'When she'd just started work.'

'One of my clients dated her. He said she usually has her addiction under control when she first starts work. Later in the afternoon, she'll begin disappearing, saying she has to "powder her nose." She's not joking. She returns from the "powder room" a different person – energized, organized, and smiling. Once, my client saw her come back with white powder on her nose. She told him it was powdered sugar. He didn't buy that excuse. By two or three o'clock, her pupils are usually dilated. She has problems with a runny nose and an occasional nosebleed. If she's not careful, she's going to have a bad case of cocaine nose.'

I shuddered at the thought. I'd seen those.

'That's a shame, Monty. She's so pretty.'

'In a darkened bar, Angela. For now.'

The conversation had taken a gloomy turn. 'I did get something from my time with Brenda,' I said.

'She suggested I interview the phone service voice artists and find out which women had had a fling with Sterling – and a good motive to kill him. She saw him with three different women. She couldn't give me any names, but one was Asian, one was black, and the third was a quiet white woman. The last one didn't flirt with him at all. In fact, they argued. I suspect that was Diana, the mother of the sick little girl, Abigail. I was about to start watching the interviews that the TV reporter did with all the women protestors to see who the other two were when you called.'

Monty nodded. 'That's a good start.'

Our server returned. 'How was your dinner?'

'Delicious,' I said. 'Compliments to the chef.'

The server smiled as he removed my empty plate. 'I'll tell my wife she has a fan. Anything else I can get you?'

'The check,' Monty said.

I pulled out my purse, but he held up his hand. 'Dinner is on me. I invited you, remember?'

'Then let me leave a tip.'

'Nope. My treat.'

'At least let me do something.'

Monty turned deadly serious and looked me in the eye. 'Then help me, Angela. Help me save Camilla.'

TWENTY-SEVEN

The next morning, I woke up refreshed and ready to work. After a quick breakfast, I planned to go through the online TV news reports about the protesting phone sex workers. I had to save Camilla.

My plans were interrupted when my work cell phone rang. It was Jace, with a new investigation.

'A woman OD'd at the Four Star.' Jace sounded like his old self. I was relieved.

I knew better than to ask for details on a cell phone. I changed into my oldest DI suit and sensible shoes.

I laugh when women investigators in TV shows wear heels, short skirts, and sexy plunging necklines. Nothing could be further from reality. If the investigator had to crawl around on musty carpets, like I'd be doing, she'd be risking disease. It's possible to pick up athlete's foot from dirty carpets. If she had to run or move fast, she'd sprain her ankle in high heels. As for the low neckline, she could be bitten by flies and other creatures that infest decomposing bodies – or wind up with them in her bra. And that's just for an indoor investigation.

Few death scenes are as glamorous as they appear on TV. Right now, I was about to visit the squalid Four Star Motel. The Four Star, built in 1947, began as a handsome art moderne motel with sweeping curves and attached garages for each room. When the interstate was built, the new hotels along the highway took its business, and the Four Star became a hot-sheet motel. It also became a local legend, and even married couples would go there on a lark for a little illicit fun.

Now I was in the parking lot of the dingy hotel. The white stucco had faded to a cracked, dismal gray, and the cheerful turquoise trim was peeling off. Yellow crime scene tape blocked most of the lot.

I squeezed my car in next to a cop car, and Mike, the chatty uniform, let me past the tape and gave me the skinny about the victim.

'Oh, man, this one's a beauty,' Mike said. 'I expect at least one divorce before it's over. A pretty girl died of a nasty OD. The maid found her this morning in room fourteen.'

'Did you know the victim?'

'I knew *of* her. Brenda Burkett,' he said. 'The bartender at Solange.'

'Oh.' I wanted to feel bad that she was dead, but I didn't feel anything at all.

'Did you drink at Solange, Mike?'

'No, too rich for my blood, Angela. But Brenda was sort of famous.'

I didn't ask why. Instead, I said, 'Was Brenda alone when she died?'

'We think someone was in the room with her when she started to OD, and hightailed out of there.'

'Any witnesses?'

Mike laughed. 'Are you kidding? At this place? As soon as the first cop car showed up, the folks in here scattered like scalded roaches. They won't be back to this sin spot any time soon.

'I do know this. Whoever was with Brenda when she died, he panicked and cleared out in a hurry. Some married doctor. Left behind his business card and more. Jace and Nitpicker will tell you the whole story.'

Mike handed me a pair of booties and said, 'I don't know why you need these in that filthy room, but you know the drill.'

I signed the scene log, rolled my DI case across the cracked asphalt to room fourteen, and put on my booties at the doorstep. The odor slapped me in the face – moldy men's locker room mixed with the smell of death.

Jace met me at the door. The Jace I knew, with his boyish face and the clothes his wife picked out for him, all pressed and clean.

'It's Brenda,' he said. 'She died hard.'

Brenda's nearly naked body was on the sagging bed. The thin grayish-white sheets were knotted and twisted, revealing the stained mattress. Brenda had thrashed around, vomited, and lost control of her bowels and bladder. Her long red hair was matted with vomit and other fluids. She wore only black panties. Tossed on a rump-sprung blue armchair were a green dress, a small purse, and black strappy sandals.

My favorite tech, Nitpicker Byrne, was dusting a rickety blond wood nightstand. 'Lucky you,' I said. 'You get to wear a Tyvek suit.'

'In this place,' she said, 'I'd rather wear a hazmat suit with a breathing apparatus. But hey, I get all the glamorous assignments.'

'Is that white powder on the nightstand what I think it is?' I asked.

'Yep. Probably what's left of an eight-ball of blow.'

I knew an eight-ball was an eighth of an ounce of cocaine. 'More than enough for her to OD on,' I said.

'Could be,' Nitpicker said. 'Or the coke could have been unusually pure. Either way, she partied like a rock star – and died like one. We're fairly sure she wasn't alone. A bottle of Perrier-Jouët champagne was in the trash basket. The dude popped for the fancy flowered bottle, which is at least a hundred and seventy-five bucks. He wiped the bottle clean but left his prints in three places: on the toilet when he lifted the seat, and the handle when he flushed. He also left his prints on the TV remote.'

'You're sure those are his prints? There must be hundreds of prints in here.'

Nitpicker wiggled her gloved fingers. 'Trust the master. The toilet and the TV remote always get your man.' She winked. 'There isn't a male alive who won't insist on controlling the remote.'

'This dude left us even more,' she said. 'He dropped a used condom by the bed and didn't pick it up, so we have DNA. The fool even left his business card behind. Used it to chop the coke and the card fell under the nightstand.'

'Who's the lucky man?' I asked.

'Doctor Marvin Xavier Turner, board-certified ENT.'

'I know him,' I said. 'At least, enough to say hi to him. He's supposed to be a top ear, nose, and throat specialist. He's a mild-looking man with thin gray hair and a receding chin. Hardly the type to go for a coke party at a no-tell motel.'

'There is no type, Angela,' Jace said. 'How old is he?'

'About fifty,' I said.

'A dangerous age for a man,' Nitpicker said. 'Midlife crisis time – when men start thinking about hot cars and wild women.'

'I can't believe Doctor Marvin would let Brenda die,' I said.

'I can. He's married with two kids,' Jace said. 'And using coke. If this becomes public, he could lose his family and his medical license. He's not going to risk it all for a party girl.'

'How do you know he took off when she started getting sick?' I asked.

'We don't,' Jace said. 'Maybe he came out of the shower and found her dead. Who's to say he didn't leave before she OD'd?'

'Then why would he panic and run?' I asked.

'Maybe he had a hospital emergency and had to leave in a hurry. If he bought the coke, and we can prove it, then Doctor Turner is in big trouble. But that may be impossible to prove.'

'He could have called nine-one-one after he left,' I said.

'His call could be traced. Instead, he left that woman alone and the maid found her dead at ten this morning.'

'It's possible the adulterous ENT left when Brenda started having the symptoms of an overdose – rapid heartbeat, sweating, clammy skin, among other things,' Nitpicker said.

Jace finished up for her. 'Can the ENT be in trouble for not calling for help? Not really. There's no way to prove she was alive and his failure to call caused her death.'

'Ah-choo!' I gave a mighty sneeze.

'Careful,' Nitpicker said. 'Don't blow away any evidence.'

'Time for me to get to work. The mold in here is getting to me.'

Brenda was lying on her right side in the fetal position. The body was completely stiff – full rigor mortis. That usually took place eight to twelve hours after death, depending on many factors, including the temperature. The room's air conditioner was set at a chilly sixty-six degrees, which could have slowed the rigor. I photographed the thermostat and recorded the ambient temperature, which was a degree warmer.

Next, I photographed the body, taking the usual shots. Because the body was in full rigor, and lying on the right side, both Jace and Nitpicker had to help me move it upright and then on its left side.

I started by examining the victim's head. She had pierced ear lobes and I described her diamond earrings as 'yellow-metal earrings with one clear white stone and yellow-metal posts.'

Next, I checked her nose. 'I think Brenda may have a case of cocaine nose. This bump here on her nose could be a collapsing septum. We'll know more after the autopsy.'

I photographed the nose, concentrating on that nasal bump and then close-ups of both nostrils, noting traces of white powder and blood in both. The decedent had a one-inch trail of dried blood running down from her right nostril.

I looked for burns or irritated areas around her mouth, in case she had ingested something corrosive. Nothing.

Her face, arms, torso, and legs were smeared with feces and vomit. I measured the areas and took samples of both. She had dark patches of livor mortis on her right side. That's where the blood settles after death. It also indicated her body hadn't been moved since she died.

I noted and photographed the location of the coke on the nightstand. There was no vial or container in the trash. 'Brenda is supposed to be a habitual user,' I said. 'Where's her stash?'

'Bet we'll find it in her purse.' Nitpicker spread out a sheet of paper and carefully emptied Brenda's purse. She found a driver's license, cell phone, credit card, small hairbrush, and lipstick.

Nitpicker checked the lipstick. 'A lot of cokeheads use a lipstick tube for their stash.' This one contained nothing but orange lipstick – the same color Camilla found on her cheating husband's shirt. At the bottom of the purse was a small plastic bag of cheap hard candies with colorful waxed-paper wrappers.

'Aha! Found it!' Nitpicker held up the bag with gloved fingers, took out one candy, and showed us. 'The ends of the wrappers are glued shut, and the contents feel soft, not hard like this candy is supposed to be. That's got to be her stash.'

'Don't open it,' Jace said.

'Wouldn't think of it,' she said. 'But this is real nose candy.'

We both photographed the phony candies. They would go to the lab unopened for analysis.

I covered Brenda's hands with brown paper bags and sealed them with evidence tape. I filled out the rest of my forms, except for next of kin. I'd have to check with Solange for that.

That was it. We zipped her stiff, uncooperative corpse into a black body bag. While I waited for the morgue van to take Brenda away, I thought about the last time I saw her. She'd been at home behind the bar at Solange, alive and vibrant, mixing the perfect martini and hunting for a rich husband.

I wondered if that's why she had the coke party with Dr Marvin X. Turner at this seedy motel. Was it a last-ditch attempt to snag a rich husband?

The plan failed. Dr Turner had bolted, leaving Brenda behind for death to claim her.

TWENTY-EIGHT

Working the scene of Brenda's death was like being trapped inside a sweaty gym sock. It was a relief when we finished at one thirty and I stepped outside for fresh air.

Jace joined me and asked, 'Since you know Doctor Turner, will you go along with me when I talk to him?'

'I don't really know him that well, Jace. It's not like I've been to his house for dinner.'

'Please, Angela? You understand this place better than I do.'

I couldn't resist Jace. 'I should go anyway,' I said. 'Doctor Turner was probably the last person to see Brenda alive, and I have to interview him for that information.'

Dr Marvin Xavier Turner's office was a five-minute hop from the sleazy motel, in a much better part of town. The one-story brick office building was as modest and unassuming as Dr Turner seemed to be. Jace and I parked in the lot. The office door was unlocked, and when we went in, the waiting room smelled like microwaved food. At the sign-in window, a sixty-something receptionist whose name tag said *Shirley* was eating nuked pasta. Her thin blonde hair was pulled into a stubby ponytail.

She stuck her fork in the pasta. 'Doctor Turner is not seeing patients until two o'clock.'

'Good.' Jace showed his detective badge. 'Buzz us in and we'll talk to him now.'

'I can't. He's eating lunch,' the receptionist said.

'Buzz us in or he'll go out in handcuffs and we'll question him at the police station.'

Shirley reached for the phone, but Jace stopped her with steel in his voice. 'Do. Not. Call. Him. Buzz us in. Now.'

Shirley did, trembling with fear.

'Where is he?' Jace asked.

'The door at the end of the hall. I—'

Jace cut her off. We marched in on Dr Turner, seated behind his massive dark desk piled with charts and files. The doctor was munching on a thick, drippy sandwich piled with white meat of some sort, lettuce and tomato.

'Hi, Angela.' The doctor gave me a tentative smile with a smear of mayo at the edge. 'I'm at lunch. I can't talk now. Shirley, my receptionist, should have told you and your friend that.' His potato-plain face was flushed with annoyance.

Jace showed his badge and said, 'I'm surprised you have any appetite after last night.'

Dr Turner's lips were thin to begin with, but now he folded them in. He blinked through his round, rimless glasses and tried to bluff. 'I'm not sure what you mean.'

Jace loomed across the desk. 'Cut the bullshit, doc. I'm talking about your cocaine-fueled frolic at the Four Star.'

'I wasn't. You can't. No one saw—'

Jace cut off his blustering. 'We don't need witnesses, Dr Turner. You incriminated yourself. You left behind three sets of prints, and we know they're yours because your hospital requires the medical staff to have background checks. Two sets of prints were from the toilet, so I hope you washed your hands before you bit into that sandwich.'

Dr Turner dropped the sandwich as if it was covered in slime. Now he tried to brazen it out. 'So what if I did go there?' I bit my lip to keep from laughing. The chinless doctor, with his careful comb-over, looked ridiculous trying to sound tough.

Jace picked up the framed photo of the doctor with his pretty wife and two blonde teenage girls and handed it to the man. 'They might be upset to know that their husband and father was at a hot-sheet hotel with a redhead.'

I'd always liked Dr Turner before this episode. Now it revealed the weasel under that Milquetoast facade.

'My family will get over it.' The jerk gave a smug smile.

'Brenda Burkett won't. She's dead.'

Dr Turner looked gobsmacked. 'She can't be. She was alive when I left.'

'Congratulations, Doc. You just confirmed you were shacked up with Brenda.'

The doctor tried to rescue what was left of his dignity. 'I wasn't "shacked up," as you so crudely put it. Ms Burkett wanted a private consultation.'

Jace's face was red with outrage. 'You were consulting her privates, all right.'

I blinked in surprise. Jace wasn't usually this risqué. Maybe he really was tired of the Forest rich getting away with murder.

'Nothing untoward happened.' Dr Turner sounded self-righteous.

'Oh, yeah? We've got a condom that says otherwise. And it has your DNA in it. We definitely know you were doing the nose part of your ear, nose, and throat routine. We found what was left of your eight-ball.'

'I have no idea what an eight-ball is.' Dr Turner was fidgeting like a little kid.

'It's what you're behind right now,' Jace said. 'You're in big trouble, Doc. You can lose your license for buying coke.'

'She bought the coke. I've never used it before. I gave her the money for it. A thousand dollars.'

Jace laughed. 'She robbed you, Doc. You could get an eight-ball around here for five hundred and sixty dollars or less.'

Any last shred of respect I had for Dr Turner vanished. First, Jace tricked him into admitting he was with Brenda, then the doctor said he gave her the money for the fatal coke. The doc was dumber than a box of hammers.

'Did she buy the champagne, too?' Jace said.

'No, I got a good price at Total Wine.'

'Nice,' Jace said. 'Infidelity on a budget. You were obviously called away in a hurry last night. What time did you leave the motel?'

'About ten thirty. A patient was having trouble breathing after her rhinoplasty. I had to rush to the ER.'

I took out my iPad and noted that information.

'Why are you writing that down, Angela?' The doctor's voice was sharp.

'Because you were the last person to see Brenda alive,' I said. 'And judging by the rigor mortis, that's about the time

she died.' I knew my statement about time of death could be
wrong, but it was worth the risk.

'No!' He sounded frantic. 'You don't know that. She could
have had someone else in the room after I left.'

'Let me restate that, Doctor Turner,' I said. 'You were the
last *known* person to see Brenda alive. Our forensic expert
found no evidence that she invited someone else to join her.
And she was dead or dying when you left her.'

'No, no. I swear she wasn't dead.' Sweat was popping out
on the doctor's forehead, and his eyes were wild.

'What state was Brenda in when you left?' Jace asked.

'Relaxed,' he said. 'I believe the word is "mellow." And
satisfied.'

Yeah, right, I thought. A balding, fifty-something man with
a paunch is going to be the last of the red-hot lovers.

'Are you sure?' Jace began pounding him with questions.
'You didn't notice if Brenda had any signs of anxiety? High
blood pressure? Fever? Sweating? No irregular heartbeat? No
trouble breathing?'

Now sweat was pouring off the doctor. He ran his hand
through what was left of his carefully combed hair. 'No, no,
no, and no, detective. She was perfectly healthy. I left her the
rest of the coke. I really didn't enjoy it that much. And now,
if you have any other questions, I'd like to call my lawyer.'

Too late, I thought. *You've already told us what we needed
to know.*

'Save the lawyer for when I bring you in for questioning
next time, Doc,' Jace said.

'Detective, I may be an adulterer, but I am not a killer.'

There was a tentative knock on the doctor's door frame.
Shirley was standing in the doorway, wide-eyed and wringing
her hands. Her voice was almost a squeak. 'Excuse me, Doctor.
Your first patient is here.'

I wondered how long she'd been there, listening.

When Jace and I got to the parking lot Jace said, 'He's
lying, Angela. Did you see him fold in his lips? He was holding
back information.'

'He was also fidgeting like a little kid who needed to use
the john,' I said.

'Another sign he was lying,' Jace said. 'Doctor Turner was in the room when Brenda was dead or dying, and he didn't try to revive her.'

'Can't we get him on that? Charge him with manslaughter?'

'What he did wasn't illegal, and we can't prove it anyway. That's just wrong,' he said. 'He's going to get away with it.'

I remembered Shirley lingering by the door. 'Don't worry, Jace. He'll get what's coming to him. I'm pretty sure his receptionist, Shirley, heard all about his coke-fueled adventure. The gossip mills will start grinding. Mark my words.'

I hoped my pronouncement was right. Our next stop was Solange, to see if Brenda had any family. At the restaurant, we asked for the manager. The receptionist said, 'Gloria is behind the bar. Our bartender didn't show up.'

Gloria was a slender blonde of about forty, pouring scotch for a gray-suited businessman. She was attractive but harried. Jace showed his badge and asked if he could speak to her in private. She called a server to work the bar, and we followed Gloria to her office.

'How can I help you, detective?' she said.

'Does Brenda Burkett work for you?'

'She did, but she didn't show up today. I'm getting ready to fire her. What's going on?'

'Brenda was found dead this morning,' Jace said.

Gloria caught her breath for a moment, then said, 'I'm sorry. Did she OD?'

'Why do you say that?' Jace asked.

'She was a good bartender, the best martini-maker in the Forest. That's why I kept her on, detective. But she had a serious coke problem.'

'How long did she have this problem?' Jace asked.

'I knew she used occasionally, but since she turned forty, she used it more and more. At work, she would be broody and difficult, and then disappear into the restroom and come out smiling. I've been in this business long enough to know the symptoms of coke addiction. I tried to get her into treatment – even offered to pay for it myself – but she refused. The last time I made the offer, she laughed at me.'

'Did she have a problem with men?' Jace asked.

'What kind of problem?'

'Do you know if any of her dates hurt her or abused her?'

'No. She was a bit of a free spirit, but she was single and that was her business.'

'Does she have any family?' Jace asked.

'One sister. She's married. Penelope Powers. She has an office in the Chouteau Forest Lawyers Building downtown. They aren't very close.'

Jace thanked her. We started to leave when Gloria said, 'Detective, I really am sorry about Brenda. She'll be missed.'

The Chouteau Forest Lawyers Building was a blue glass cube that reflected the architecture of other buildings. The office of Penelope Powers, Esq. was on the third floor. Everything in the waiting room was white, including the receptionist, who had white hair and a white suit. Jace said he had to see Ms Powers about a personal matter. Jace and I took white chairs and thumbed through magazines in the stark, white waiting room for half an hour before Jace got restless.

'I'm going snow-blind in here.' He went up to the receptionist and flashed his badge. 'I need to see Ms Powers immediately.'

The receptionist's face turned even whiter when she saw Jace's credentials. 'Yes, sir, I'll go back and remind her.'

Jace and I followed the receptionist to Penelope's office. It was as cold and pale as an ice palace: drifts of white orchids on glass tables, white lamps, a bare glass-topped desk with a white laptop, and Penelope herself, in all black with blood-red lipstick. She was about fifty, with dark hair and a bitter mouth.

'Stephanie, I told you I didn't want to be bothered.' She frowned at the receptionist.

'I told her to, Ms Powers.' Jace showed her his badge. 'I want to talk to you about your sister.'

'What's she done now?' Penelope sounded put-upon.

'She died.'

Penelope showed no emotion. We waited in the growing silence until she finally said, 'OD'd, no doubt.'

'Yes,' Jace said.

Penelope sighed. 'I'm not surprised, Detective. I'm sorry my sister is dead, but she's been heading that way for years.

I've bailed her out of one scrape after another. She was impossible. I finally gave up.

'Our parents left us each a nice sum of money. I took the money and made something of myself. Brenda blew hers on parties, cars, and clothes until she wound up a bartender.' She said the word as if tending bar was something shameful.

'She made a mean martini,' I said.

'She was an embarrassment. I couldn't take my clients to the best restaurant in town when my cokehead sister worked there. She picked up men, too. Married men.'

'Yes, well, we all have faults,' I said. *Even you, iceberg.*

'I am the death investigator for her case. I need some demographic information.'

Fortunately, Penelope could answer all my questions. She was comfortable rattling off numbers and statistics. Brenda had just turned forty in February, and I wondered if that had made her frantic to find a husband.

When I finished, Jace said, 'Anything else you'd like to know about your sister's death, Ms Powers?'

'Yes. When can I have her cremated?'

TWENTY-NINE

Jace and I left the lawyer's ice cave, grateful for the warm, soothing sun and the bright splashes of red and pink impatiens lining the walkway. I never felt more grateful for those ordinary little flowers.

'I'm starting to feel sorry for Brenda, Jace. At least, I understand why she turned to drugs.'

Jace mimicked Penelope, '"I took the money and made something of myself."'

'Yeah, an iceberg,' I said. My cell phone rang. I waved goodbye and answered the call in my car. It was Monty, with news of Camilla.

'She's just had surgery on her arm,' he said.

'When can I see her?'

'Not today. She's barely out of the recovery room. But she's doing fine, the doctor says. She needs her rest. Sterling's funeral is in two days, Angela, and then we'll have to send Camilla back to that hell hole. Once she's in jail, it will be even harder to get her out, and with a broken arm, she'll be more vulnerable.'

'I know, Monty. I plan to spend the rest of the day and tomorrow, if I'm not called into work again, trying to help Camilla. Are you sure your private investigator can't find anything?'

'Already used him, Angela. He sent me a whopping bill for nothing. He doesn't have your touch. You know the backgrounds of these people and the subtleties of life in the Forest. I'm thinking of firing him. By the way, Mrs Ellis wants you to call her. As soon as possible. She sounded frantic.'

'Sure. I'll call her now.'

Oh, lord. I promised to help Mrs Ellis with Sterling's funeral and I hadn't done a darn thing. I called Camilla's housekeeper immediately. 'Thank you for calling, Angela. I couldn't find your phone number.'

'How can I help?'

'Just about everything is under control for the funeral, dear,' she said. 'The flowers, the service, the food, and the reception. I do need you to do one thing for me. One little favor, please, and right away.'

Her voice changed. It was both hesitant and wheedling. Whatever she was going to ask, it couldn't be good.

'I need you to go to the funeral parlor and check on Mr Chaney's body. It has to be done today.'

'What do I have to do?'

'Camilla wants to make sure her husband is fully dressed in his black Tom Ford suit – shirt, tie, vest, socks, and shoes. You can't trust undertakers. When my dear mother died, the undertaker wanted to wrap Mother's body in a sheet! She was supposed to meet her maker in a bedsheet – completely naked underneath! I told them absolutely not. She was buried in her favorite polka-dot dress and heels.'

I wondered about wearing heels for all eternity, but at least Mrs Ellis's mother wouldn't have to walk in them.

I stopped the flood of memories by asking, 'So I'm just supposed to see that Sterling is properly dressed?'

'Yes. That's all. The Chouteau Forest Funeral Home is open until nine tonight. I'd go myself, but, well, you're used to looking at dead bodies.'

People always said that about me. But I never got used to looking at dead people. When I was working, I felt sorry for those who died too young, or suffered, or died without dignity. I felt physically sick when a child was murdered. I knew those weren't the right responses and they would take their toll on me. I could control my physical responses to a decaying body. But I never got used to looking at dead bodies. Death was the ultimate mystery, and the only way to know the answer was to cross to the other side.

When I knew the deceased, it was much worse. Still, I'd promised I'd help.

'Who do I ask for at the funeral home?'

'Thomas Graves,' Mrs Ellis said. 'He's the director.'

'Seriously? His name is Graves?'

'Oh, yes, he spelled it for me.'

'It's like he was born for the job,' I said.

'Well, he did take over the business from his father,' Mrs Ellis said. 'Thank you so much, dear.'

I hung up and called Chris. He wanted me to come to his house for pizza. He also offered to go with me on my grim chore to see Sterling Chaney's body. I thanked him, and said I'd come over as soon as I finished. I knew I'd be in no shape to do any more work on Camilla's problem after I saw Sterling's body.

On the way to the funeral home, I passed the Forest Bakery and bought a triple-fudge cake for dessert.

At last, I pulled into the funeral home parking lot. The Chouteau Forest Funeral Home and Chapel did its best to make sure its clients exited in style. The two-story white building had an impressive rotunda and a sidewalk protected by green awnings. Inside, I was greeted by a gray-suited man with a face like a mournful cod. The chandelier overhead lit his growing bald spot.

The Cod's voice was like a soft, cemetery wind. 'Which loved one are you here to see? We have two slumber chambers.'

Already, I was seriously creeped out. I made my voice louder than necessary. 'I'm here to see Mr Graves about Sterling Chaney. I'm representing Mrs Chaney.'

The Cod wrung his hands and said, 'Oh, yes, oh my, yes. Quite an impressive casket for his final rest. Let me show you to Mr Graves's office. It's right behind this door here.'

He opened a pair of mahogany doors, walked a few steps across the hall, and knocked on a door marked *Private*. 'Mr Graves, a visitor to see you about Mr Chaney.'

Thomas Graves was a whole lot less creepy than the Cod at the door, though he did have the only pencil-thin mustache I'd seen outside of a movie. I introduced myself as a friend of Mrs Chaney who was helping with Sterling's final arrangements.

'Yes, yes, I've been expecting you. He's in a private room that is not being used for viewing at this time.'

Graves was tall – very tall – and thin to the point of, well, I didn't want to say cadaverous, but he was one skinny guy. And the black suit didn't make him look any heftier.

I followed him down a hall papered with blue forget-me-nots, and into a pale-blue parlor. Sterling's casket was even bigger than I remembered. About the size of a refrigerator, except in shiny gold-colored bronze. A small spray of roses looked lost on its lid.

'Magnificent, isn't it?' I could hear the awe in Graves's voice.

'That's one word for it.' I could think of others. Gaudy. Ostentatious. A waste of money.

'The loved one has been embalmed,' Graves said.

'I thought embalming isn't required for burial in Missouri,' I said.

'That's true. But the law says burial must take place within twenty-four hours of death if the loved one is not embalmed. Mrs Chaney did not want any cosmetic work on her husband, but we tried to arrange him as well as possible, considering his, ah, condition.'

I longed to say, 'His condition is he's dead and lost his head,' but I held back my crude words for Camilla's sake.

Graves carefully removed the small spray of six red roses, then fiddled with the gold casket. Katie had said the red velvet interior was 'ruched, draped, flounced, and pleated like some Victorian lady's dress.' I thought it looked more like the stage curtains at a grand theater, with the deceased at center stage.

The undertaker had done a good job with Sterling, under the circumstances.

His battered head had been cleaned up and his hair styled. The head was slightly turned so the damaged side mostly rested on a red velvet pillow.

'His head was reattached to his body?' I asked.

'Oh, yes. Mrs Chaney requested that service.'

I was glad Sterling wasn't slathered with that horrible make-up undertakers use.

I always have a problem with viewing dead people that I knew. They look like themselves, but they don't, all at the same time. They seem strangely flattened.

I didn't see any trace of the drunken, unfaithful Sterling in this person, except for his red nose. His hands were crossed, and he was wearing thin black gloves, probably to cover the injuries on his hands. He was definitely wearing his Tom Ford suit that was 'black as a bill collector's heart' with five-button cuffs on the jacket. His white shirt had the pointed collar with the silver collar pin that Sterling was so proud of. And he was wearing polished black shoes.

For a brief moment, those shoes reminded me of the young, debonair Sterling at his wedding, arms open to greet his bride, and a tear slid down my face at the thought of that doomed marriage. I tried to wipe it away so the undertaker wouldn't see it. Then I nodded to Thomas Graves and said, 'You did a good job. I'll let Mrs Chaney know.'

The Cod was showing two mourners into Parlor A, so I didn't have to talk to him.

I fled that house of death as quickly as I could. In the parking lot, I called Mrs Ellis and told her that Sterling was dressed in his finery. Then I raced to Chris's condo, carrying in the chocolate cake. He set the cake box in the kitchen and, between kisses, said, 'Our pizza is on the way. I ordered our usual: half sausage and half pepperoni.'

Chris smelled so good. I ran my fingers through his hair and held him. He was becoming my rock and my refuge.

'Bad day?' he asked.

'Yes. I needed to see you.'

The pizza arrived ten minutes later. I was flushed and my lips were slightly swollen. I carried the cake upstairs, along with plates, napkins, and cutlery.

An open bottle of red wine and two glasses were waiting on the nightstand.

Chris arrived, bearing the pizza box. We ate pizza and drank wine while he made me tell him about my day. He believed that talking about my job was therapeutic, especially the gruesome parts. Maybe he was right. Anyway, I didn't mind. I told him about Brenda's death scene, the visit to Dr Turner, and Brenda's soulless sister. I ended with my visit to the funeral home to make sure Sterling went to his reward in Tom Ford.

After that, we started on the cake, which was scrumptious.

Soon we were both giggling. We spent the rest of the night celebrating that we were alive and in love, proving that randy Andrew Marvell was right: 'The grave's a fine and private place, but none, I think, do there embrace.'

THIRTY

My work cell phone rang at eight thirty the next morning. It was Katie. 'Untangle yourself from Chris,' she said. 'You need to come in for the autopsy report on Brenda Burkett.'

'How did you—'

Katie interrupted me. 'Know where you were? Hah! I know you bought a triple-fudge cake at the Forest Bakery before you went to the funeral home, then drove to Chris's condo. He ordered pizza, and you never left.'

I wasn't the brightest bulb in the chandelier in the morning, especially when I was slightly hungover. 'Astounding. The CIA has nothing on the Forest gossips.'

Katie snickered. 'Good thing you live a law-abiding life. Bring three coffees. Jace is bringing doughnuts.'

Good thing I'd plugged in my work phone before I fell asleep last night. Chris hurried downstairs and I ran for the shower. He brought a mug of hot coffee upstairs, and I was dressed and ready in half an hour. I was glad I kept a few things at Chris's place, including a fresh blouse and a clean DI suit. Especially after I'd crawled through the no-tell motel yesterday.

I kissed Chris goodbye, stopped at Supreme Bean for three Supremes to go, and was at Katie's office at nine thirty. Jace was already there, perched on Katie's desk, next to a box of a dozen cake doughnuts. The two of them were eating powdered sugar doughnuts.

'You have white powder on your tie, Jace,' I said. 'And I don't think it's part of Brenda's stash.'

Jace quickly brushed off the sugar, and both he and Katie reached for the coffee.

'Thanks,' she said. 'I'm desperate for more caffeine.'

I virtuously chose a plain cake doughnut. Last night's

triple-fudge cake had temporarily satisfied my sugar craving. After a couple of doughnuts and coffee, Katie gave us the details of the autopsy.

'No surprises here,' she said. 'Brenda had a serious coke habit. So bad she had a hole in her septum.' I knew that was the cartilage that gave the nose its shape.

'Why does snorting coke damage the nose?' Jace asked.

'The nose has a fragile blood supply,' Katie said. 'Coke closes off the blood vessels, and the septum's tissues get less oxygen. That causes the septum lining to die. Once that happens, the lining can't support the cartilage underneath it, and it dies, too. So it's a chain effect. That's how our decedent got a hole in her septum. Her nose was on the verge of collapse.'

'Too bad. She was so pretty,' I said.

'Not for much longer,' Katie said. 'Even at this stage, my guess is it would have taken more than one surgery to restore her nose.

'Brenda didn't have an easy death or a quick one. It probably started with a headache and maybe hallucinations. Her heart must have felt like it was coming out of her chest. Eventually, she had a hemorrhagic stroke. That's what killed her.'

'The man who was with her said she was fine when he left at ten thirty that night,' Jace said.

'I sincerely doubt that,' Katie said. 'I suspect he wanted to get out of there as fast as he could. One of the symptoms of a cocaine overdose is paranoia. If she was talking crazy, he probably bailed out of there in a hurry.'

'Have you heard from her sister Penelope?' Jace asked.

'Another piece of work,' Katie said. 'She can't wait to claim Brenda's body. I expected to find her sitting on the morgue doorstep this morning.'

'Penelope never recognized her sister's unique talent. Let's toast the Forest's finest martini-maker.' I raised my coffee cup.

'To Brenda,' we said, and touched cups.

'And may her cold-hearted sister get what's coming to her,' I added. 'Penelope wants to cremate Brenda and dump her like a full ashtray.'

'It will be like she never existed,' Jace said.

'I'll remember that martini.' I could almost taste it.

But I never would again.

THIRTY-ONE

After my grim morning at the morgue, I drove home, determined to help Camilla. The best way to start was to watch the TV news stories about the phone sex workers' protests. Which of those women had had a fling with Sterling – and a good motive to kill him? Who could have killed the manager, Larry? Was it the same woman or two different ones?

I made a pot of coffee and watched the interviews with the reporters. And I remembered Brenda the bartender's words: *'Try the girls who worked at his phone sex place. He'd bring some of them here to impress them. Most were starry-eyed at being in the Forest's most expensive hot spot. He was all over them, like an octopus. The valet said he'd bang them in the parking lot. One visit here and he never brought them back again. So you wanna know who could have killed him? Every woman who worked for him.'*

I could almost see Brenda's greedy fingers trying to grab my fifty-dollar bill.

Brenda said one of the women was Asian. From watching the tapes, I guessed that was Suzi Chin. She had long, straight hair and a nice figure.

Also, an outraged Mrs Ellis said Suzi came to the Chaney house and *'started talking about how she was falling in love with him. She left love notes on his pillow – which I found – and wrote "SC + SC = LOVE" on the bathroom mirror in a lipstick heart. Took all morning to scrub that nonsense off.'*

Two protestors were Latina. Brenda never mentioned any Latinas. Five were black. The TV reporter had interviewed Jenny Brown, a slender black woman with long braids and brown eyes. Sterling gave her the princely sum of five bucks a day to use her 'Southern mammy voice' or talk 'gangsta.' Jenny had found Larry's body, and I'd interviewed her at the Sterling Service office.

I saw two more black protestors in the group. One was the voluptuous Linda Connelly. Sheila Grafton was the one who was pregnant. She might be a candidate, but she looked to be about eight months gone. Did Sterling take her to Solange before she was pregnant? Did he impregnate her? If so, her impending baby would join the lucky sperm club.

There were also two black women who seemed to be in their fifties. Attractive and gray-haired, they were conservatively dressed. I was pretty sure they didn't have flings with Sterling.

There was one more person that Brenda had mentioned: '*A white lady. Looked like a cracker . . . Sterling wasn't playing grab-ass with her. She was trying to convince him of something, but I don't think it worked. She left here angry.*'

If that woman was a phone sex worker, I bet it was Diana Dunn, arguing for health insurance for her little daughter, Abby. She didn't look like a cracker to me, but Brenda wasn't kind.

I looked up the addresses for all the women. They lived in the working part of town. It was twelve thirty. I decided to start with Jenny Brown. Her apartment was in a sunbaked brick shoebox near the highway. There wasn't a single plant for relief. What passed for a lawn was covered with small white rocks that glared in the sun.

Jenny was home when I knocked on her door. She remembered me from Larry's death investigation and invited me in. Her long, narrow living room was painted a cheerful blue. Framed pictures of Jesus, Martin Luther King, and President Obama were on the walls.

Jenny was wearing a long, white summer dress that contrasted beautifully with her dark brown skin. She was even prettier in person than on TV. Her coffee table was piled with nursing school catalogues.

'I'm going back to school.' She smiled. 'Being a nurse has been my dream, and now I can realize it.'

'So you're taking advantage of Camilla Chaney's offer to go to school.'

'You bet I am.'

'Then will you help me? I'm trying to save Camilla. She's

in jail for her husband's murder, and I don't think she killed Sterling.'

'I'll do anything. Camilla is the only person who's ever given me a chance. Have a seat. Would you like something to drink?'

Jenny brought me a bottle of cold water, we both sat on her gray living-room couch and got to work. 'Did you go to Solange with Sterling?' I asked her.

'Yes, I did.' She looked down at her nails, artfully painted blue with small palm trees. 'I wanted to see what it would be like to have lunch at the best restaurant in town. I was so stupid. I wore my best dress and had my nails done so I'd look nice. He picked me up in that Ferrari of his, and I admit that part was fun.' Her eyes sparkled at the memory. 'When we got to the restaurant, the receptionist said our table wasn't ready yet. Sterling said, "Would you like a drink in the bar?"

'We sat at a table in a dark corner. The bartender came over and took our orders. He wanted a martini and I asked for a Coke. After the bartender left, Sterling put his arm around me. I was very uncomfortable and tried to move away. He said, "You know, that bartender makes the best martinis in town. Why don't you order one?" I said I was Baptist and I didn't drink alcohol. He made some crude joke about why Baptists don't have sex standing up. I've heard that one a million times.

'Then he whispered in my ear, "You're the cutest little chocolate drop. I hear girls like you are hotter than hell." That's when I stood up and walked out. Didn't say a word. I called an Uber from the lobby and hid in the ladies' room until it arrived. Then I went home and cried.'

'I am so sorry,' I said.

'Why? You didn't do it.'

'I'm sorry you had to go through that.'

She looked at me with those big brown eyes. 'There isn't a woman alive who hasn't been through some version of that. Tell me it's never happened to you.'

'It has. More than once.'

'Well, then, welcome to the tribe, sister.'

We laughed and started going through the other possible names.

'OK, you didn't kill him. What about Linda Connelly?'

'Maybe. If she went to lunch with him, she didn't tell me about it. We're not exactly friends.'

'Could Sheila Grafton have killed Sterling?'

'No way, Angela. Sheila is about to deliver any day now. She's married and loves that man to pieces. She'd never go with a player like Sterling, not even for lunch. You can cross her off your list right now.'

'That was easy. There were two other women, both in their fifties with gray hair.'

'Two women in their fifties?' Jenny looked puzzled.

'They were picketing at the Chaney house. On TV.'

'Oh! You mean the Sonders sisters, Martha and Leah!' She started laughing.

'What's so funny?'

'Martha and Leah are church ladies. The backbone of the Mount Zion AME of Chouteau Forest. Sterling would have a better chance of making it with Beyoncé than those two.'

Jenny was still giggling, and I looked at her.

'I'm sorry,' she said. 'I'm just thinking about Sterling trying to do the wild thing with those two ladies. By the time he peeled off their layers of clothes and got to their corsets, he would have given up out of exhaustion.'

'I had a couple of great-aunts like that,' I said. 'Aunt Marie wore this corset with whalebone stays that must have been bullet-proof. I never figured out how she managed to have six kids.'

'Probably delivered by UPS,' Jenny said, and we both collapsed laughing.

OK, it wasn't that funny, but it was a laugh we both needed.

'How did two church ladies wind up working for a phone sex service?' I asked.

'Martha needs the job to take care of her two grandchildren. Her pastor said as long as she didn't *do* any of the sinful things she was talking about, she could be forgiven. I don't know why Leah works there, but I bet it's for similar reasons. She wears a leg brace under her long skirt.

'On their breaks, they both read the Bible. I guess it combats all the sin they hear. Don't judge them, Angela. They're way older than fifty. They've had hard lives and they need the money. You only took that job if you were desperate.'

Now I felt bad about laughing at the women. I changed the subject.

'What do you think of Suzi Chin?'

'Not much. She really went after Sterling. She told me their love was fated because they had the same initials – SC.'

'I know she wrote their initials in lipstick on the mirror in his bathroom,' I said. 'Ticked off Sterling's housekeeper no end. Apparently, he took Suzi to his house.'

'Was Camilla at home?'

'Don't know, Jenny, but they had separate bedrooms in that huge place.'

'Rich people.' Jenny shook her head. 'I'll never understand them.

'Suzi told me she quit using birth control when she was going with Sterling. She said he would marry her when she gave him a son.'

'But Sterling didn't want children,' I said.

'I told her that, but Suzi said any man would change his mind when he held his son in his arms.'

'Instead, Sterling dumped her,' I said. 'Ending her big plans.'

'Sounds like a motive to me,' Jenny said.

'There was one more employee who supposedly went to Solange with Sterling. The bartender described her as white and "a cracker." Said she and Sterling argued. I'm guessing she was talking about Diana, who was angry she wasn't getting health insurance.'

'That would be my guess, but Diana would never risk doing anything that might get Abby taken away from her. Besides, she did get her health insurance, after all.'

'Any idea how Abby is doing?'

Jenny shook her head. 'No, I didn't stay in touch with her mother.'

'Are any of the voice artists going to Sterling's funeral?' I asked.

'Most of us. To make sure he's in that coffin for good.'

'It's closed casket,' I said. 'But I checked on it for his wife. Sterling is definitely in it.'

'Then we'll be there to make sure the cheapskate doesn't crawl out of that gold casket.'

'Maybe we should call Diana and tell her about Sterling's funeral,' I said.

'Good. Let's not deny her that pleasure,' Jenny said. 'I'll get her phone number.'

I called Diana from Jenny's living room. 'The call went straight to voicemail,' I told Jenny. 'But at least Diana has the information.'

I went back to my questioning. 'Sterling's car was tampered with,' I said. 'Do any of these women know enough about cars to tinker with the brakes and airbags?'

'Linda Connelly. She told me she changed her flat tire on I-55. I said that sounded dangerous, and she said she knew her way around a car blindfolded. Diana's father was a mechanic. No way Martha and Leah would know anything about cars.'

'What about Suzi?' I asked.

'Suzi? She wouldn't get her hands dirty messing with a car. However, she might persuade some man to do it and pay him with sex. She's that calculating.'

'So, as murder suspects, we have Suzi and Linda Connelly,' I said. 'I'll talk to them both.'

'Angela, if you do that, be careful. Those women are tough. They've both been in prison.'

'Even Suzi?'

'Yes. She did time for assault with a deadly weapon. And Linda bragged about putting a woman in the hospital when she was in prison. You know Linda went to prison for beating a man to death. Do you carry a gun, Angela?'

'Me? No.'

'How about a knife?'

'No, what do you think I am?'

'Someone who has no idea what she's getting into,' Jenny said. 'Don't you have any protection?'

Now I felt foolish. 'Well, I have pepper spray.'

'Show me.'

It took a minute or so while I dug around in my purse before I fished out the black canister.

'Uh-huh, I thought so,' Jenny said. 'If one of those women attacked you, you'd be dead by now. You can't tell an attacker, "Excuse me. Could you please wait while I find my pepper spray?" Take that pepper spray and put it in your jacket pocket, where you can get it in a hurry. Go ahead, do it.'

I did. Jenny was right. Maybe I could get Chris to go with me when I talked to the women. At the very least, I'd check in with Katie.

'One more question.' Now I sounded like Columbo. 'Do you know which women would want to kill Larry, the manager?'

'None of us liked him,' Jenny said. 'But he was kind of a loser, with his video games and witchy wife. We all knew he was blackmailing some of the men who used the service. I'd say one of them killed him.'

I thanked her and stood up to leave.

'Angela, promise me you'll keep that pepper spray in your pocket until Sterling's real killer is arrested,' Jenny said.

'Sure.' I headed for the door.

Jenny stepped in front of me. 'No. Don't brush me off. You're stirring up a lot of trouble. Promise me you'll keep the spray in your pocket. Even if you're just going to the grocery store.'

It seemed a small gesture, and Jenny had been a big help.

'I promise.'

THIRTY-TWO

The afternoon sun was so hot, my shoes stuck to the parking lot's asphalt. Jenny was right to demand that I carry pepper spray in my pocket until Sterling's killer was arrested. Someone had tampered with Sterling's Ferrari, and they didn't know who else was going to ride in it. Erin had been killed, too. Someone that callous was doubly dangerous.

It was only three o'clock, and I thought I had time to talk to Linda Connelly. But not before I arranged back-up. Curvy Linda had killed one man. No way would I face her alone.

I couldn't call Jace because he'd already locked up Camilla as the killer. This was no longer his case. Katie didn't answer her phone. That left Chris. He got off work sometime this afternoon. Three o'clock? Three thirty? I wasn't sure.

I was relieved when Chris answered his phone. As soon as I told him what I wanted, he said, 'You want to see Linda Connelly? Are you nuts?'

Now my voice was cold enough to freeze his fingers on his phone. 'I am not nuts. I'm trying to help my friend.'

Chris sounded contrite. 'I know that, Angela. I'm sorry. But you have to be careful. Linda Connelly is a convicted felon.'

'I know that.'

'Do you know why she went to prison?'

'She beat a man to death.'

'She beat her landlord to death. She couldn't pay the rent, and he suggested a crude solution, saying she could work it off on her back. Linda picked up a marble ornament on the hall table and beat him with it. Almost pounded his head flat.'

'Good,' I said. 'He deserved it.'

'That's what the jury thought. Her trial resulted in a hung jury. Linda was offered a plea deal for voluntary manslaughter with five years in prison. She took it. She's smart as well as deadly.'

'I just want to talk to her.' Now I sounded like I was wheedling.

He turned mocking. 'You want to ask her if she committed a double murder. And she's going to say, "Oh, yes, Angela. I did it. I confess. Please take me to prison again so I can pay for my crimes."'

He'd added a falsetto imitation of a woman's voice. That was the last straw.

'I don't have to listen to this.' I pressed the 'end' button on my cell. Too bad it wasn't an old-fashioned handset and cradle. I would have loved to slam it down. Maybe they should make an 'angry phone call' app with that sound.

I sat in Jenny's parking lot, steaming. Even with my car's air conditioning blasting at me, I didn't cool down. To hell with Chris. I was going to Linda's apartment. It was only six blocks away. I should be there in five minutes.

Except I wasn't. A bad accident at the corner blocked traffic for almost a mile. When my car finally crept up to the scene, I saw a fire truck and two ambulances, along with a burned-out Jeep. Did someone die? Would I have to go to work on another death investigation? I was still on call until midnight.

Mike, the uniform, was directing traffic. I pulled into the center lane and asked him, 'Any fatalities?'

'No, Angela, both drivers are going to the hospital, but they'll survive. We don't need you.'

'Good.'

Mike held up his hand and waved me back into the line of traffic. Soon I was free of the bottleneck and on my way. My cell phone rang, and I checked the caller's name. Chris. I didn't answer. Another call. Chris again. The heck with him.

Finally, I turned down the street to Linda's apartment complex, the Belfour Terrace. It was a dismal collection of four dingy yellow-brick buildings, all ten stories tall. Some apartments had boarded-up windows. Others had bed sheets on the windows instead of curtains. Several apartments had old couches on the walkway instead of outdoor furniture.

The narrow entrance to the complex was blocked by a Chouteau Forest cop car. Chris. He got out of his car and came over. He had his ticket book out.

'Are you going to arrest me?' I was furious.

'Don't have to. You're the most arresting woman I know.'

He gave me that irresistible grin and said, 'Angela, I'm sorry. I should never have talked like that to you. As soon as you hung up on me – and you were right, I behaved like a perfect ass – I came over here. I knew you'd drive straight to Linda's apartment complex.'

My anger was cooling a bit.

'You're not only loyal, Angela, you're brave. Sometimes too brave. Please let me go with you. I am really sorry.'

He seemed contrite. After that apology, I was ready to forgive him. Although I hated to admit it, he was right. It was dangerous to see Linda without back-up.

I smiled at him. 'Thanks, Chris, but you're wearing your uniform. Linda will never talk if you're with me. Wait here. If I don't come out in half an hour, come get me.'

'Half an hour? Angela, this woman is on the sixth floor. You could be dead by the time I get up there.'

'How about this? I'll call your cell right now, then keep it connected and put my phone in my jacket pocket. You'll be able to hear us talking. If the conversation starts to go bad, you can run to the rescue.'

'OK.' Chris sounded reluctant, but at least he agreed. He moved his car away from the entrance and parked it around the corner. I called him on his cell phone, and we conducted a couple of tests to make sure my idea worked. After two tries, he said he could hear me, even if I kept my phone in my pocket.

I was ready. I had my back-up in one pocket and my pepper spray in another.

I parked my car next to the main door of Linda's building, between a sun-blasted 1980s Buick and a rusting pickup. Snow drifts of trash collected in the gutters, and brown plastic grocery bags fluttered in the tree branches like trapped souls. This complex was a blight on the Forest. I wondered why it was allowed to exist in its rundown condition. Maybe it belonged to some local bigwig with plenty of pull.

I entered the narrow lobby, furnished with a chipped black-lacquered table piled with stacks of free newspapers and take-out menus. The once-white walls were covered with graffiti and the floor was scuffed yellow tile.

The elevator stank of urine. It bumped and swayed its way up to the sixth floor so slowly I began to panic that I'd be stuck in it.

At last, the door opened. More scuffed yellow tile. The mint-green walls were decorated with dirty handprints. I saw the fire stairs at the end of the hall. I could run for them if my interview went bad.

I heard a baby crying in one apartment and smelled cabbage cooking in another. Latin music was blasting out of the third.

Linda's apartment, 615, was in the middle of the hall. I could hear the TV and hoped Linda was home.

I knocked on the door, and soon I heard chains sliding off and locks clicking. Linda must have checked the peephole and decided I looked harmless.

Linda did not. She was tall – taller than me, and I'm six feet tall. She wore tight jeans and a tank top. Her hair was in cornrows. Linda was a light-skinned black woman. Coiled around her right biceps was a snake with long bloody fangs. On her left biceps was the tattoo of a snarling panther. On her ring finger was a gold wedding band.

'What do you want?' Linda's tone made me feel like a bucket of muck dumped on her doorstep.

'I'm here to talk about Camilla Chaney.' My voice was an embarrassing squeak, like a teenage boy who hadn't reached puberty.

'Yeah? So? What do you want to say?'

I looked past her shoulder into the apartment. What I could see was clean and neat. On a well-polished table in the entry was a marble statue of a black panther. I wondered if that was the statue she used to beat up her landlord.

'Camilla is charged with murdering her husband.'

She glared at me fiercely. 'What's that got to do with me?'

I took a step backward to avoid the heat of that glare. 'I think she's innocent.' My voice sounded a little steadier.

She crossed her arms. 'Again, what's that supposed to mean to me?'

'I'm trying to find out who killed him.'

'Good for you. Now run along.'

'I'm asking people where they were the day before Sterling was murdered.'

'Why?'

'Because someone tampered with his car.' I gulped. I couldn't help it.

Now I heard rage in her voice. 'And you think *I* killed him?' She took one step forward and looked me in the eye. I took two steps back, but it wasn't far enough. She thumped me on the chest with her finger.

'I didn't kill him.' *Thump.*

'You wanna know why?' *Thump.*

'Well, do you?' *Thump.*

I managed to nod yes.

Now Linda screamed in my ear. 'Because Sterling Chaney drove a Ferrari. And there's nowhere in the Forest – not even here in this shithole – where a black woman like me could get near a Ferrari without someone calling the cops.

'You listen to me, bitch. I don't care if Queen Camilla is in jail. I knew lots of innocent people who were locked up when I was in prison, and nobody cared about them. Her highness sat on her ass while we worked long hours in that job talking to jerk-offs, and what did we get? Barely enough money to scrape by. All I can afford is this rat hole, while she lives in a frigging mansion. So, if she's been arrested, that's too damn bad. Because she can afford the best lawyers. When I got hauled in by the cops, I had to use a public defender. Don't expect me to shed any tears for her. Understand?' *Thump.*

I nodded again, then gathered my courage and said, 'She did give you a settlement and a chance to go back to school.' My voice sounded mouselike. Linda was a lioness.

'I don't *need* school. I'm using my money to open a body shop with my wife. Yes, *wife*. So don't get any stupid ideas that anything was going on with Sterling and me. I'm gay and I told him so the first time he hit on me.'

I eyed the fire stairs door at the end of the hall.

'Now, any other questions?' Linda asked.

'Uh, no.'

'Then get your skinny white ass out of here before I call

the cops.' She reached for something on the table with the marble panther, and I sprinted for the fire stairs. To hell with my dignity. I wanted out of there.

I flung open the door and raced down two flights of steps until I ran into Chris, coming up the stairs.

'Angela!' He wrapped his arms around me. 'Tell me you're OK.'

'Yes, of course.' I sounded much more confident now that I was away from Linda and with him. 'When did you decide to come after me, Chris?'

'As soon as I heard her roar, "And you think *I* killed him?"'

'She did sound pretty scary,' I said. 'And she was definitely angry.'

I kissed him. 'Thanks for being my back-up. I needed you.'

'Damn right,' he said.

'What time is it?'

He checked his watch. 'Four twenty.'

'Will you go with me to Suzi Chin's house?'

'No. I'd like to take you home and cook for you. I'll be your back-up tomorrow, but tonight I just want to be with you.'

'But Sterling's funeral is the day after tomorrow,' I said. 'Camilla has to go back to that awful jail.'

'You can look for Sterling's killer tomorrow. We both have the day off. Come with me.'

And so I did.

THIRTY-THREE

The next morning, I woke up in Chris's bed to the smell of bacon – and waffles. At least, I thought it was waffles. I brushed my teeth, washed up, slipped into my robe and hurried downstairs.

Sure enough, bacon was frying in Chris's favorite cast-iron skillet, and the waffle iron was open on the kitchen counter, with a big bowl of batter next to it.

'Good morning, love.' He kissed me. I enjoyed the scratchy feel of his whiskers. 'Hope you like blueberry waffles.'

'Love them. Almost as much as I love you.'

He laughed and poured me coffee. It was a soft, sunshiny morning, and we ate our breakfast waffles with warm maple syrup outside on his balcony. After the hearty breakfast, we went back to bed and made love, and then fell asleep in each other's arms.

It was two o'clock when we woke up. I looked at the bedside clock. 'Chris! I need to talk to Suzi, and we're running late.'

While Chris showered and dressed, I called Mrs Ellis to find out if she needed help with the plans for Sterling's funeral.

'No, dear, everything is taken care of. You did the hard part, seeing if he was properly dressed inside his coffin. I couldn't do that, no matter how much I love Camilla. I'll see you tomorrow at the church. The funeral is at ten.'

Same time as his last funeral, I thought.

By the time I was dressed and ready to go, it was three o'clock. We took my car.

'Where does Suzi live?' Chris asked.

I told him the address of Suzi's apartment and we were there in ten minutes. Suzi's place was way better kept than both Linda's and Jenny's apartment buildings. She lived in a neat Tudor-style built in the sixties, with plenty of flowers and shade trees.

Suzi lived on the second floor in apartment C. I knocked

on the door. No one answered. Chris knocked harder. Finally, an older woman with tightly permed gray hair poked her head out of the door of the apartment next door.

'I'm Myra Mason. The building manager. Are you looking to rent two-C?' she asked.

'No, I'm looking for Suzi Chin. I thought she lived here.'

'That one.' Myra made a face. She clearly did not like Suzi. 'She used to live here, but she skipped out on me, owing two months' rent. Moved in with some man, no doubt. Left the place in a mess. I've just cleaned and painted it.'

'Do you know where Suzi went?'

'If I did, I wouldn't be out two months' rent.'

'Do you know the name of the man she's dating?'

'Can't keep track of them all. She should have had a revolving door on that apartment. Let me call Mrs Keller.'

Myra left us standing outside what used to be Suzi's apartment. Fifteen minutes later, she came back. 'Mrs Keller says she was dating a guy named Sam Herron. He works at the Forest Bank on Gravois. She suggests you check with him.'

I thanked her. Myra said, 'Would you do me a favor? If you do find her address, would you let me know?' She handed me a business card, and I tucked it in my purse.

When we were back in my car, Chris said, 'Are you going to give Suzi's address to Myra if you find it?'

'Sure. I don't owe Suzi anything.'

Sam Herron was a loan officer at the bank, a blond hunk in a gray business suit. Chris and I talked to him in his cubicle, keeping our voices low.

'I dated Suzi for a while,' Sam said, 'but we split up about six months ago. Last I heard, she was dating a broker at the local Merrill-Lynch office. His name was . . . let me think . . . Zander. Zander Daniels.'

It was just after four o'clock when we tracked down Alexander K. Daniels in his office. The market was closed, and he took a little time to talk to us. 'Suzi? She left me a month ago. Moved in with some guy who is opening up the new Ferrari dealership in St Peters. His name? Ken somebody. Can't think of his last name, and I really don't want to. I'm trying to forget everything about Suzi Chin.'

Zander was about thirty and good-looking in a conventional, preppie way: blue eyes, strong jaw, short hair, straight nose. I couldn't tell if Suzi had broken his heart or hurt his feelings when she dumped him.

St Peters was an up-and-coming suburb an hour or so north of the Forest.

Chris and I thanked Zander for his time and went back to my car. 'Let's leave your car here,' Chris said, 'and go for a walk in the park across the street. I'll get us some cold water. What kind of ice cream do you like?'

'Rocky road,' I said.

Chris bought two bottles of water and I got two scoops of rocky road, a rich blend of chocolate ice cream, marshmallows, and walnuts, in a sugar cone. Yum.

We sat on a bench under a big maple tree. I kept licking my ice cream so it wouldn't drip. When I got it down to cone level, I said, 'Zander was a big help. Suzi wanted to kill Sterling, so she moved in with Ken the Ferrari dealer. He did her dirty work.'

'Whoa, whoa,' Chris said. 'What's her motive?'

'She wanted Sterling to leave his wife and marry her. She thought they were destined to be lovers. She told Mrs Ellis she was in love with Sterling. He got scared when she became clingy and dumped her.'

'OK,' Chris said. 'But why would she murder him? Because she couldn't have the man she wanted?'

'Yes.'

'Where's your proof?'

Damn. He would mention that. 'I don't have any. Not yet. But the police could go over that Ferrari and check for Ken's fingerprints.'

'Even if the techs do find Ken's prints, so what? He could have worked for the dealer where Sterling bought his car. He could say Sterling hired him to check out the car before he bought it.'

I bit into my cone with a loud crunch. Chris kept talking.

'And how are you going to tie Sterling's murder to Suzi? She sounds like she is tough and smart. She goes through men like I go through socks.'

'But that's good,' I said. 'If she's left Ken, he might be happy to testify against her. Maybe he'd let us look around his home.'

'Might? Maybe? Angela, you have nothing,' Chris said.

'What about motive?'

'Maybe. But what if Suzi told someone, "Good riddance. I am so over Sterling. Why should I waste the best years of my life going after some middle-aged married man, when there are too many hot young guys out there?"'

'Means, possibly. But right now, we can't tie this Ken to Suzi. There's not a shred of proof. We don't even know Ken's last name.'

'But he should be easy to find,' I said. 'We can find the site of that new Ferrari dealership. There should be records.'

'If. Might. Maybe. Should,' Chris said. 'We still have to go looking for this Ken and Suzi. We haven't found either one of them.'

I crunched the last of my cone resentfully.

'We can't do anything else today,' Chris said. 'It's almost five o'clock. The government offices will be closed, and the highway to St Peters will be clogged with cars. Let's devote another day to finding them.'

I took a sip of water, then said, 'Tomorrow is Sterling's funeral. I'll have to be there. For Camilla. After the funeral, she'll have to go back to jail in protective custody – which is basically solitary confinement.'

'Angela, it will be OK. You know Monty. He'll fight for her, I promise. He'll do everything in his power to prove that jail is unsafe and have Camilla staying at her home. Mark my words. She'll be wearing an ankle bracelet in no time.'

I wished I believed Chris, but I was losing hope. Jace, the detective I respected most, had arrested an innocent woman, and I'd failed to help her.

THIRTY-FOUR

I went home to my place, feeling discouraged. Chris and I didn't have a fight. I just wanted to be alone tonight.

First, I called Monty to ask about the procedure for Sterling's funeral.

'Does Camilla want me to ride to the church in the limo again?' I asked.

'You can't ride with Camilla to the funeral this time, Angela. She will be in a sheriff's van with four deputies for her security detail.'

'Four! For one small woman with a broken arm?'

'The sheriff is worried that Camilla might be too close to people if any fights break out.'

'Fights? Who's going to be fighting at this funeral? Sterling doesn't have any family.'

'Don't forget Sterling's unpredictable drunken friends.'

'Oh. Right.'

'The sheriff didn't want Camilla to go to the funeral, but she has that right under Missouri law. Camilla has to pay for the security detail. And they're not just protecting her. They have two other objectives besides keeping Camilla safe. They have to keep her from escaping, and protect others from her.'

'Camilla would never try to escape,' I said. 'And why do they have to protect other people from Camilla?'

'They don't. Not really. But in the eyes of the law, she's a murderer.' Monty automatically corrected himself. '*Alleged* murderer.'

'Also, the security detail has to make sure nobody passes her any contraband and that she doesn't try to pass notes or anything to other people.'

'Will her hands be cuffed in front or back?'

'Neither,' Monty said. 'She has her left arm in a sling. Her right arm will be cuffed to a waist chain.'

'A waist chain? Are you kidding?'

'No, I'm not. She can't be cuffed in front because of her sling. And if she was cuffed to a deputy, that would hinder his ability to respond if there was trouble. I did petition the court to let her wear a black dress to the funeral instead of jail scrubs.'

'Well, that's something.'

I must have sounded angry because Monty snapped back, 'You're damn right, it is. And I was lucky to get that. The judge said I could have Camilla's dress delivered to the jail and it will have to be inspected before it goes to her. The procedure is similar to getting a suit to a prisoner to wear to court. She's not allowed to wear heels, though.'

'Why not?'

'They're considered a weapon.'

'Oh, for heaven's sake. Tell me I'll at least get to sit next to her.'

'No way. The security detail wants to keep Camilla separate from everyone at the church and the graveside. I'm not sure you'll even get a chance to talk to her.'

'What about at the funeral reception?'

'Camilla is not permitted to go to that. One more thing, Angela. The media will not be allowed inside the church. Father Winthrop agreed to that. He doesn't want Sterling's funeral turned into a circus. The Forest Inn also agreed to keep them out. But the media will be outside the church and at the cemetery.'

'Thanks for the warning. My response will be "No comment."'

'Good. I'll see you tomorrow.'

The morning of Sterling's second – or real – or final – funeral was hot and sunny. I was dressed in my best black pantsuit, a white silk blouse, and heels. As I was going out the door, I remembered Jenny's words: '*Promise me you'll keep the spray in your pocket. Even if you're just going to the grocery store.*'

I wasn't going to the grocery store. I was going to a funeral and four sheriff's deputies would be there. But a promise was a promise. I went back upstairs, fished the pepper spray out of my DI suit, stuck it in the pocket of my jacket, and hurried to my car.

I got to the church early, about nine thirty, and ran the gauntlet of reporters slinging questions at me. One asked, 'Are you a friend of Sterling or Camilla?' Another wanted to know: 'Do you think Camilla killed her husband?' I tossed out a 'no comment' and ran for the safety of the church.

It was dark and cool inside, and the organist was playing a mournful version of Bach's *Sheep May Safely Graze*.

The church was filling up already. On the left side of the church, I recognized a clutch of Sterling's bar buddies, including George, the red-nosed drunk who tried to take a selfie of Sterling and himself with the gold casket. From the look and sound of them, his barfly friends had already been drinking. I recognized some of the female funeral-goers from before. They were busy glaring at Sterling's drunken pals. In the back was a knot of the Sterling Service 'voice artists,' no doubt making sure Sterling would soon be six feet under. Jenny Brown gave me a wink as I passed her, and I patted my pocket where the pepper spray was.

The first two pews up front on the right were roped off. Mrs Ellis sat alone in the third pew, wearing a black dress and black summer straw hat.

I walked up the aisle and sat next to her. 'I'm so glad you're here, Angela,' she said. She patted my hand and tried to smile. Monty was the next to arrive. Mrs Ellis and I scooted down in the pew, and the lawyer sat next to us.

Suddenly, there was a murmur through the church. All eyes – including mine – swung toward the back. Camilla entered the church, guarded by four sheriff's deputies: one in front, one on either side of her, and one in back. All men. All muscular. Without her heels, Camilla looked smaller and somehow diminished. Her hair was pulled into her usual chignon, but she did not wear a hat.

Still, Camilla stood straight, and she wore the waist chain and handcuff as if they were accessories. Her face was deathly pale, and she wore no jewelry, not even her wedding ring. My eyes teared up when I saw my friend.

As she was escorted up the aisle, George staggered to the end of his pew and screamed, 'You bitch! You killed my friend!'

There was an audible gasp in the church.

The four deputies tensed, hands on their holsters. George tried to spit on Camilla but hit the closest deputy instead. That deputy bent George's arm back and said, 'You're under arrest for assaulting an officer.'

Another deputy appeared from nowhere, and George was quickly frogmarched out of the church.

Camilla and her escorts were settled in their seats when Sterling's gold casket was carried in. This time it was not covered with the enormous spray of red roses. I found out later that Father Win had insisted that the undertakers remove the flowers on the casket. Episcopalian funeral rites preferred only modest flowers on the altar. The gaudy glory of the casket was covered with a traditional white pall.

Shortly after that, Father Win came out and began the service.

'We are here today to find comfort in the truth of Scripture,' he began, 'and especially to surround Sterling and Camilla with our love, our faith, and our prayers.'

He hit Camilla's name extra hard. I thought there was defiance in those opening words. And support for Camilla. At least, I hoped so.

Father Win continued, 'We see within the pages of the Bible a compassionate God who is touched with the feelings of our infirmities. As it is written in the Gospel of Matthew, "Blessed are they that mourn: for they shall be comforted."'

Father Win spoke briefly but eloquently and finished with those lovely words from the Gospel of John. 'Jesus said, "I will not leave you comfortless: I will come to you."

'Comfortless means "orphans – ones without help,"' Father Win said. 'It has been said that God never sees His children die. He only sees them come home. And today, Sterling Chaney is coming home.'

The congregation sang 'A Mighty Fortress Is Our God.'

The service ended when the rector moved to the foot of the casket and sprinkled it with holy water while he said, "'Give rest, O Christ, to your servant with your saints, where sorrow and pain are no more, neither sighing, but life everlasting.'"

Father Win led the procession out of the church. Camilla, leaning on one deputy, swayed as if she might pass out. I looked at Monty and said, 'Is she going to be OK?'

'They'll take care of her, Angela. Don't worry.'

But I did, anyway.

The hearse and the sheriff's van led the funeral procession, and the rest of us followed to the Chouteau Forest Cemetery. It was an old cemetery with marble mausoleums, weeping angels, baby lambs on the children's graves, and other grim Victorian statuary.

Sterling was being buried in a newer section, a hilly area with towering shade trees and modern gravestones insisting the dead were 'Beloved Husbands' and 'Dear Wives,' whether they really were or not.

At the graveside, two sheriff's deputies stood on each side of Camilla. I was directly behind Camilla. The other mourners spread out around the grave, including a cluster of Sterling's blitzed buddies. They seemed restless and bristling with rage. I hoped they wouldn't make another scene. I could see Jenny and her co-workers in the back row. Twelve bagpipers arrived. The flowers were back on Sterling's gold casket, and it shone brightly in the summer sun. It blinded me from seeing everyone, but I could make out several black-clad figures in the distance. The media was spread out along the edges, recording the ceremony, and at least one police officer was doing the same thing.

Father Win began the prayer, 'Everyone the Father gives to me will come to me. I will never turn away anyone who believes in me . . .'

When he finished, we started reciting the words of the Lord's Prayer. We were at 'and lead us not into temptation' when suddenly there was a metallic scream at the top of the hill, followed by a horrific clanking and grinding.

Everyone turned toward the hilltop, even the four deputies and Father Win. Finally, someone said, 'They're digging a grave at the top of the hill.' That announcement was followed by nervous laughter.

One of Sterling's bibulous buddies – Vince Fowler, a notable Forest wastrel – screamed, 'Damn you, Camilla! You couldn't even schedule Sterling's funeral properly. His burial sounds like a damned construction site. You did that on purpose, you greedy bitch!'

The backhoe screeched again, adding to the noise as Sterling's swarm of barflies joined their irate friend, all of them screaming insults and epithets at the widow. The guards were focused on the rowdy group, in case they attacked.

The bagpipers started in with 'Amazing Grace.'

Under the ungodly mechanical screams and the skirling bagpipes, I thought I heard a shriek – more like a wail. I turned and saw a woman running toward us, holding something in her hand.

'That's right, go ahead and laugh,' she said. 'Complain about the noise. They're digging my baby's grave today. And it's all your fault, Ms Rich Bitch.'

The backhoe's noise continued. As she grew closer, I recognized the woman charging toward us. Diana Dunn, Abby's mother. Did her daughter die? What happened to Diana's health insurance?

I didn't have time to find out. I reached into my pocket for the pepper spray – thank goodness Jenny insisted I bring it – just as Diana lined up to attack Camilla with a butcher knife. I whipped out the canister. And sprayed myself in the face. I'd had it pointed in the wrong direction.

Blinded, I turned the canister and sprayed again, hoping it hit the charging Diana in the face, as I fell backward against Camilla.

We both toppled over on to Sterling's gold casket, taking a sheriff's deputy with us.

THIRTY-FIVE

I t took an eternity to untangle what had happened. It finally sorted out like this . . .

After I sprayed myself in the face, I managed to hit Diana on the second try. She dropped the butcher knife she was planning to use to eviscerate Camilla, and rolled around in the grass screaming, 'My eyes, my eyes.'

When I fell on Camilla, she fell against the casket and whacked her arm. We couldn't tell if it had been broken or not. An ambulance was dispatched.

The paramedics checked Camilla's arm and said she needed to have it X-rayed at the hospital.

Then they used wipes and saline solution to help relieve my pain caused by the pepper spray. The paramedics kept telling me that the symptoms would clear up within thirty minutes.

Let me tell you, that was a really long half-hour. And my eyes stayed red and watery for hours.

After the paramedics treated my eyes, I stayed at the cemetery, sitting on a gray granite tombstone marked *Elizabeth Wagoner* and watching the action.

Meanwhile, Diana was determined to confess. It didn't matter that the police told her she had the right to remain silent. She didn't stay quiet.

'My Abby is dead,' she said. 'She died two days ago. That's her grave they're digging now, and I wish I could be in it with her. I have no reason to live.

'I killed Sterling Chaney because he wouldn't give us the health insurance, like he promised. My late father was a mechanic. I put on Daddy's old boilersuit and stuck my hair under a baseball cap. I tampered with Sterling's car when he was at the Four Star. He didn't hear me open the garage to his room. I fixed his car so it wouldn't fail right away. I didn't know that he was going to pick up Erin O. McBride and finalize the settlement that day, so I killed an innocent woman. That's another reason I don't want to live.

'I killed Larry the manager, too. He's the one who delayed the insurance – him and his lazy ways. He played video games instead of doing his job. I don't regret killing him at all.

'When my Abby died, I blamed Camilla. She didn't try to get insurance for us, and when she finally did, it was too late. My Abby was too sick. She didn't survive the surgery. Camilla deserved to rot in jail, but I knew her fancy lawyer would get her off scot-free. That's the way it works for the rich. I planned to kill Camilla today, so she'd never be able to enjoy her money and her freedom.'

She held out her hands. 'That's all. You can put on the handcuffs and take me to jail now. I don't care anymore.'

After Diana was led away, Camilla said, 'That poor woman.'

'Poor woman nothing. She tried to kill you,' I said.

'But she didn't,' Camilla said. 'She's lost everything.'

'And you're going to be free,' Monty said. 'It will take a day or two to straighten things out, but you're going to be OK. In the meantime, you can stay in the hospital. In fact, you should go there now.'

'I will,' Camilla said. 'But I'd like to finish my husband's service. I can't go through a third funeral.'

The paramedics said the delay would be fine, and Father Win resumed the service.

We gathered around the golden casket and recited the Lord's Prayer again. The backhoe on the hilltop growled and screeched as it dug the grave of Abby Dunn, the young girl that Sterling killed with his own thoughtlessness. The girl whose impending death caused his own.

Over the noise, Father Win said, 'Rest eternal grant to Sterling Chaney, O Lord.'

'And let light perpetual shine upon his soul,' we answered.

We went back and forth with the ancient, beautiful prayer

until Father Win gave the penultimate line. 'Let us go forth in the name of Christ.'

The burial service ended with a heartfelt 'Thanks be to God.'

EPILOGUE

Sterling Chaney's murder and burial were the stuff of legends. Teenagers scared themselves silly with the tale of the headless Ferrari driver.
His life left behind a trail of destruction.

As for George, Sterling's drunken friend who missed spitting on Camilla and accidentally hit the sheriff's deputy, well, the spit really hit the fan. The deputy had had a quarrel with his teenage son over unlawful drinking that morning. When the deputy was attacked by the tipsy George, he made sure the red-nosed boozer paid.

George was arrested and charged with assault, disorderly intoxication, disorderly conduct, and an 'unlawful funeral protest.' In other words, 'any action that is disruptive or undertaken to disrupt or disturb a funeral or burial service.'

George spent a very uncomfortable year in jail and paid a thousand-dollar fine. His friends who disrupted the burial service got the same sentence.

Word got around (OK, maybe Katie and I helped spread it) about Brenda Burkett and her cold-hearted sister, Penelope Powers. Penelope did not even bother to have a memorial for the Forest's premier martini-maker, and that offended her many fans. Penelope's business dropped off steeply, and she lost her practice. She now works for a law firm that handles traffic tickets.

Shirley, the office manager for Dr Marvin Xavier Turner, board-certified ENT, was indeed listening at the door when the specialist confessed to his coke-fueled fling. She couldn't resist spreading this juicy gossip, and soon it was all over the Forest. Dr Turner's wife found out and was shocked by his debauched behavior. She promptly divorced him.

Dr Turner's practice declined. He is now working at a walk-in clinic.

I also found Suzi Chin's address and gave it to her former landlady, Myra Mason. It turned out Suzi had moved on and moved out of the Ferrari dealer's house and was now living in Ladue, another upscale area, with her latest lover. He generously paid the five thousand dollars Suzi owed Myra, as a parting gift. She was last seen drinking white wine in the bar at Solange.

As for Roberta Perkins, who loved her designer labels, she was heartbroken when her husband Larry died because they couldn't close on that new million-dollar house in the Chouteau Forest Estates. After the Sterling Service's manager died, Roberta discovered that Larry did not leave her with a pension, and only a measly ten thousand dollars in life insurance. Worse, her husband left behind several unhappy blackmail clients. To avoid a police investigation, Roberta had to return their money.

She was forced to sell her pretty house in Toonerville, and now lives in a down-market apartment complex near Jenny Brown. She works at a designer resale shop.

Speaking of down-market apartments, Linda's awful apartment complex, the Belfour Terrace, turned out to be owned by Henrietta Du Pres Du Pont. Repeated complaints to the Forest code enforcement bureau were ignored, until the St. Louis newspapers were tipped off. They gleefully printed photos of Henrietta's mansion and the rundown Belfour Terrace along with a story headlined: 'High Society, Low Rent. Chouteau Forest Society Queen Slums It.'

This gave Henrietta's many enemies ammunition to force the troublemaker off their committees. Plus, Henrietta had to pay thousands in fines and several million to fix up the apartment complex.

The media also had a snarky good time when I pushed Camilla onto her husband's casket. My funeral pratfall photo was headlined: 'Chouteau Forest Death Investigator Accidentally Solves Death Investigation.' I was glad I didn't get the credit for solving Sterling's murder, since I wasn't supposed to be looking into it in the first place. The video of me lurching blindly into Camilla ran for several days on local and national TV, until it was replaced by a video of a surf-boarding pup.

Some good did come out of all this death. Monty sued the Chouteau County prison system. The investigation resulted in Earlene, the dangerous bully, being sentenced to twenty more years. She will now be kept out of the general prison population. The two guards who stood by when Camilla was severely beaten were arrested, charged with negligence, and fired.

Monty also sued the system for damages when Camilla was injured. She received a million dollars.

Camilla wanted to give me the money, but I asked that she give it to Eldon McIntyre to restore the Forest's Avalon Theater to its former glory. The old theater is now one of the highlights of downtown Chouteau Forest. Eldon's mother was there for the grand reopening, and I have a free lifetime pass.

Camilla Chaney was completely exonerated and is now a very rich widow. She went back to college to get her teaching degree, and she enjoys teaching students with reading disabilities. She also runs the Camilla Chaney Foundation, which supports causes dear to her heart.

As for my heart, it's just fine, thank you. I'm enjoying my romance with Chris Ferretti. Sometimes I think about Katie's warning, that I'm 'sleeping with one man while wearing the wedding ring of another.' As to whether I want to take off Donegan's ring, much less let Chris replace it with his own ring, that's a problem for another day.

I am blessed with love, laughter, and good friends. My life is peaceful.

Until someone else dies in the Forest. And another mystery begins.

THE INSIDER'S GUIDE TO CHOUTEAU COUNTY PRONUNCIATION

Missourians have their own way of pronouncing words and names. We're called the Show Me State, and you don't tell us how to say something. The French were among the first settlers, but we resist Frenchifying words.

Chouteau is *SHOW-toe*.

Du Pres is *Duh-PRAY*.

Gravois is *GRAH-voy*.

Detective Ray Greiman is *GRI-mun*. His name is mispronounced German.

So is my name. It's pronounced *VEETS*, and rhymes with *Beets*.

Missouri can't even decide how to pronounce its own name. The eastern part, which includes St. Louis, calls itself *Missour-ee*. That's how Angela pronounces the state's name. In the west, which has Kansas City, it's called *Missour-uh*. Politicians have mastered the fine art of adjusting their pronunciation to please whichever part of the state they're in.

Elaine Viets